I0705835

The Golden Witness

a 509 Crime Story

by Colin Conway

The Golden Witness

Copyright © 2024 Colin Conway

Cover Design by Rob Williams

ISBN: 978-1-961030-20-6

Original Ink Press, an imprint of High Speed Creative, LLC
1521 N. Argonne Road, #C-205
Spokane Valley, WA 99212

Visit the author's website at colinconway.com

What is the 509?

Separated by the Cascade Range, Washington State is divided into two distinctly different climates and cultures.

The western side of the Cascades is home to Seattle, its 34 inches of annual rainfall, and the incredibly weird and smelly Gum Wall. Most of the state's wealth and political power are concentrated in and around this enormous city. The residents of this area know the prosperity that has come from being the home of Microsoft, Amazon, Boeing, and Starbucks.

To the east of the Cascade Mountains lies nearly two-thirds of the entire state, a lot of which is used for agriculture. Washington State leads the nation in producing apples, it is the second-largest potato grower, and it's the fourth for providing wheat.

This eastern part of the state can enjoy more than 170 days of sunshine each year, which is important when there are more than 200 lakes nearby. However, the beautiful summers are offset by harsh winters, with average snowfall reaching 47 inches and the average high hovering around 37°.

While five telephone area codes provide service to the westside, only 509 covers everything east of the Cascades, a staggering twenty-one counties.

Of these, Spokane County is the largest with an estimated population of 506,000.

...a "golden" witness—someone who saw the event clearly, could explain specifically what happened with certainty, was able to identify who the actors were, and most importantly, was completely independent and disinterested in the event itself or the participants.

- *The Worst Kind of Truth*/Frank Zafiro

The
Golden
Witness

a 509 Crime Story

DAY 1

Chapter 1

Spokane Police Officer Ron Rowe turned onto College Avenue. He scanned the neighborhood as his patrol car crept forward.

Three brown-skinned children played in an unfenced yard while an overweight white man lay nearby on a beach towel. He wore swim trunks and sunglasses and seemingly paid no attention to the kids. The man's bronzed skin glistened under the midday sun, a telltale sign of too much tanning lotion.

The children noticed Rowe's patrol car and excitedly waved when he passed by. He was about to return the gesture, but their neighbors diverted Rowe's attention.

Two black men leaned on a chain-link fence. They held beers and watched Rowe with alert eyes. The officer checked the house numbers behind the men—2106. This was a double block, so the location he sought was still several lots away. Rowe nodded at the two men, but they turned disdainfully away and sipped from their cans.

The officer's attention slid further down the block.

It was a Tuesday afternoon, and no women were outside. Rowe thought it a troubling sign for any neighborhood when a plurality of men remained home during the work week. Society had flipped its priorities when men tended to children while women went to work. Hell, some men didn't even care for their offspring when they stayed home. They simply didn't work.

This neighborhood needed gentrification, Rowe thought, a sweeping influx of investor interest, but it was The Zone. The smart money, the careful money, mostly stayed away from this part of town. Even with the recent increase in property values the city had experienced, this area couldn't escape the black eye given it decades earlier.

Out-of-state investors occasionally bought in The Zone with dreams of quick-flip paydays. The Kendall Yards development to the south provided optimism for many of those interlopers. Yet, hope didn't thrive in this neighborhood.

Rowe pulled his patrol car to the curb. He tapped the Mobile Data Computer (MDC) to alert dispatch he was on scene. When Rowe exited the car, he quietly closed the door—a habit borne from his years on graveyard.

Another patrol car rolled up. Lucas Jefferson climbed from the driver's seat and gently closed his door. Jefferson was black, once played linebacker in college, and was Rowe's best friend. They often joined each other on calls.

Rowe headed toward the other officer. "You believe this shit?"

"What a day."

At the start of their shift, dispatch sent Rowe and Jefferson to a domestic violence call. A woman had stabbed her boyfriend in the stomach for allegedly flirting with the woman's mother. All three were stumbling drunk, yet it was barely breakfast time for most of the city. Jefferson arrested the woman and transported her to jail. Rowe rode with the man in an ambulance to the hospital to capture any excited utterances, especially in the event he died from his wounds. Neither Rowe nor Jefferson thought that likely, but it was best to be careful.

The mother later attacked Jefferson as he exited the jail. She was upset over her daughter's incarceration. Jefferson apprehended her, too, then immediately walked the matriarch inside and booked her.

That was just the start of their day.

Rowe led the way toward the target house. He scanned the neighboring homes and let the inside of his forearm brush his Glock with each step. It was a conscious habit whenever approaching a location while on a dubious call such as this.

Jefferson motioned down the street. "You notice the Dead Boys?"

Rowe glanced in the direction his friend pointed. "The guys drinking beers?"

"That's Fast Freddie Gilmore and Keenan Mack."

"I thought the Dead Boys disbanded after that fiasco a few months back."

Jefferson shrugged. "Guess not. The only way to get rid of cockroaches is by stepping on them."

Rowe didn't want to get into a discussion about gang members now—maybe later. Jefferson had a particular hatred for them. Rowe turned and looked at the target house. "You understand what we're dealing with?"

"Sounds like a one-oh-five."

A 105 was department slang for a crazy person. Rowe didn't know where the term originated. He'd heard it on his first night of patrol from his Field Training Officer.

Rowe couldn't count how many times he'd heard it or said it since. With the number of nut balls the department dealt with daily, officers had unlimited opportunities to use the derogatory term.

The house was an older Craftsman with a small porch and a shoddy railing. Curtains blocked cracked windows. Drying bushes and dead flowers lined a flaking white picket fence that surrounded the property. Yellowing grass and patches of dirt masqueraded as a lawn.

"A Felony Flats special," Jefferson said.

Most patrol officers called this neighborhood The Zone. For whatever reason, Jefferson always preferred the nickname the civilians used.

Rowe stepped through the rickety gate and headed up the uneven pathway. The closer he got to the house, the less he liked this call.

A woman had dialed 911 to report a murder. Usually, dispatchers and officers greeted this revelation with great care. However, the woman claimed she witnessed it on her computer. Dispatchers stated the woman sounded hysterical.

Rowe thought the call seemed less like a homicide investigation and more like a welfare check. Another 105, he thought, this one likely watching YouTube. Rowe stepped to the right of the door; Jefferson moved to the left. The fabric was missing from the screen door. Rowe reached through the opening and knocked. It opened before he could tap a third time.

The golden-haired woman standing there was wrong for the house. She was also wrong for the neighborhood. Naomi Stapleton stood a foot shorter than Rowe. The MDC said she was twenty-five, but she looked several years older. It had to be the make-up and fake eyelashes.

Rowe didn't remember what the computer reported as her weight, but it couldn't have been much. The black workout bra and Lycra shorts revealed a lean body. Blond hair cascaded over her left shoulder.

Naomi's eyes flooded with relief. "Finally."

"Spokane Police," Rowe said. "You called?"

"I did." Naomi slapped the screen door's lever, and it popped open. She motioned for the two officers to follow her deeper into the house.

The front room resembled many homes in The Zone. Ratty couch. Broken-down recliner. Clustered on the coffee table were a greasy pizza box, two Big Gulps, and a half-eaten carton of cookies. A red plastic bong, cloudy from repeated use, sat on the floor.

A large flat-screen TV and the latest PlayStation were in the corner. The cardboard boxes for both devices were still in the room. A first-person shooter game was paused on the television's screen. Rowe saw it advertised during NFL games last season but couldn't recall its name.

Rowe reassessed Naomi. She was pale with dirty, bare feet. Her toenails were painted red, but the coloring had chipped. Maybe she belonged in the neighborhood after all.

The sound of rushing water came from another room.

"Who else is here?" Jefferson asked.

Naomi waved her hand toward the hallway. "My boyfriend."

"Call him out."

"Guille," she shouted, pronouncing the name *Gill-ē*. "Come here."

Both Jefferson and Rowe reached for their guns.

The water stopped. A moment later, a light-skinned man stepped around the corner. He wore khaki pants and

Timberland boots, but no shirt. Tattoos covered the man's thin upper body. An image of a gun peeked out from above his waistband. He wiped his hands with a small towel.

"Yo," he said proudly. "That shit's motherfucking destroyed." He stopped when he saw the cops. His face hardened and his hands went into the air.

"He didn't do anything," Naomi said.

Rowe held out an arm to keep her back.

The boyfriend's gaze cut to Naomi, and his eyes narrowed. "What'd you do?"

Naomi lifted her hands in frustration. "I had to."

"I said no." The boyfriend shook his head. "Now look."

"What's your name?" Jefferson asked.

"Guillermo." He lowered his arms. "Guillermo Messi."

"Middle initial?"

"None." Messi's lip curled. "And I ain't got no warrants. You can believe that."

"Birthdate?" Jefferson said.

Messi told him.

Jefferson reached for his shoulder microphone to call dispatch for a name check.

Rowe faced Naomi. "Tell me what you saw."

"A guy got shot in the head." She held two fingers to her temple. "Pow. Pow. Just like that."

Messi clicked his tongue against the back of his teeth. "What'd I say?"

Rowe pointed at the boyfriend. "Shut it. We'll get to you soon enough." He turned his attention back to the woman. "Where'd it happen?"

"My studio." She started past Rowe, but he grabbed her.

"Is there a body in there?"

"No," she said. "It happened on my computer."

Rowe exchanged a glance with his partner. "Keep an eye on the boyfriend."

Jefferson's head was cocked so his ear remained near his shoulder microphone. He nodded an angular agreement.

Ron Rowe released Naomi, and she walked into the hallway. The boyfriend glowered at her as she passed by. Messi tried the same attitude on Rowe, but the officer didn't put up with it.

"Give us any trouble," Rowe said, "and you'll wait in the back of a patrol car."

"It's my house."

"Not while we're here."

Messi broke eye contact. "Whatever."

"That's what I thought."

Naomi waited at the end of the hall.

The first room Rowe passed was messy. A queen-sized bed was unmade, and clothes were strewn about on the floor. Even from the hallway, it smelled like stale sweat and old sex.

Rowe went by the bathroom next and paused. A laptop computer floated in the tub.

"It's back here," Naomi said impatiently.

In the last room, the curtains were closed, and the lights were off. White string lights hung around the largest wall, giving the room a surreal glow. A twin-sized bed stood opposite a small desk. A fluffy comforter covered the bed and multiple throw pillows were stacked near its head. A large-framed picture with the words *Play Time* hung on the wall in place of a headboard. Two vibrators sat on the nightstand.

On the floor, in front of the bed, was a ring light with a camera in the middle. It appeared to have been recently tipped over since it was still illuminated.

The desk was bare except for the end of a power cord likely meant for the laptop. Rowe looked back toward the bathroom. He flicked the light switch, and the room brightened.

"This is my studio," Naomi said.

Rowe had a good idea of what she did in her studio, but he kept his opinion to himself. "Tell me what happened."

She pointed at the bed. "I was there. And he was there." She pointed at the desk.

"On the computer?"

"That's right, and somebody walked into his house and—" Her eyes went wide. "I can't believe I saw that."

"Did you get a good look at who did it?"

"You better believe it." She stepped forward and pointed at a spot on the desk where the laptop had been. "The shooter leaned down and looked right into the camera." Naomi paused. "At me."

"Why did he do that?" Rowe asked.

"Probably because I was screaming." She rolled her eyes. "I didn't handle it very well, especially when he said he'd find me."

"He said that?"

Naomi nodded. "'We will find you.' That's what he said. Just like that."

"Were you recording?"

Her face scrunched. "What? No. Gross. Never."

"Who was the guy?"

"I don't know. I'd never seen him before."

"No," Rowe said. "The dead guy."

Naomi's brow furrowed. "Oh, yeah. Sorry. Nick. His name was Nick."

He frowned. "Is that his real name?"

She shrugged. "That's the name he told me. I don't know if it's real."

Rowe hadn't removed the notebook from his pocket yet. He still wasn't sure how real this call was. The whole story might be a hoax.

"But he had a screen name," she said.

"What was it?"

Naomi shrugged. "I don't remember."

Of course, Rowe thought.

"It was like five random numbers and a couple letters. Didn't mean anything to me. It probably didn't mean anything to him either."

"Do you know where Nick was from?" Rowe asked.

She nodded. "Chicago."

"That narrows it down."

"It does?" Naomi appeared confused.

Rowe left her in the back bedroom and returned to the bathroom. He lifted the computer from the tub. Water cascaded from its insides. He set the laptop on the toilet and let water continue to leak out. The screen was cracked, and several keys were missing from the keyboard.

Naomi stuck her head around the corner. "Do you have any more questions?"

"Why'd you put it in the water?"

She straightened. "That was Guille's idea. He said no one could track us if we ruined the computer."

Rowe grunted and studied the wet device. Water continued to dribble out of the USB ports.

Naomi stepped into the bathroom. "We didn't have a hammer or anything to break it, so Guille slammed it on the ground then dunked it. Seemed like a smart idea."

"Except now we don't have much to work with."

Naomi cocked her head. "You know his name is Nick, and he lives in Chicago. You said that was enough."

Rowe motioned for her to step back so he could leave the restroom without brushing against her. A moment ago, he thought she was an attractive woman. Now, he didn't want to be close to her.

She moved out of his way. "Did I misunderstand what you said?"

Back in the living room, Jefferson shook his head. "No wants."

"I told you," Messi said. "My shit's clean."

Rowe walked by the two men on his way to the front door.

"What do we have?" Jefferson asked.

"A mess."

"Where you going?" his partner asked.

Officer Ron Rowe looked back. "To call a sergeant."

Chapter 2

Detective James Morgan sat backward on the folding chair and rested his arms across its top. He lowered his chin onto his forearms and stared out of the second-floor window.

Across the street was The Hempstead, a four-story apartment building with a reported thirty units. The structure was built in 1913 as a Single Room Occupancy hotel with shared restrooms. Later, it was converted to low-income apartments. Morgan had responded to the building as a patrol officer for complaints of drugs, prostitution, and domestic violence.

However, its history as a police nuisance seemed to have stopped when it was sold over a decade ago to a limited liability corporation with plans to convert the apartments to condominiums. It remained untouched and had sold twice since then. The current owner was Riverside One LLC, a Wyoming limited liability corporation, named after the street it resided on.

"Let's call the fire marshal," Detective Nayla Senai said.

She sat behind a camera with its telephoto lens pointed at The Hempstead's front door. Senai wore a loose-fitting shirt to hide her gun and badge. Tight black jeans hugged her legs and wrapped snuggly around the tops of her combat boots. She spread her long legs to accommodate the camera's tripod. Morgan might have found the pose suggestive if he didn't respect the woman more than anyone else on the department.

Senai was originally from Ethiopia. She overcame a tough childhood to become one of the best detectives in the department. As far as Morgan was concerned, she could be—*should be*—a Major Crimes detective. He believed the department overlooked Senai because of her history with the Criminal Task Force (CTF) along with the stigma of growing up in an African nation. Otherwise, the department would have fallen over itself to promote a competent black woman for no other reason than to show how progressive it was.

The two detectives were in a vacant apartment the CTF had rented for two months. It was more than Morgan wanted to spend because it affected the team's annual budget. He had hoped the landlord would allow them to use the unit out of civic loyalty, but the jerk threatened to lease the apartment to another interested party. Morgan wouldn't forget how the guy treated SPD. He knew there would come a day when the landlord needed something from the department. Downtown landlords always needed some police help—it was just a matter of time. Morgan would be there to make sure SPD got its metaphorical pound of flesh when it happened.

Right now, the apartment only contained a couple of folding chairs, Senai's camera equipment, and a nearly empty trash can.

"What's the fire marshal going to do?" Morgan asked. His head bounced as he spoke because he hadn't moved his chin from his arms.

"A health and safety inspection will get us into the building."

"The common areas, maybe." Morgan's head continued to bounce. "But that's it. We won't get into any apartments."

"It's a start."

Morgan exhaled heavily. "It's a start," he agreed.

Maybe they should involve the fire marshal. However, Morgan believed if they showed too much attention to the building, whatever was occurring inside would stop and the activity would move elsewhere.

Sometimes, it was better to stand in the shadows and observe.

The CTF had tried to learn the names of the Riverside One partners by using the Wyoming Secretary of State's business search website. Unfortunately, all they discovered was a Chicago attorney listed as the registered agent. Contacting an attorney about the LLC was tantamount to calling the fire marshal—the LLC partners would know the cops were sniffing around.

The Criminal Task Force had been in the proverbial shadows for several days now, watching The Hempstead. A tip from a prostitute had turned Morgan onto the building.

"Something strange is going on there," Morgan's source had said. "Nobody ever leaves. Everything is sent there. Food, women, you name it."

"Who's paying for it?" Morgan had asked.

His source didn't know because she hadn't gone into the building. She'd learned about it from a friend who'd been hired to go inside. The source's information had proved to be true so far.

Morgan initially sat off The Hempstead for several hours. No one left the building. He returned the next day, and it was the same situation. He also never saw anyone enter the building. Lights were on in the units, the shades were drawn, and shadows moved about. In all his years on the department, Morgan had never seen anything like it.

He could have gone up and tried the door, but Morgan thought discretion was the better course of action. Now, the entire CTF watched the building, and it remained unchanged. Shadows walked through units behind drawn shades, but they had yet to see anyone enter or leave the building.

Morgan's attention drifted away from The Hempstead to a homeless man pushing a grocery cart filled with junk. A bungee cord held a blue tarp to the lower portion of the basket. The plastic fabric fluttered in the breeze. The man was at the far end of the block. His head bobbed with each laborious step.

Senai leaned into the camera. "Courtney looks good."

"He looks like a bum."

She pulled back from the camera's viewfinder to eye him. "That's not politically correct."

Morgan grunted. "So don't tell him."

Officer Courtney Earley was a large man. During his college days, he played defensive end for the University of Montana Grizzlies. He might have lost some of his playing weight, but he wasn't losing his height.

After three days without deepening intel, Senai decided to put someone on the street. Even though the tip came through Morgan, she was put in charge of the operation by the CTF sergeant.

Morgan was still on the administration's hot seat after a stunt led to a citywide debacle with the downtown junkie population. He had promised a snitch a get-out-of-jail-free card in exchange for some extra effort. Morgan never expected his promise to get so wildly out of hand. He got a suspension for it.

He didn't hold a grudge because Senai supervised the operation. They often shifted leadership responsibilities. They were both detectives, and the team was structured to spread the workload.

Senai opted to put Earley in the homeless outfit because of his beard. She thought he'd make an excellent derelict. Morgan would have gone with one of the other CTF officers because he thought Earley's size was detrimental.

"I know you're worried," Senai said, "but he's doing a good job."

A portable radio on the windowsill crackled. *"Big man's on the move,"* Officer Jeremiah Strange reported.

Strange was stationed down the street in an old pickup used for surveillance. The rust bucket was known around the department as the Rolling Dumpster. Underneath the hood, the engine was in tiptop shape, courtesy of Fleet Services. However, the body looked like its name implied.

The radio squawked just before Officer Adrian Thorn replied, *"All quiet on the western front."*

Thorn sat at the opposite end of the street in a partially souped-up Chevy Nova. It was primer gray with patches of Bondo filler applied to the front and rear quarter panels. When it got up to speed, the Nova rattled and vibrated so badly it had earned the nickname Shaky Jake.

A rusty pickup and partially renovated muscle car were ubiquitous for most areas in Spokane County. They blended into the poorer neighborhoods like toothless smiles and mullets.

Morgan removed a bag of salted peanuts from his jacket pocket. He tore it open and dumped some nuts into his palm. He extended the bag to Senai. She shook her head.

"Have some," he said. "They're healthy."

"They're covered in salt."

He clutched his fist around the bag. "That's why they're good."

"You're going to die if you keep eating that way."

"You keep saying that." He tossed some peanuts into his mouth.

Earley meandered along the sidewalk. He stopped, shouted at no one in particular, then reached into the cart and threw a bottle into the street. It exploded.

"He deserves an Oscar," Senai said.

"The boy is one oar short of a full rowboat." Morgan tossed more peanuts into his mouth.

When Earley neared the entrance to The Hempstead, he approached the front door. The portable radio crackled. "*No guards inside,*" he muttered, as if trying to hide the movement of his lips.

"Any cameras on the front door?" Senai asked.

"*No idea.*"

Earley's body jerked, and the glass windows shook. Even though Morgan couldn't see it, he figured Earley was tugging on the door handle.

The camera clicked repeatedly next to Morgan's ear. "Look at him go," Senai said. "He's going to tear that door off its hinges."

"*Heads up, big man,*" Strange transmitted. His voice registered no excitement. "*Movement coming from the east.*"

"*I got them,*" Thorn added. "*What's the play?*"

Two white men in tracksuits—one red, the other green—trotted across the street. Which building they had come from, Morgan couldn't see. He'd work on that problem later.

Morgan shoved the peanuts back into his pocket before grabbing the radio. "Courtney, call the ball."

Earley stopped shaking the door. "*Stay put,*" he mumbled. He turned and wobbled back to his cart. He grabbed its handle just as the men in tracksuits arrived.

They were both in their early thirties and lanky men. Both were bald with tattoos on their necks and hands. Even from this distance, Morgan could tell they were the type for trouble.

Senai remained hunched behind the viewfinder. The camera continued to click near Morgan's ear. "I've got them," she whispered.

The man in the green tracksuit waved his hands while he spoke.

Earley tried to push his cart away, but the man in the red suit shoved it back.

Green Man grabbed Earley and slapped him three quick times. Twice with the open hand, once with the back. The undercover officer didn't respond, though. Earley kept his arms down.

Morgan hollered, "Whoa!" and jumped to his feet. He grabbed the folding chair with his free hand and threw it to the side of the room. It clanged shut when it landed. He stood near the window, careful not to block Senai's camera.

Red Man shoved the cart into Earley's gut, and the big man buckled. Green Man continued shouting and waving his hands above Earley's head.

"*Are we going?*" Thorn transmitted.

It took incredible willpower for Morgan to respond with, "Stand down."

"*I'm getting out on foot,*" Strange said. Anxiety laced his voice.

"Don't get involved," Morgan ordered. "Stay in your car."

Red Man pulled the shopping cart away from Earley and pushed it down the sidewalk. It careened wildly until it collided with a parked Honda. The car's alarm sounded and the brake lights flashed.

Green Man grabbed Earley's coat and slapped him once more. He stuck his finger in the undercover officer's face and said something. Then the lean man spun Earley and kicked the big man in the ass.

Both men in tracksuits yelled and pumped their fists as Earley shuffled away toward his cart. They did this for a couple of moments before crossing the street.

Morgan activated his radio. "Find out where they came from."

"*Got it,*" Strange said. "*I see it.*"

Courtney Earley pulled his cart away from the Honda. He reached into it and found a bottle. He chucked it into the middle of the street and it exploded.

"Best performance," Senai muttered.

Earley lumbered off to the west, yelling to himself as he went.

"Let's wrap it up," Morgan said into the radio. "Everyone meet back at HQ."

Chapter 3

"That's when I stepped outside and called you," Ron Rowe said.

Sergeant Megan Ledbetter stood with her thumbs hooked into her duty belt. She was a larger woman with short blond hair and intense eyes. Ledbetter was in her mid-forties and known as the Nut Crusher. A scar ran from her right temple down to her ear, a result of a knife attack earlier in her career.

Lucas Jefferson stood in the doorway of the house. His head swiveled back and forth, keeping an eye on the occupants while watching Rowe's interaction with the sergeant.

"What do you want from me?" Ledbetter asked.

Rowe shifted his stance under her withering stare. He was still getting used to working with the sergeant. To clean up their reputations as hot dogs, he and Jefferson had moved to day shift at the beginning of the year. Unfortunately, they were assigned to work with Ledbetter, a notorious ball buster, especially for hard-charging types. He thought working with a woman supervisor would have been easier—so far, he was wrong.

"I want your opinion," Rowe said.

"About?"

"The situation."

Ledbetter's gaze shifted to Jefferson. He avoided her judgment by looking into the house. She faced Rowe again. "You read the bible, Ron?"

Rowe snickered and immediately regretted it. The sergeant's face hardened.

"Got a problem with the good book?" she asked.

"No."

"I hope not." Ledbetter's eyes swept about the yellowing grass. When her attention returned to him, she said, "There's a proverb that says if you give a man a fish, you feed him for a day."

Rowe heard it when he was a kid. He didn't want to be lectured at a crime scene.

"But if you teach a man to fish," the sergeant continued, "you feed him for a lifetime."

Rowe decided right then he liked male sergeants better. They would have just told him what he needed to know. Why Ledbetter had to go through a dog and pony show, Rowe didn't know.

She must have read the confusion on his face because she said, "I'm teaching you to fish."

"All right."

Ledbetter crossed her arms. "What do you think you should do?"

Rowe was a senior patrol officer. He had seven years on the job. This wasn't his first time around the block. If he wanted to bounce a case off a sergeant, he didn't need that supervisor to make him feel stupid. His face grew warm.

"Well?" Ledbetter asked.

"I don't see the problem in asking for your opinion."

She furrowed her brow, not bothering to hide her irritation. "Why do you need my opinion?"

He motioned toward the house. "I don't want to waste a detective's time."

"That's very nice of you, but the detectives aren't your worry. Bury them with cases for all I care."

Rowe stared at her. He wasn't about to break eye contact.

"Your job is to serve the citizenry. The woman in there said she witnessed a murder. Was her claim credible?"

"I think so."

"*You think* so?"

He winced.

Ledbetter asked, "What would move your opinion in either direction?"

"Some follow-up questions, I guess."

She stared at him.

"Follow-up questions," he said with finality. Rowe regretted calling for a sergeant now.

"If you're satisfied it's credible...?"

Rowe opened his mouth but stopped before he spoke. He took a moment to consider his answer. "I'll take the computer and log it into evidence. Then I'll write a report and let the detectives decide what to do with it."

Ledbetter raised an eyebrow. "Anything else?"

"No, ma'am."

"Good," Ledbetter said. She paused, as if considering something. "Don't log the computer into the property room. Take it directly to the digital lab. If there was a murder somewhere else, we don't have time to let the damn thing work its way through the system."

With that, Sergeant Megan Ledbetter slapped his shoulder once. "Happy fishing." She strode toward her car.

Rowe turned and looked at Lucas Jefferson. They had more work to do.

***

Ron Rowe returned to the back bedroom with Naomi Stapleton. He put the broken laptop on the desk. A little water leaked from inside, but she didn't seem to mind.

"Just to clarify," Rowe said. "You were on the bed."

"That's right." Naomi pointed to where she had been.

"And Nick was here." Rowe's hand hovered over the laptop.

Naomi nodded. "At his desk."

"You could see his desk?"

She shrugged. "Not really, but I assumed that's where he was sitting. I could see a bed behind him, so he wasn't sitting in his kitchen."

"What was he doing?"

Her eyes widened.

"I need you to tell me," Rowe said.

"He was jerking it." She mimed the way a man masturbates.

"So, he was naked?"

"That's normally how guys jerk it."

Rowe figured challenging her assertion might make him look like a perv, so he let it go. His gaze drifted to the two vibrators near the pillows.

Naomi followed his attention. "Questions?"

"You did that while he did his thing?" Rowe hated how his question sounded.

"You don't know what was going on?"

"I do, but I have a report to write."

She put her hands on her hips. "How detailed do you want it? Is 'Nick jerked off while I masturbated' enough? Or do you want it more graphic?"

Rowe's face warmed, and he looked down to jot her answer into his notebook. "Would you have a picture of Nick?"

Her expression soured. "Why would I have that?"

Rowe could think of lots of reasons, the least of which was blackmail, but he kept those thoughts to himself. Instead, he said, "Describe Nick."

"He's white. Probably thirty-five. He had a tattoo and an accent."

"What kind of accent?"

"Russian."

Rowe titled his head. "You said he was from Chicago."

Her face pinched. "Russians can't live in Chicago?"

"Was his English good?"

"Pretty good, but he still sounded like those old Arnold Schwarzenegger movies."

"Schwarzenegger isn't Russian."

Naomi waved a single hand. "You know what I mean."

"What about his tattoo?" Rowe asked. "Do you remember anything about it?"

"It looked cheap, like a prison tattoo."

He was about to ask her how she knew what those looked like, but he remembered Guillermo Messi was in the other room. Many of his tattoos looked as if they were made with inferior ink.

"Was there anything in Nick's bedroom you remember?"

"Only the Jesus cross on the wall. I always thought it was a bit weird seeing that behind him. I'm not religious, so it didn't bother me too much."

Rowe wasn't religious either, but he couldn't imagine a cross hanging over anyone's shoulder while masturbating.

"How many times have you and Nick had private calls?"

Naomi's head bounced as she thought. "We just started doing them. This was maybe our fourth. Or fifth. Not too many."

"What about the other guy?" Rowe asked. "Can you describe him?"

"The killer? He was white, too, but scary with crazy eyes. And he was definitely Russian."

"Why do you say that?"

"Because when I screamed, he leaned in and studied the camera. Then he asked, 'Who are you?' Like the way Arnold talks. But I kept screaming, and he closed the laptop. That's when I ran and told Guille."

"And you called the cops?"

"That's right."

"Do you think you can identify the killer if you saw him again?"

Naomi nodded emphatically. "A hundred percent. No, a thousand percent. I'll never forget that face."

Rowe fished a Victim's Rights Card from his breast pocket. He wrote the incident report number at the top of it, then handed her the card. "I'm going to file a report. It should get assigned to a detective."

"Nick seemed like a nice guy," Naomi said. "I hope you find whoever did that to him."

"I need to take your laptop. It's evidence now."

She waved it off. "Have it. It's not like I can use it anymore."

* * *

Lucas Jefferson asked, "Where were you when this went down?"

"Right there." Guillermo Messi pointed at the paused video game. "Killing motherfuckers."

"While she was working?"

Messi smirked. "A pimp ain't in the room while a bitch is working a john."

"You're a pimp?"

The boyfriend lowered his head. "Not if it gets me arrested."

Jefferson fought back a smile. Guillermo Messi was like countless dirt bags he'd encountered on the street—tough around their buddies, tougher around their women, but pussies when the cops showed up. "So, what happened?"

Messi motioned toward the rear of the house. "Naomi was back there with one of her regulars—"

Jefferson interrupted. "You know his name?"

"Hell yeah, I do. Dirty Feet Nick, the weird motherfucker."

"You know all of them that follow her?"

Messi laughed. "There's no way I could know them all. Ol' girl's got 'em lined up for days. Shelling out ten bucks a month to see what she's offering. Pervert sons of bitches."

Jefferson tilted his head. "What was she offering?"

"Her cooch, what else? But baby girl hooks 'em with her feet. Some want more if you get what I'm saying."

"This Nick was different?"

"Him and about ten others. They all want private shows with her on the regular."

"She did that? One on one?"

Messi sneered. "Listen, a bitch does what's good for the business. You know what I mean? She shows her feet and pussy to a thousand guys. She can show it to one more. Money's money. Even for a guy who likes dirty feet."

"Dirty feet?"

"People are into weird shit. Nick wanted her feet dirty. Don't ask me why. She'd walk around outside without her shoes on before they got together." Messi snickered. "Made me feel good about the stuff I like."

Jefferson didn't want to know what Guillermo Messi was into. "So, Naomi witnessed a murder?"

"She came running in here, all naked and shit. Totally freaked out. Said some guy walked into Dirty Feet's room and shot him in the head. Two times." He mimed firing a gun twice. "Then Naomi said the shooter looked into the camera and mean-mugged her. Totally freaked her out. It took me like five minutes to calm her down."

"That's when you destroyed the computer?"

Messi tapped the side of his head. "I had to, yo. Like, what if that guy could figure out where we were? I grabbed her laptop and smashed it on the floor, then I drowned the fuck out of it. No one is getting anything off it now."

"Pretty smart," Jefferson said without cracking a smile.

"Tell me about it." Messi beamed with pride. "I dropped my phone in a toilet once and it never worked again." He thumped his chest. "I knew what I was doing. Ain't nobody tracking anything off that computer."

Ron Rowe walked into the living room. He carried a laptop in his left hand. Naomi Stapleton followed closely behind.

"Yo," Messi said. "Where you taking that?"

Rowe stopped near the front door. "It's evidence."

"You can't have that. It's ours."

"If you make us write a warrant," Rowe said, "we will. But it's going with us one way or another."

"Let them have it, baby." Naomi slipped her arm through Messi's. "I can't use it."

Messi sneered. "Fine. Whatever. Besides, if they hook it up, maybe the killer will follow it there and get the surprise of his life."

Jefferson lifted an eyebrow. He didn't entirely understand technology, but he was pretty sure that wasn't how it worked.

Messi turned to Naomi. "Wouldn't that be hilarious, yo?"

She smiled. "As long as he gets caught."

Rowe said, "We're out," as he passed by his partner. He left the house without further word.

Jefferson nodded to Messi, but the man was already cooing to Naomi about how smart he was for dunking the laptop.

It was time to leave.

Chapter 4

When Morgan walked into the Criminal Task Force office, he immediately looked for Courtney Earley. It was a quick search since no walls separated the team. They operated in a bullpen fashion with six desks. One for each team member and one for the sergeant. All in the open. Morgan loved the camaraderie it built. It felt like his days in the Marine Corps.

"Where's big man?" Morgan asked.

Adrian Thorn turned from the three-drawer cabinet he was digging in. He was a rangy pale man with long, stringy hair that fell to his shoulders. He wore a mechanic's shirt with a dark oval on the left breast where a patch had been torn off long ago. His faded jeans had holes in the knees and his boots were scuffed. "We dropped him at the main building so he could grab a shower. He'll be over in a minute."

The CTF office was in the Monroe Court Building, a structure just east of the Public Safety Building. Only a couple of SPD functions remained in the MCB—the Criminal Task Force and Volunteer Services. At one point, the department housed many ancillary functions in the MCB, but most had moved to the city-owned Gardner Building on the other side of the Public Safety campus.

Morgan liked being away from the rest of the department, as it allowed him to feel different. On some days, he felt special because of their remote location. On others, he felt like an outcast. He liked the latter better because it gave him a chip on his shoulder. Morgan knew he'd gotten lucky with the CTF assignment, and he'd do anything to hold on to it as long as possible. He had no aspirations for a promotion or to transfer to another team.

Morgan dropped into his chair. "How'd he seem?"

"Fine," Thorn said.

Jeremiah Strange reclined in his chair with his feet on his desk. He wore a Black Barons baseball jersey, black jeans, and a new pair of Air Jordans. He'd recently taken to wearing his hair in cornrows. A case file lay open on Strange's lap. "Courtney's been hit before. He'll handle it like a champ."

Nayla Senai leaned around her computer. "You worried about him, Morgan?"

Morgan *was* worried, actually. The big man had been shot during a CTF raid. He recovered physically, but Morgan wondered how Earley would do the next time the chips were down. Since then, the detective had kept a watchful eye on the largest member of his team.

But Morgan didn't want the others to know about his concerns. He eyed Senai. "You ID those tracksuits?"

"They're Russians," Strange said. "Or dagos. Only those jackals wear those faggoty outfits."

Thorn shoved the drawer back into the cabinet. "You can't say that. It's offensive."

"Which part?" Strange said.

"All of it."

Strange looked to Nayla. "Is that true?"

"Yes," she said. "It's all offensive."

Strange eyed Thorn. "When did you become such a pussy?"

"Me? You're always on me to clean up my act. Then I call you on something, and I'm a pussy?"

"You're an oppressor," Strange said. "There's a difference."

Thorn grabbed his crotch. "Oppress this."

Nayla said, "You two are both offensive," then disappeared behind her monitor. Her camera sat next to the computer, and a cord linked the two. "I'm sending the pictures to Crime Analysis now. Keep your fingers crossed."

Sergeant Ken Bynum entered the office. He wore a blue T-shirt a size seemingly too small for comfort. It hugged his sculpted biceps and thick chest. Bynum always gave off the air of a happily married man, but Morgan wondered if he dressed that way to attract the attention of single women. Or unhappily married women.

Even Andrew Parker, the bodybuilding moron in Major Crimes, never dressed that way. If anything, Parker's clothes always looked like they were a size too big for him.

"Any luck on the surveillance?" the sergeant asked as he headed toward his desk.

"Courtney got his ass kicked," Thorn said.

Morgan shot him a questioning glance.

Strange lifted his hands in the air. "Dude."

Thorn appeared confused. "What?"

Bynum stopped at his desk but didn't sit. "Is Courtney all right?"

"He's fine," Morgan said. "Adrian is exaggerating."

Concern registered on the sergeant's face. "What happened, Addy?"

Thorn glanced between Morgan and Bynum. "Well."

"Well, what?" the sergeant asked.

Morgan frowned. He waved his hand in a circular motion for Thorn to continue.

Thorn shrugged. "A couple of assholes slapped him around."

Bynum stepped forward. He hovered over Morgan now. "Who were they?"

"We don't know," Thorn said.

"How's that possible?" The sergeant looked down at Morgan. "You didn't arrest them?"

Morgan stood so he could be at eye level with Bynum. "If we arrested them, what would we have gotten?"

The sergeant furrowed his brow. "We'd know who they are."

"And they'd know we were watching," said Morgan.

Bynum frowned but didn't argue the point.

"We'll identify them soon enough." Morgan pointed at Senai. "We got their pictures."

"What if Crime Analysis doesn't have them in the system? What then?"

Senai stood from behind her computer. "It was my call."

Bynum looked over his shoulder.

"It was my operation," Senai continued. "I made the call not to arrest them."

The sergeant turned back to Morgan. "Where's the report?"

"We'll get you one."

"You're damn right, you will. Courtney was assaulted. Did he fill out the incident paperwork?"

"It was a slap," Morgan said.

"Was it hard?" Bynum looked at the officers. "Addy? Doc? Was he injured?"

The two men exchanged glances, then shrugged.

"It was a slap," Thorn repeated.

"God damn it." The sergeant returned to his desk but didn't sit. "It's a policy. You get injured, we have to do the state L&I forms. If you're assaulted, you file an incident report, no matter what. They can shut us down for violating this kind of stuff. Not just the chief, but the ombudsman. That's the city council and you know the hard-on they have for us." He looked at Nayla. "No offense."

She waved it off.

Morgan flexed his jaw. He knew the man was right. Too many people were gunning to make examples of cops now. Step a little out of line, get whacked on the nose with a rolled-up newspaper investigation. Step way out of line and get smacked across the nose with a rolled-up subpoena to your court hearing.

"I don't want to be your mother on this but do your fucking jobs." Bynum flopped into his chair. He repeatedly jabbed a finger onto his desk. "I want a report from everyone on this."

"All of us?" Thorn asked.

"What did I just say?" Bynum slapped his desk and stood. "If writing a report is too hard for you, Addy, I'll get someone on this team who can, and you can find your way back to patrol."

The sergeant walked around his desk. He pointed at Morgan. "When Courtney gets back, get him to write a report and fill out the incident paperwork. Tell him to leave it on my desk." With that, Bynum spun on his heel and left the office.

"What's up his butt?" Strange asked.

"His shirt is probably too tight," Thorn said. "Gives him a headache."

Morgan settled back into his chair. Bynum's reaction was too much for this infraction of policy. Especially since the assault wasn't that bad in the scheme of things. Every cop had been slapped. There was a bigger issue at stake.

He noticed Senai watching him. She raised her eyebrows and cocked her head. Morgan didn't know what was going on with the sergeant, either. He set his hands on his keyboard. It was time to write a report.

Chapter 5

Ron Rowe entered the Gardner Building and paused in the small lobby. He carried Naomi Stapleton's broken laptop in a brown paper sack.

A murmur of activity existed beyond the lobby's white walls, but where he stood was relatively quiet. Only the hum of the building's air-conditioning unit accompanied him. A couple of uncomfortable-looking chairs and a small table with a lamp rounded out the room. Citizens usually didn't hang out there for long, so the furniture wasn't purchased for luxury.

It was rare for Rowe to visit the Public Safety Building's annex. From what he'd been told, the old property storage facility had once been on this site. After the city built a new evidence warehouse on the edge of town, it converted the Gardner Building into offices. It now housed a variety of functions essential to SPD's mission.

The woman sitting behind the Plexiglas counter didn't immediately look away from her computer. Her head turned, but her eyes lingered on the monitor, and her fingers continued to bounce across the keyboard. After she emphatically slapped the Enter key, the receptionist looked at Rowe with a pleasant smile. She had dark hair, brown eyes, and a round face. "Yes? How can I help you?"

He lifted the brown paper bag so she could see it. "Digital Forensics."

"You know where it is?"

Rowe didn't know specifically, but he had a good idea. He nodded.

The woman's hand disappeared under the counter and the side door clicked. Rowe yanked it open and stepped through. A blast of voices greeted him. It was the sound of people talking all at once, much like the experience of being at a popular restaurant.

Offices lined the outer ring of the building. Cubicles clustered together in the center. Rowe meandered toward the back. He picked up snippets of conversations as he went and heard words common around a police department.

"That's when the suspect assaulted—"

"—the maggot grabbed her outside the—"

"I'm gonna put my foot up his ass the next time—"

Rowe ignored the various conversations as he hunted for the Digital Forensics section. He'd never been there before. He'd only seen the office once while visiting a friend in the building.

He stopped at a closed door with the appropriate label. A tall, rectangular window next to the door was blocked out with brown construction paper. Slivers of light leaked out from around the edges of the paper. Rowe tried the handle, but it was locked.

An older man in his mid-sixties ambled past with the confidence of a retired gunfighter. Rowe had never seen him before and couldn't read the ID badge dangling from the lanyard around his neck because it was turned backward.

The guy grumbled, "Knock," and continued by without breaking stride. He didn't even bother to smile.

Rowe wanted to tell the old bastard, "No shit," but thought it bad form to do so where so many could hear him. Had they been on the street, Rowe would have given the guy an earful. He lightly tapped his knuckles against the door.

In a moment, a beefy white guy with a gun and badge on his belt opened the door. The man's white button-up shirt struggled to contain his massive gut. An ID badge dangled from a lanyard and rested on the man's belly. The card read Detective Mark Wickenhauser. It also had a picture that showed Wickenhauser about seventy-five pounds lighter. Rowe wondered how long ago the picture was taken.

The detective held the door with one arm while the forearm of the other rested against the doorjamb. He was a fat troll, protecting the entrance into his digital lair.

Wickenhauser's gaze dropped to the bag. "What do you got?"

"A laptop."

"Why isn't it on property?"

"There was a murder."

Now, the detective's plump lips twisted with dissatisfaction. "Log it on property. We'll get it from there." He started to close the door.

Rowe put his hand up and stopped the door from closing. "Wait."

Wickenhauser eyed Rowe's hand like a caged lion watches visitors who get too close to the bars.

"My sergeant said to bring it here," Rowe said.

The detective met Rowe's gaze, and he scowled. "Who's your sergeant?"

"Ledbetter."

"Yeah?" Wickenhauser's face relaxed. "How is Megan?"

Megan?

"She's okay," Rowe said. "I guess."

"I haven't seen her in forever. Still pretty?"

Rowe didn't react. He couldn't imagine anyone saying Ledbetter was pretty.

Wickenhauser's attention dropped to the bag. "Why'd she tell you to skip property?"

"A woman witnessed a murder."

"On that?"

Rowe nodded. He quickly summarized the events as Naomi Stapleton had explained them.

"Why's the bag wet?" Wickenhauser asked.

"Her boyfriend drowned it."

The detective snapped his fingers. "Lemme see it."

Rowe removed the computer from the paper sack and handed it to him.

Wickenhauser tilted the computer left and right as he examined it. Water dripped out and ran down his arms. The man didn't seem bothered by it. "The boyfriend did more than drown it. He smacked the shit out of it."

"Can you get something off it?" Rowe asked.

The detective shrugged. "Depends on what's inside."

Rowe liked computers fine, but he didn't understand the intricacies of them. He was a plug-and-play guy, who used them simply as a tool for work. Beyond that, Rowe liked gaming systems at home. He waited for the detective to continue.

Wickenhauser grunted several times. It was a vile sound, like a pig eating at a trough. "The processor was probably running when the boyfriend dunked it, so its likely shorted out."

Rowe shrugged—whatever that meant.

"Which isn't a big deal if there's a hard drive inside. We can remove it, clone it, and we're good to go."

"But there might not be a hard drive inside, is what you're saying?"

The detective nodded. "Maybe it's got an SSD drive instead. If that's the case, we might be up shit's creek."

Rowe cocked his head.

"Solid State Drive. Never heard of it? It's like a really big flash card. You know what those are, don't you?"

"Like cameras use?"

"That's right." Wickenhauser's lips spread in the approximation of a smile, but it was something creepy and dreadful. Had they been on the street, Rowe would have pegged the detective as someone to be wary of. Maybe he still should.

Wickenhauser continued. "If the computer shorted itself out, the SSD drive could be fried, too." He closed the laptop. "Game over."

"But you'll try?"

"Of course, we'll try. Here." The detective handed back the laptop. "You got the report number on the bag?"

"I do." Rowe slid the computer into the sack, careful not to let it break through the wet bottom. He handed the bag to the detective.

Wickenhauser clutched it to his chest like a fullback ready to break through a defensive line. "I'll get to work on it."

Rowe nodded as he stepped away from the door. He wanted to end this conversation. As far as he was concerned, if he never had to deal with Detective Wickenhauser again, it would be too soon.

"Do me a favor," Wickenhauser said.

"What's that?"

"Tell Megan I said hi."

Wickenhauser kept climbing higher on Rowe's creepy index.

Rowe headed toward the exit. He didn't bother looking back.

Chapter 6

Morgan stopped his Dodge Charger at the front of the parking lot and climbed out. The yellow glow of the Zip's Burgers pylon sign reflected off the hood of the sedan. Traffic on Sprague Avenue crawled by.

The city had recently reduced the roadway from four lanes to two—proudly announcing the accomplishment as a 'traffic diet' in the news. The administration's sales pitch included a promise that decreased lanes would not increase trip times. This was achieved by adding separate bus turnouts for passenger drop off and pick up. The redesigned roadway also included a middle lane for turning cars.

Morgan thought it was bullshit. It was some traffic engineer's wet dream. Reducing lanes didn't speed up travel no matter how many pretty new pole lights were installed along the way.

But that's how Spokane saw itself now—promise over substance.

He opened the trunk, flipped up the floorboard, and found a crumpled bag near the spare tire. It was the only foreign item inside there. He lowered the floorboard and closed the trunk.

Morgan shoved the scrunched sack into his jacket pocket and reconsidered the corridor.

A glossy coating of unsustainable hope was slathered over the brutal ugliness Morgan once held so dear. Rotting neighborhoods like the East Sprague Corridor and Felony Flats were losing their souls. The homogenization of these areas was dangerous because they destroyed where the maggots congregated.

When the house flippers and the trendy moved in, they made things messy for the cops. Gentrification brought civilians who embraced prosperity with nice-sounding words like diversity and equality. Both were concepts Morgan supported when used away from the rot.

Whenever improvement arrived, it carried two problems. It brought new, unaware victims to the old neighborhoods. It also pushed the maggots out of their established homes into different areas that might not have had a problem before the new arrivals.

Morgan had a simple mission—keep Spokane's maggot problem localized and under control.

He headed toward the fast-food restaurant. Inside, fluorescent lights bathed the interior. A radio station played, but Morgan didn't know which kind of program because a commercial for some car lot played. Three employees hustled behind the counter as they attended to those customers in the drive-thru lane.

Two junkies sat across from each other. One had thick dark hair. He wore a tattered corduroy sport coat over a Brittney Spears T-shirt. His pant leg was split from the bottom to his hip, exposing a pair of dirty white briefs. Across from him was a gaunt man with brown hair. He wore a broken pair of sunglasses. The two seemed to be in the middle of conspiring when Morgan entered. They noticed him, whispered something to each other, and quickly gathered up their burgers. The two hurried out of the restaurant.

Joey Greene was the only other person in the lobby. She sat in the third booth on the left. An unwrapped burger and soda were on the orange tray in front of her.

She was a small black woman who didn't smile at Morgan's approach. Her life on the street showed in her eyes and hope no longer lingered there. She wore a Black Lives Matter shirt with the neck torn wide to expose a shoulder. Her hair was picked into a small afro.

"Jesus, Morgan," she said. "Announce to everyone you're here, why don't you?"

He slid into the booth. "You got a problem?"

"With how you parked? Yeah." Joey motioned toward the parking lot. "You're right on the street."

"Want me to leave?"

Her eyes shifted back to him, but she remained quiet.

"That's what I thought."

Joey and Morgan had had a complicated relationship over the years. She gave him information, and he gave her dope he taxed off junkies like the two who had just slunk away.

That's how Morgan did business. He robbed junkie Peter to pay informant Paul, but he never kept anything for himself. His dipping into the pocket of those engaged in the game was always done in pursuit of information. Maggots were kept at bay by any means necessary.

The crumpled bag he carried in his pocket was some of that necessity. Inside was a balloon of heroin he had lifted after arresting a dealer. More than enough remained to book the man for distribution. Holding one balloon back to trade for information wasn't going to hurt anyone.

Joey lifted her burger and bit into it. Ketchup squirted out of the side and dribbled down her chin. Joey didn't notice, though, and continued to chew.

"Your information was good," Morgan said.

He reached across the table and Joey jerked back. Morgan paused with his hand outstretched. Joey relaxed when she realized he wasn't going to hurt her. Morgan never would, not her.

Her sudden retraction was natural, though, an unfortunate reflex due to the world in which she lived. Joey leaned forward and pushed her chin out. Morgan rubbed off the splotch of ketchup with his thumb.

"What did you find?" she asked.

"A couple of goons who smacked around Courtney."

He stuck his thumb in his mouth and sucked off the condiment. It wasn't sexual; it was expedient.

"He all right?" Her face didn't register concern. The way she asked the question was the way someone might inquire after hearing about an accident involving a famous person—with interest, but no personal investment. Joey bit into the burger again.

"Those goons were lucky Courtney didn't hit back." Morgan abruptly changed course. "Who was the girl who gave you the information?"

Joey frowned. "I told you I'm not telling. It's bad enough people know we're connected." She motioned toward the parking lot with the burger. "Then you gotta go and remind everybody."

He ignored her concern. "You haven't heard anything else about the building?"

"Nothing. And I'm not sticking my nose into it. I learned my lesson."

"Good girl."

The last time Joey gave Morgan information like this, she inserted herself into the investigation. It ended up with her brutalized, and her attackers eventually dead. That was when Courtney was shot, and Morgan found himself in the crosshairs of a Major Crimes detective and an Internal Affairs lieutenant. Both talked to Joey.

Morgan hardened his feelings toward her after that. He would continue to use her as a snitch, but he had to be careful around her. Against his better judgment, Morgan had become entangled with her and developed a confusing set of feelings. Her business was using people, and she'd gotten him to drop his guard. He should have been smarter.

"You working tonight?" he asked.

"What do you think?"

He cocked his head as he studied her shirt.

Joey followed his gaze. "Some support the cause." Her eyes returned to his. "The ones that don't believe in it—" She shrugged. "I guess they'll make me take it off because it won't stop them from doing what they want to do. They're going to pay, anyway." She grabbed her soda. "Did you bring it?"

"You promised you were quitting," he said.

"I said that?" Joey slurped from her drink. "Well, you know what they say. A girl's gotta do and all that jazz."

She was independent. No one dared put the squeeze on Joey any longer because of the shadow Morgan cast. But this wouldn't release its hold, no matter how many times he suggested it.

Her shoulders fell. "Stop holding out. We've played this game too long to know how it's going to go."

Morgan reached into his jacket and pulled out the crumpled bag. "You left this in my car."

Joey's brow furrowed. "No, I didn't."

He scowled. "Yeah, you did."

Joey set her drink down. Her mouth slowly opened and closed while she thought. "You think I'm wearing a wire or something?"

Morgan no longer knew what to think, but he wasn't about to take chances with anyone. Had they been at Joey's house, he likely would have made her strip just to be sure. "I'm saying you left this in my car."

She flicked her hand at him. "Keep it. I don't want it."

Morgan pushed the bag to her side of the table. "Then throw it away. It's yours. Like I said, you left it in my car."

Joey stared at the rumpled sack for a moment. Her hand darted out from underneath the table to snatch the ball of paper, then it disappeared back from where it came. "Yeah," she said, "maybe I did." Her expression quickly hardened. "You know I would never do nothing to rat you out."

He no longer knew that, but he wanted to believe it. Morgan's feelings were still confused, but he would never again forget what she did for a living.

She used people.

Just like he did.

Chapter 7

"You still mad at me?" Naomi Stapleton asked.

She stood at the edge of the living room with her arms crossed.

Guillermo Messi reclined on the couch with his feet up on the coffee table. His concentration was on the large screen television and the video game he played. The explosions and gunfire were so loud, she wasn't certain he'd heard her.

"Guille."

His face pinched. "What?"

"You hear what I said?"

He leaned right and ducked as if to avoid incoming fire. "Yeah."

"Well?"

Guillermo paused the game and faced her. "You done already?"

They'd gone to Best Buy together and bought a new laptop. She'd spent the last couple of hours setting it up and getting her various accounts reconnected.

Guillermo wanted her to do another session on OnlyFans but her heart wasn't in it. Her head was still on the earlier incident.

"I haven't started," she said.

"Why the fuck not?"

"Because I'm worried."

His brow furrowed. "About?"

"If you're still mad at me."

Irritation splashed over his features, and he turned back to the game. The explosions and gunfire started again.

Naomi stepped forward. "Talk to me."

He paused the game. "What for?"

"I want you to stop being mad."

"No." He shook his head. "I told you not to do that shit, but you went and did it anyway. I owe you for that." Guille pointed the controller at her. "You invited trouble for yourself was all you did."

"What kind of trouble can I get in with them?"

Guille tossed the controller to the couch. "I guess this ain't happening." He reached for the bong. "You tell me, genius. What kind of shit did you have on your computer?"

"Nothing."

He raised an eyebrow. "Really?"

Naomi turned her palms upward. "I didn't have anything on there except my work stuff."

"So you're cool with a bunch of cops seeing your pussy now?"

She stiffened. "Why would you say that?"

"Because you got pics on there, don't you?"

Naomi did have nude pictures of herself. Mostly she streamed videos now, but she sent her fans occasional photographs—gifts, she called them—to keep them engaged.

Competition in the OnlyFans world was fierce, and she needed to find ways to stand out. Some of the other women in the space sold their underwear and socks. Naomi hadn't gotten to that level, but she imagined someday she might—if she was lucky.

Guille's lip curled. "Tell me you didn't have any pictures of us fucking?"

She shook her head. "We only streamed the one time."

He pointed the lighter. "If some cop sees my dick, I'm gonna lose my shit. I didn't sign up for that."

Naomi didn't point out that cops watched porn, too. Her friend, Kennedy, knew police officers subscribed to her account because she talked to them about it.

Guille lit the bowl and inhaled deeply. He held the smoke in his lungs for several seconds before exhaling. He pointed the lighter at her again. "When them cops find those pussy pics, you can damn sure believe they'll use that shit against you."

"But did we have to destroy my computer?"

He slammed the bong on the coffee table and jumped to his feet. "You think what I did was wrong?"

"No."

Guille flexed his shoulders. "You think it was stupid?"

"I didn't say that."

"You didn't have to." He threw the lighter, and it hit her in the bicep.

Naomi winced and grabbed her arm where it hurt, but she didn't leave the room. She knew better than that.

"I know when you think you're better than me." Guille stomped closer. His face reddened. "You better get yourself in check, bitch."

"What'd I do?"

His hand shot out and snaked its way into her golden hair. He twisted and pulled her near him. "You know what you did. I saw you looking at them cops. You think you can get away from me by waving that coochie for them?"

"That's not what I did."

He twisted his fist and jerked her lower. "Don't lie. Tell me the truth."

Tears formed in her eyes. He wouldn't believe the truth. She loved him and would never leave him, but Guille liked to pretend he was her pimp. Her neck hurt from being contorted at this angle, and it felt like he was about to yank her hair out.

"Yeah," she whispered.

"Yeah, what?"

"I thought I could get away."

He smirked. "That's what I thought."

His fingers released her hair, and she straightened.

Naomi wiped the tears from her face. "Guille, I would never—"

He slapped her. The blow surprised her, and she fell to the floor. He'd never hit her in the face before.

Guille leaned over her. "Get your ass back in the studio and start earning again. Stop with the tears. Ain't nobody buying them."

She rubbed her cheek and stared up at him.

"Don't come at me with no bullshit during my game ever again!" Spittle covered his lips as he yelled. "Got it?"

"I'm sorry," she whispered.

"Sorrys don't pay the bills."

They stared at each other for several long seconds. Outside, a car missing a muffler drove by. The refrigerator kicked on and hummed loudly from the kitchen.

Guille's face softened, and he stepped back. "Get up."

Naomi struggled to her feet. He grabbed her elbow and helped her the last bit.

"Yo," he said. "I'm sorry about that." He carefully fussed with her hair. "You know how I get sometimes."

She stared at him, afraid the tears might return.

Guillermo pulled her hand away from her cheek. "It's not so bad. A little makeup will cover it fine." He kissed her where it stung. "You'll look great. Better than those schleps deserve."

Naomi sniffled.

"Have you tried the new computer?"

She nodded.

"It works good?"

Another nod.

He grabbed both shoulders. "Everything is gonna be great."

"Everything is gonna be great," she parroted.

"Your fans haven't got to see much of you today, have they?"

The incident with Nick had thrown the day sideways. It was sad the guy had died, but as Guille had pointed out, she had a business to run.

"Why don't you go in the studio for a bit?" His voice was gentle, and Naomi noticed he wasn't ordering her now.

"I'm hungry," she said. Her voice sounded like a little girl's.

"I know. We'll get something in a bit." Guille rubbed her arms. She winced when his hand went over the spot hit by the lighter. "Got you good with that, huh?"

"Stings a little."

"My temper. I'll try to be better."

"I know."

He rubbed her arms some more, and she tried to hide her discomfort.

"Why don't you work for a bit? Not long, okay? Just give them a taste so they don't forget about you. Then we'll order some delivery. You can get your favorite."

She smiled. "From Lunar Pizza?"

He nodded. "Of course."

That was why she loved him. He allowed her to have her way on so many things.

Guille reached for the bong, then picked up the lighter from the floor. "Here. Why don't you relax?"

She took a long hit. While she held it, Guille gazed longingly into her eyes.

"You're a good girl."

Naomi Stapleton exhaled and smiled. That was the Guille she knew and loved. His attitude became erratic after she started the online sex work. It seemed to get worse after he began pretending to be her pimp.

"Now, go back and give them a show," he said.

Guille took the bong and lighter, then returned to the couch. He flopped into his previous spot and took a quick hit for himself. Next, he grabbed the video game controller and the explosions and gunfire returned.

Naomi's grin slowly faded. Her man was right. The show had to go on.

Chapter 8

James Morgan pressed a security fob against the entry pad and entered the apartment community's weight room. To be more exact, he should call it the Fitness Facility, which was written on the glass door, but that always sounded wimpy in his ears.

Light jazz music played over a set of hidden speakers. It was the same station piped into the community center's office lobby. Morgan didn't care for music and would have been fine with silence.

A few residents were there at that hour. One ran a heavy-footed pace on a treadmill, its whirring a comforting sound. Another man stood before a wall-length mirror and curled free weights, his face red with exertion. The last resident, a woman, worked on the Universal Machine.

He'd seen them all there before, but only one made him smile—the woman, Vivian Basler.

When she stood, she was nearly as tall as he was. She'd rounded the corner of her forties a year or two ago. Vivian always looked as if she stepped out of a fashion magazine and right now was no exception. She wore a tight-fitting shirt that read Trust the Process, yoga pants, and running shoes. Her short blond hair was hidden underneath a carefully tattered denim baseball hat.

Morgan walked over to the weight bench and flopped down. He grabbed the empty bar and did twenty slow presses to warm his chest muscles. He wouldn't have when he was younger, but wisdom came with age. That was a tale he liked to tell himself.

After the quick stretch, he grabbed a couple of 45-pound plates and put one on each side. Morgan lay back on the bench and hefted the bar off the rack.

He was on the eighth rep when Vivian walked over and stared down at him.

Morgan paused in his pressing. "Not going to say hello?"

"You're in the middle of a set."

"Doesn't stop me."

"I see that."

He pushed out his ninth and tenth reps, set the bar back into place, and sat up. That's when Morgan noticed a light sheen of sweat on Vivian's forehead. Dopamine spiked in his system when he wondered what her perspiration tasted like.

Vivian fought back a smile, as if she could read Morgan's thoughts. "It's nice to see you, too."

Before he could respond, she headed back to the Universal Machine. She straddled the seat and reached up for the pulldown bar.

Morgan went for two more plates—another pair of 45-pounders.

When he stole a glance at Vivian by way of the full-length mirror, she caught him looking. His heart raced, and he felt foolish, like a schoolboy with his first crush.

Morgan had longed for Vivian since the first time they met in the community's indoor pool. The two had become friends, but neither stepped over the line to suggest something more. Morgan always resisted crossing over the line. It wasn't fear that held him back.

He slipped the additional plates onto the bar and settled underneath it. Once he positioned himself, he lifted it off and began his second set.

Morgan loved living in the community because he'd met many lovers there over the years. His life was chaotic, and he no longer had an interest in going to a bar to meet women. He'd done that in his younger years. Now that he was in his early fifties, women were merely a pleasant diversion.

He pressed his eighth repetition and set the bar back onto the rack.

Morgan's days were numbered at the police department, so he wanted to make every moment count. Sooner or later, he would age out. Someone in the administration would determine he didn't matter anymore, and they'd force him to retire or move to a less strenuous job. Until that day, CTF would always remain his priority.

Because of that, women remained a distraction—a beautiful means to an end. He used the apartment community to fulfill that need. That's how he met his last girlfriend, a redhead far too young for him by society's standards. The girl knew what she was getting into by his reputation around the community. She decided to challenge him, nonetheless. She was full of energy and pleasant curves. However, she didn't like the push and pull, the game Morgan played with all women.

Most women couldn't stand the game.

Morgan sat upright and looked at Vivian.

She dabbed her face with a small towel. She didn't pay any attention to him. He felt slightly disappointed. He hoped for a little conversation. At the very least, a glance his way. Maybe a little smile. Morgan stood and headed for the plate rack and grabbed a pair of 25-pound plates. He slid them onto the bar.

As he lay on the bench, Morgan realized Vivian was playing the game he loved. She'd come over and said hello, then walked away, leaving him wanting more.

With a grunt, he lifted the bar.

Vivian Basler was the one woman who Morgan would throw everything away for. She was the only one who understood the game better than he did. They'd never even kissed, but he knew he'd lay down his life for her. James Morgan was certain he loved her.

She appeared above him again and broke his thoughts.

"Why are you ignoring me, Jimmy?"

Vivian was the only one who could get away with calling him that. The nickname sounded like fingernails on a chalkboard, but through her lips it sounded like silk on bare skin.

The bar and its plates suddenly felt heavier than they should, and it was only the third repetition. It was 275 lbs. He was going for six reps; he could always do that number.

Morgan groaned. He paused with his arms fully extended. "I'm not ignoring you." His voice sounded strained.

He pushed out the fourth repetition. His chest muscles felt like they were going to explode.

Vivian hovered over him. "I'm over there and you continue to ignore me."

"You're crazy," he wheezed. He caught a whiff of her perfume. She smelled wonderful.

The bar settled onto his chest.

Vivian studied him as he broke rhythm. A smile slowly formed. "Trouble getting it up?"

He pushed. The weight felt heavier than it had in years. He squirmed underneath it. His feet slipped on the ground.

This was only his fifth repetition. There was no way he was getting six tonight. Not with her standing above him.

"Need some help?" she asked.

"No," he gasped.

The barbell wavered from side to side as it rose and his arms shook. Morgan's legs found their footing, and he arched his back. Every fiber in his body strained to get the weight off him. His arms finally extended, and the bar fell backward, clunking loudly into place.

Morgan sat up. His chest burned, and he breathed heavily.

"You should be careful," Vivian said. "You might give yourself an aneurysm."

He stood so he could face her. "How's business?"

"It's been better," she said.

Vivian managed a group of webcam girls. They were mostly foreign and in their early twenties. Vivian set them up with their own apartments and oversaw the operation. She was a digital madam. Years ago, she ran her own webcam business, but stopped when she discovered the lucrative nature of managing others.

Morgan had thought about looking her up on the internet, in hopes of finding a picture or video of her. But he always stopped himself. He didn't want to see her that way. He didn't care that she'd done the webcam gig, but he wanted her sexuality to remain a secret. It was part of the push and pull. The unrealized allure. The never-captured surprise.

"Still losing girls?" he asked.

"Most realize they can go out on their own so they think don't need me. They don't know how to manage their money or their impulses."

"What happens when they do learn to control those?"

Vivian shrugged. "I've prepared for that eventuality."

Morgan thought about a follow-up question, but Vivian wandered back to the Universal Machine.

He could pursue her in hopes of continuing the game, but there were rules to the push and pull. Morgan had to be careful not to show too much interest. Vivian already knew he liked her too much.

Morgan slipped off the 25-pound plates to do another set at the reduced weight. He settled onto the bench and lifted the barbell into place. He did six reps, the last two were exceptionally hard, and he struggled not to cry out in exertion.

When he sat upright, he glanced toward the Universal Machine. Vivian was no longer there. He looked around the Fitness Facility, but she'd slipped away while he was under the bar.

Morgan shook his head ruefully. She'd left him wanting more.

It was the push and pull, and Vivian Basler always won.

DAY 2

Chapter 9

Detective Damien Truscott's desk phone rang. The number on the small ID screen showed his supervisor, Sergeant Ryan Yager, was calling. Truscott didn't bother leaning back in his chair. He couldn't see Yager's office from where he sat.

He picked up the receiver and announced his name.

"Go see Lieutenant Brand," Yager said.

The Major Crimes supervisor, Truscott thought. There was no way the administration was transferring him out of Property Crimes. Not after he'd just gotten demoted from the Special Victims Unit.

"What for?" he asked.

"They need some help."

"Why me?"

Yager scoffed. "Anyone else would say 'thank you.'" He hung up.

Truscott abandoned the report he was writing. He'd done some follow-up that morning on a residential burglary but was unable to locate a suspect. It was mostly a cover-his-ass report; the type many detectives did to show they worked even when they developed no new leads. The department was still a government agency, and like all government agencies, it wanted to create one thing—paperwork.

He passed through the Major Crimes office. Several of the detectives ignored him. Camaraderie existed within the police department, but it wasn't a blanket attitude. Instead, it was like a junior high school. Small cliques ruled the hallways and long-established pecking orders were maintained.

Truscott once felt like a popular jock, the guy who had a lot of friends. Now, he felt like the kid caught eating paste—or worse.

Detective Andrew Parker looked up from his desk. He lifted his chin by way of a friendly gesture, then returned to studying a binder splayed open on his desk. It was the only display of friendliness Truscott received in the MC bullpen.

Lieutenant George Brand hunkered behind his computer, the monitor lights reflecting off his round spectacles. He was a large, bald man with an accountant's demeanor. Truscott always thought him wrong for the department, but somehow the man made it through the academy and years on the street.

It was a neat office. A hutch stood behind the desk with binders and books competing for prominence. Awards were precisely aligned on the walls. A square clock hung in the middle, as if marking time until a new accolade could take its place.

Truscott tapped the door frame.

Brand looked away from the computer. "Thank you for coming." He lifted a file from his desk. "I wanted to talk with you about this before I emailed it."

"What is it?" Truscott grabbed the file and sat in one of the chairs.

"I'm assigning you a case."

Occasionally, a loser case landed in the purview of Major Crimes. Whether for a lack of evidence, witness credibility, or many other possibilities Truscott didn't want to consider, the cases were destined to go nowhere. The department had a duty to investigate them, however. Putting an experienced homicide detective on them was deemed a waste of valuable resources.

Property Crimes detectives weren't so highly valued.

"It came in yesterday," Brand continued. "A woman witnessed a homicide."

Truscott scanned the file as the lieutenant spoke. He could already see the problems. The responding officers were Ron Rowe and Lucas Jefferson, a couple of meatheads who wrote shitty reports. Truscott had opportunities to follow up on some of their past reports and knew he'd have to be careful. The officers had a habit of leaving out important details, getting barely enough to justify probable cause. Since no arrest was made, who knew what they left out?

Brand droned on, but Truscott looked up when he heard something about Digital Forensics. "What's that?"

"The laptop. It's with Digital Forensics now."

Truscott closed the folder. Maybe this case wouldn't be such a dog after all. He waved the folder. "Can I have this?"

Brand motioned for him to take it. "It's yours."

Truscott stood. He saluted the lieutenant with the file. "I'll do my best."

"Don't waste too much time on it. Give it a once over, then write a report. Let Chicago PD handle it."

***

The phone rang in his ear while Damien Truscott continued to scan the opened file on his desk. The reports Rowe and Jefferson wrote were better than he expected. Perhaps they had grown as officers. Or maybe they had a more attentive sergeant this year.

After reading about the damage to the laptop, Truscott worried there might not be anything salvageable.

The phone continued ringing in his ear. How many was that? Truscott wondered. Four? Maybe even five. When would someone answer Rowe's call?

While in SVU, Truscott had learned the Digital Forensics team was amazing, but there were still limitations to their wizardry. They couldn't do all the crazy antics shown in the movies or on television shows. An investigator couldn't plug a USB cord into a suspect's computer and immediately reveal every aspect of an individual's life in 256 colors or on a three-dimensional display.

On the eighth ring, the phone connected.

"Homicide," a woman wearily announced.

Truscott asked, "Is this the Chicago Police Department?" He immediately cringed.

On his computer monitor was the phone number for the Chicago Police Department's Homicide Division. He had looked it up. So, why did he just ask the woman if it was CPD?

He blamed distraction since he was thinking about computer forensics.

"Homicide," the woman repeated.

"Yeah, this is Detective Truscott with the Spokane Police Department. I'd like to speak to a supervisor."

"Hold."

The phone started playing a song about drinking pina coladas. Truscott didn't know the lyrics, but he'd heard it before. It was a tune his dad listened to during Truscott's childhood.

Truscott tried to focus on the file, but he found himself enjoying the song and singing along with the part about getting caught in the rain. He closed his eyes and listened to the lyrics of the second and third verses. The singer eventually revealed the woman who walked into the bar called O'Malley's was his old lady. Truscott thought that was a nice twist.

Disappointment shot through him when the song broke before it ended. He wanted to hear the chorus once more, but he could probably sing it by heart now.

"Sergeant Lowden," a gruff male voice said over crinkling paper.

Truscott introduced himself.

"You caught me in the middle of my lunch," Lowden said, "so I'm gonna eat while you talk. You got a problem with that?"

He'd forgotten about the two-hour time difference. "No, I'm good."

Paper rustled near the microphone, and the sergeant moaned slightly as if he enjoyed what he was tasting. "What's this about?" Lowden asked through a mouthful of food.

"I'm following up on a report."

Lowden coughed. "Where'd you say you were?"

"Spokane."

"Where's that?"

"Washington."

"D.C.?"

"State."

"Oh," Lowden said. "Seattle."

"The other side of the state."

A keyboard clacked as Lowden asked, "What do you want with us out there?"

"A woman said she witnessed a murder."

"We got enough of our own," Lowden said. "Thank you very much."

"She said she saw it on the internet."

The sergeant snapped his fingers. "Gonzaga! I knew Spokane sounded familiar. I just googled it." Paper crumpled again.

"Yeah," Truscott said. "They're royalty out here."

Lowden's lips smacked as he chewed. "They bust my bracket every year. Either I pick them, or I don't, but they fuck me no matter what I do."

"So, about this murder?"

"You said she saw it on the internet?"

"That's right."

Lowdown slurped a drink. "She nutso or something?"

Truscott put his elbows on his desk and rested his head in his open hand. The other continued to press the receiver to his ear. "The officers who responded seem to think she's stable."

"We get more than our share of loonies reporting murders."

"Listen," Truscott said. "All I want to know is if you guys processed any homicides yesterday."

Lowden laughed, then coughed. It sounded as if he were choking. This went on for a minute.

"You okay?" Truscott asked.

"You're kidding?" Something thunked near the sergeant's phone. Did he just put his lunch down? Was it that heavy? "We got killings coming out our ears."

"How many did you have yesterday?"

"Listen to you." Lowden clucked. "How many did we have yesterday? A helluva lot more than you guys in Spokane. I'll tell you that much." A keyboard clacked. "For your information, we had three."

"Were any of them a guy named Nick?"

Lowden didn't respond. The line remained open because Truscott could hear various people talking in the background.

"Hello?"

"Is that all you got for me?" Lowdown asked. "Tell me you didn't interrupt my meatball sando for a guy named Nick."

"He's a white male, approximately thirty-five."

"Named Nick."

Truscott realized how weak his information was, so he added, "Probably short for Nicholas."

The paper crinkled near the phone. "Or Dominic."

"Right."

"Or Nicodemus," Lowden said through a mouthful of meatball sandwich.

Truscott sighed. "Nobody is naming their kid Nicodemus."

"Or maybe it was short for his last name. Like Nicholas."

"I already said that."

"But you were thinking first name. Tell me I'm wrong."

Truscott didn't bother to hide his irritation. "Was anyone with a name like that killed yesterday?"

"No," Lowden said.

"Let me ask you this. Was anyone murdered in front of his computer?"

"You thinking his computer zapped him?"

Truscott pinched the bridge of his nose. "Like maybe someone came up from behind and double-tapped him in the back of the head."

"We ain't got nothing like that on our files."

"There you go," Truscott said.

"There you go."

"Thank you for your time, Sergeant."

"Hey," Lowden said, "do me a favor."

"What's that?"

"Keep them Zags outta my bracket this year."

The sergeant hung up without saying goodbye.

Truscott stared at the receiver. He thought people only did that in the movies.

Chapter 10

"We got a hit," Nayla Senai said.

Morgan turned from his computer to look at her. "On what?"

She leaned around her monitor. "On the pictures I sent to Crime Analysis yesterday."

They were the only two in the Criminal Task Force office. The sergeant was at an administration briefing in the Public Safety Building, and the rest of the team were on separate projects. Only Courtney Earley had gone back to watch The Hempstead. He was in the vacant unit across the street.

"What'd they say?" Morgan asked.

"They identified both men. Sergei Golubev and Mikhail Semyonov."

"Couple of Russians?"

"Eastern Europeans," she corrected.

Morgan rolled his eyes. He never wanted to offend Senai or her heritage. Morgan went out of his way to be careful with her after the way he was raised. His father and grandfather brought him up in the hate, and he wanted desperately to keep that indoctrination at bay. However, Morgan had no love for the Russians. Those lessons remained from his time in the Marines, and there was no way that was ever getting out of his system. He wouldn't try to remove his disdain for the commies if given a choice.

In Morgan's book, Russia was America's mortal enemy. If people wanted him to be politically correct about that, they could shove it up their traitorous asses.

"They got records?" Morgan asked.

"Healthy ones," Senai said. "You name it and they've done it or been accused of it."

"You got addresses?"

"We do."

Morgan stood and walked over to Senai's computer to check out their pictures. Golubev was the man in the red track suit. Semyonov was the man in the green. "Maybe we should introduce ourselves. See what's happening in their world."

"Sounds like a plan."

"Contact Adrian and Doc," Morgan said. "Have them watch Sergei and Mikhail. Let Courtney know we've identified them."

Senai nodded.

"If they start to move, have them call for a stop."

"Right."

"But tell them to give the Russians time to get away from their homes so it doesn't look purposeful."

Senai frowned. "It's not my first rodeo."

"You ever been to a rodeo?"

The attractive woman of Ethiopian descent stared at him.

Morgan smirked. "I didn't think so."

"I can still say it."

"Sure, you can. It's a free country." He headed toward the door.

"Yes, it is." She stood to better see him. "Where are you going?"

"To talk with SIU."

"Why?"

"To play nice."

He paused at the door to see the expression on her face. It was rare to see Senai dumbfounded.

The Spokane Police Department's Special Investigations Unit resided in the Gardner Building. Years prior, SIU had been in the Monroe Court Building. However, their relocation was part of the department's consolidation into the repurposed evidence storage building.

Morgan appreciated the department's gang unit being so far away from CTF. His team often stepped on SIU's metaphorical toes. Sometimes, Morgan even stomped on them. Had the gang unit been across the hall, it would have made for uncomfortable times. As it was, whenever Morgan went too far, Sergeant Trevor Hackworth picked up the phone and chewed Bynum out over observing lanes of operation. Since the move to the Gardner Building, at least he could no longer come down the hall to do it in person.

At the lowest level, it was territorial pissing. At its highest, it was empire building. Morgan didn't care, though. He had a job to do—keep the maggots at bay. If that meant bumping some of his compatriots out of his way, he'd do it.

He paused in the Gardner Building's lobby. The receptionist looked up and her eyes briefly widened. She regained her composure, swallowed hard, and looked over her shoulder.

Her name was Rebecca Maupin. She had a round face, agreeable hips, and a boring, inattentive husband. She and Morgan had met a couple of years back at a probation party. Every new class of rookies threw one. Morgan always made a point to stop in and say hello. Rebecca was more than a little friendly to Morgan that night and he'd accepted her advances. He treated her the way he thought a disregarded wife wanted. Since then, she barely spoke to him.

She buzzed him through the security door without waiting for him to announce his purpose for being there.

He grinned at her, and Rebecca's cheeks flushed. She looked away. Morgan grabbed the door and entered the secure facility.

In his office, Sergeant Hackworth sat at his desk and bent over a report. He clutched a brown felt-tip pen in one hand and rubbed his bald head with the other. His face contorted with concentration.

He was an intense man. Under other circumstances, Morgan believed the two might have liked each other. As it were, they were two pit bulls often fighting over the same piece of meat.

Morgan asked, "You ever hear of two commie bastards named Sergei Golubev and Mikhail Semyonov?"

Hackworth looked up with a scowl. "The fuck?"

He repeated the names.

The sergeant snapped the cap onto the pen. "What of them?"

"So, you have. What can you tell me about them?"

"Why do you want to know?" Hackworth crossed his arms. He pulled his shoulders back to flex his chest.

The growling over the same cut of steak had started, Morgan thought. He hoped the two Russians were worth it.

"We're watching them," Morgan said.

"What for?"

"We like their fashion sense."

Hackworth's lip curled. "Funny. No, really."

"They're involved in The Hempstead."

"That piece of shit on Riverside?"

Morgan nodded. "That's the one."

"What are they doing with that?"

"We don't know. That's what we're trying to find out."

Hackworth cocked his head. "Why are you here?"

"I just said."

"No. Why are you *really* here?"

Morgan spread his hands. "Can't a guy play nice?"

"Not you."

"What kind of trouble are we going to get when we contact them?"

Hackworth briefly pursed his lips, then he brought the one lower between his teeth and gnawed on it. "Sergei's not so bad. He's full of bluster. Mikey's the one you gotta watch."

"Why's that?"

"He thinks he's a big shot. Push him too far and he might snap."

"Who do they work for?"

The sergeant shook his head. "No one as far as I know. They used to run their own crew, but a couple years ago, they fell off our radar. I'm surprised you're even looking into them."

"Why's that?"

"They're low-level trouble. Hardly worth your effort. What has the mighty CTF sunken to?"

Morgan shrugged. "I guess we're picking up the crumbs left behind by SIU."

"That's what we do. Wiping villainy from the streets so you don't have to."

"A regular crew of superheroes."

"Jealousy looks good on you." His attention dropped back to his paperwork. "See yourself out."

Morgan zigzagged through the cubicles. He said hello to a few folks he knew. It was always good to keep relationships in a variety of departments. He never knew when he might need a friendly ear or a helping hand.

His cell phone buzzed, and he pulled it from his pocket. It was a text message from Courtney Earley.

COME SEE ME. I GOT SOMETHING FOR YOU.

Back in the lobby, he pulled the security door closed behind him. Rebecca turned, saw him, and immediately straightened. Her eyes darted about, afraid to look at him too long.

Morgan approached the Plexiglas. "How've you been?" he asked.

She leaned in and whispered. "I can never do that again."

"It was your idea."

Rebecca's hand stroked her neck. Her mouth opened and closed as if she were a fish struggling for air. "It was wrong."

"Of course it was," Morgan said. "But you know how to get a hold of me if you ever change your mind."

"I can't," she hissed. She glanced about, seemingly worried someone might see them talking.

He smiled. Even though he'd been without a woman for a while, Morgan really didn't care if Rebecca wanted another roll in the sack. He only wanted her to call. If she did, Morgan wasn't sure he'd agree to see her.

By the look in her eyes, he knew she would call. Maybe not today. Perhaps not tomorrow. Someday soon her husband's inattentiveness would reach an intolerable level again. That's when Rebecca would reach out. He knew that for certain.

Morgan tapped the counter. "I'll talk with you soon."

Chapter 11

An explosion jolted Naomi Stapleton from her sleep. Her body jerked, and she kicked her feet. She lifted her head from her pillow and reached for Guille, but he was gone. There was another explosion and more gunfire.

"Ugh," she groaned and dropped back onto the pillow.

He was playing that stupid game again. She wished he'd stop. It's like he wanted to do that more than anything. Even sex couldn't lure him away from the controller. He tried to talk her into blowing him while he played, but Naomi wasn't having any of that. What did she get out of it besides a sore neck?

"Turn it down!" she hollered.

She grabbed his pillow and held it over her head, squeezing it so it wrapped around her ears. That muffled the sound, but she could barely breathe. Naomi tolerated it for several moments but eventually yanked the pillow from her face and slammed it back to his side of the bed.

What time was it? Naomi wondered. She rolled over and grabbed her phone from the nightstand. 9:32 a.m. She flopped onto her back. What the hell was Guille thinking? They never got up that early.

She lifted the phone above her face because she'd noticed something—a missed call. With a tap of her thumb, she opened the call history. Two calls had come in from a blocked number. The first was about an hour ago, the second came thirty minutes later. Naomi turned off her ringer when she went to bed—Guille insisted she do it, so it didn't interrupt his sleep.

She lowered her hand and rested the phone on her stomach.

Whoever had called from a blocked number hadn't left a message; they couldn't because Naomi never set up her voice mail. Why should she? Her friends texted. Only Boomers called. Her mother and grandmothers called. Bill collectors called; well, they used to before she started earning with OnlyFans.

Naomi lifted the phone again and reconsidered the call history. Maybe it was the cops, she thought. Guille once told her they called from blocked numbers. Were they calling because the officers forgot something?

She set the ringer to buzz and closed her eyes.

An image of Nick flashed in her head. Physically, he was a vile man—short and pudgy. He had a bulbous nose and his eyes bulged behind thick, dark-rimmed glasses.

Naomi never saw him below the waist, and she was thankful. Nick sat near his desk and his body trembled and shook as he touched himself. He cooed nice sentiments—complimentary words Guille never said. They were comments no man had ever said to her.

"If you were my woman, I would worship the ground you walked on."

She knew what Nick said was ridiculous, but she liked it, nonetheless. He paid her to play with herself while he jerked off. It was sex at its crudest.

"You are the finest princess I have ever seen."

No man had ever called her a princess. Not even her father when he violated her. He hadn't even called her that the night before he killed himself. Even though Nick was physically repulsive, she liked it when he called her a princess. She wanted to be thought of that way by someone.

Guille only called her his bitch since he started with the pimp nonsense. She tolerated it because she wanted him to feel good about himself.

The phone buzzed in her hand and the ID screen announced another blocked call.

Her eyes cut to the door. Explosions and gunfire continued to come from the living room.

She swung her feet from the bed and padded to the door. As quietly as she could, she shut it.

Guille hadn't wanted her to report the murder to the police. He made his feelings clear last night when he slapped her. How would he feel if she answered the phone right now and it was the cops?

The phone buzzed again in her hand.

She thought about the cooing words Nick had said. "You are the finest princess I have ever seen." The man didn't deserve to die that way.

Her thumb swiped across the screen. "Hello?" she whispered.

"Naomi Stapleton?" His voice was masculine, full of confidence.

"Uh-huh." She hurried back to the bed and hopped onto it.

"This is Detective Truscott with the Spokane Police Department."

"Uh-huh," she said. Her eyes remained on the doorknob. If it turned, she'd hang up immediately.

"Are you okay?"

"Yes," she said.

"You're whispering."

"My boyfriend is sleeping."

"I'd like to come and reinterview you both about the incident that occurred yesterday."

She cringed but didn't look away from the door. "That's not a good idea."

"Why not?"

"He's not happy I called."

"Your boyfriend doesn't want you to talk with the police?"

"Uh-huh." She covered her mouth.

Explosions and gunfire continued from the other side of the door. She canted her head to check for shadows. Guille had a wireless controller. He could play and walk around the house. If he heard her talking, he might move closer to the door.

"What about you?" Detective Truscott asked.

"Huh?"

"What about you? Do you have a problem talking with the police? I'd really like to know what happened."

"That would be fine," she whispered.

"Would you come to the department and talk with me here?"

She straightened. What if Guille saw her at the police department? What if one of his friends saw her going in? What would she say then?

"No. Not there."

"How about I buy you a coffee?" Truscott said. "We could meet at Starbucks or something."

She leaned over and checked for more shadows. The noises from the game continued.

Sitting with a policeman seemed unnecessarily dangerous. If Guille found her with another man, he would go nuclear. If he discovered the man was a cop, who knew how bad it would be?

"Can you meet me at a grocery store?" Naomi asked.

"I'll meet you anywhere. Which one?"

"The Safeway on Northwest Boulevard."

"Fine," Truscott said. "When?"

"In an hour?"

"That's good. Where should I meet you?"

"Near the eggs," she said and hung up.

Naomi swung her feet off the bed and walked out of the bedroom. In the living room, Guille reclined on the couch. He wore only his boxer shorts, and his feet were on the coffee table. The video game seemed extra loud now.

He glanced at her. "You're finally up."

"Thanks to your game," she muttered.

Guille leaned as he ducked away from an incoming rocket. "What's that?" he asked.

"Nothing."

Naomi walked into the kitchen, opened the refrigerator, and pulled out the carton of eggs. It was half full. She turned and stared at the back of Guille's head. "I'm going to make some eggs," she said over the simulated gunfire. "Want some?"

"Huh?"

"Want some eggs?" she said louder.

"Yeah. Bacon, too."

Naomi opened the carton and turned it over. The eggs dropped and splattered over the floor.

"Shit."

"What?"

"I dropped the eggs."

Guille glanced over his shoulder. "Fucking klutz."

Naomi grabbed some paper towels and the trash can. Now, she wouldn't be questioned when she went to the grocery store. In the entire time they'd known each other, Guille had never gone with her.

Chapter 12

Morgan unlocked the apartment door, but it only opened a few inches before a security chain stopped it.

"Big man," he said through the narrow opening. "Let me in."

"Hold on," Courtney Earley called.

Heavy footsteps crossed the apartment until Earley came into view. "Sorry about that."

The door closed and Morgan heard the chain slide back before it opened again.

Courtney Earley stood in the doorway. He was several inches taller than Morgan. He had broad shoulders, a softening midsection, and a long scraggly beard. He wore a black Metallica T-shirt, blue jeans, and biker boots.

"Skittish?" Morgan asked.

"If you really want to know, I was in the head."

"So, you put the chain on?"

"I like my privacy. My gut is acting up."

Morgan patted Courtney's stomach as he walked by. "I've got no idea why."

The big man shoved Morgan in the shoulder, which slammed the detective into the wall. "Those in glass houses, fat man."

Morgan shook the ringing from his head. "Respect your elders."

"Don't poke the bear."

"Easy, Smokey." He squeezed Earley's upper arm. "What did you want to show me?"

Earley motioned Morgan to follow him toward the window. Two chairs were where Morgan had sat with Senai yesterday, but on top of the tripod today was a cell phone. Senai had taken her camera back to the station. "They got some groceries this morning."

Morgan cocked his head. "Groceries?"

Earley nodded. "From Black Sea Market. It's a Russian store on Mission."

"How do you know that?" Morgan asked.

"That it's a Russian grocery?"

"And where it was located."

"I googled it. How do you think?"

Earley detached the phone from the tripod. "This whole business gets weirder."

"Anybody come out of the building?"

"Not yet."

"Did the delivery guy go inside?"

"Hold on," Courtney said.

The big man's fingers danced over the phone. In a minute, a video started. "Here you go," Courtney said. He held the phone so both could see.

A delivery van with the Black Sea grocery logo splashed on its side sat in front of The Hempstead.

"I didn't get it started until the van had already stopped," Courtney said. "At first, I thought it was going to pass by."

Morgan grunted.

From the lower right of the screen, two men in tracksuits trotted toward the back of the van—Sergei Golubev and Mikhail Semyonov.

The driver got out of the van and waddled toward the back. He was a portly man with a rosy complexion. His white T-shirt was a size too large, and his jeans drooped around his waist. Compared to the lean men in tracksuits, the driver appeared as if he might have been left in the sun too long and melted.

The three men briefly talked, then they all laughed.

"Looks like they're friends," Courtney said.

Morgan nodded.

Golubev pulled a phone from his jacket and called someone. Semyonov and the driver continued to talk. When Golubev finished his brief conversation, the driver moved to the van's roll-up door. The men in tracksuits stepped back, and their hands went to their waistbands. Nobody jumped out and Golubev and Semyonov relaxed.

Courtney pointed at the cell phone. "This is where it gets interesting."

The three men each grabbed a plastic carton from the van and carried it to the front door of The Hempstead.

There was motion inside the building now. Someone opened the front door from the inside. A second person carried a stack of empty cartons out and placed them on the sidewalk. They were exactly like the ones being unloaded from the van.

"What the hell?" Morgan whispered.

Courtney said, "They're getting restocked."

The two men inside The Hempstead grabbed the cartons full of groceries and placed them inside the building's lobby. They didn't exchange any words with Golubev, Semyonov, or the driver.

"How many cartons come off the van?" Morgan asked.

"In all, twelve."

Morgan frowned. "How many people do you think twelve cartons of food will feed?"

"Depends, I guess. Is that a week's worth of food or a single day?"

"Gotta be more than a day," Morgan said. "This is the first delivery we've seen."

Earley shrugged. "We've only been up for a couple of days, but we're not watching it twenty-four/seven. Maybe we missed a previous delivery. Let's say it's three days."

On the small screen, the driver placed the empty crates into the van, then yanked the door back into place.

The men inside The Hempstead locked the door and began shuttling the crates of food away. Morgan presumed they were taking it to an elevator.

Golubev and Semyonov walked offscreen, and the van drove away in the opposite direction.

Courtney stopped the video. "What do you think?"

Morgan's gaze lifted to the apartment building across the street. He rubbed his chin and let his mind ponder a variety of possibilities.

He kept coming back to one, and he didn't like it—a Russian gang had set up an operation inside The Hempstead.

If true, they'd stumbled onto a hornet's nest. Morgan and his team had handled pests before, but this one felt eerily similar to the gang house they'd found in the East Sprague Corridor. It ended up with Courtney shot and Morgan in the front sights of an Internal Affairs lieutenant and a Major Crimes detective. Both leads came from Joey Greene.

Morgan wanted to talk to her again.

"You think there's an army in there?" Courtney asked.

The question interrupted Morgan's thoughts.

"An army?"

"Someone delivered prostitutes and groceries," Courtney said. "Doesn't that sound like they're taking care of an army?"

Morgan stared at the apartment building.

Earley continued. "Maybe not a literal army, but twelve cartons of food is a lot. Maybe it's a platoon or something?"

"A squad," Morgan said. "A platoon would eat that much food for lunch."

"You think we should interview the delivery guy? Shouldn't be hard to find him at that little grocery store."

Morgan shook his head. "If we're doing it my way, I say we don't tip our hand. Not yet, anyway. Let's keep watching."

Earley raised an eyebrow. "Shit. Senai. What do you think she'll want to do?"

"Show her the video and ask. It's her show."

"Yeah." The big man's shoulders slumped. "I forgot."

"I won't tell her you texted me first."

Earley smiled. "Thanks, man. I didn't do it on purpose."

"I know."

Morgan patted his shoulder. "But you better get her involved ASAP."

Chapter 13

Detective Damien Truscott parked in the lot and walked toward the front of the Safeway. Had this been an actual emergency call, he would have parked along the sidewalk curb, perhaps even the fire lane. But there was no exigency to his visit.

Traffic zoomed by on Northwest Boulevard, an arterial that cut diagonally through the city's north side. A large pickup with ridiculous twin exhaust pipes extending above the cab roared down the roadway. An American flag was propped up in its truck bed and whipped wildly.

Several citizens eyed Truscott suspiciously as he crossed the parking lot. Three homeless men clustered near the front of the building. One of them muttered, "Five-oh."

Truscott entered the building and proceeded toward the dairy section. An attractive blond woman walked aimlessly about. She wore a black sports bra, pink pajama bottoms, and flip-flops. She carried a red basket with both hands. Inside was a carton of eggs.

"Naomi Stapleton?" Truscott asked.

She quickly appraised him. Determining something, she crossed one arm across her chest and locked her hand behind the other arm which still held the basket. "They let cowboys be detectives now?"

Truscott wore a sport coat over a plaid shirt, blue Dockers, and cowboy boots. He knew some in the department mocked how he dressed, but he wasn't going to change for them.

He held out his hand and introduced himself.

Naomi's eyes darted about the store, and Truscott pulled his hand back.

"Is there somewhere else you'd like to go?" he asked.

"No," she said. "We gotta talk here. Guille thinks I'm getting eggs."

Truscott searched for signs of domestic violence. Her makeup was heavily applied, but it appeared there might have been some bruising on the left side of her face. "Are you all right?"

Naomi glanced about again. "Guille didn't want me to report the murder, that's all."

"So, he'd be upset to know we're talking?"

She looked at him now. "That's an understatement."

"You didn't know the victim's name?"

"Nick," she said. "I already told the other cop this. Didn't he tell you?"

Truscott smiled kindly. "He wrote a report. I need to clarify a few points."

Naomi dropped the arm crossing her body. "Let's walk. We probably look weird standing here." She started down the nearest aisle.

Truscott pulled his notebook from his jacket. "What else can you tell me about Nick?"

"He lived in Chicago."

"What did he look like?"

She stopped and checked out a box of Lucky Charms. "You believe the price of stuff now? Crazy, huh?" She eyed the detective. "He looked like a white guy. Sort of losing his hair."

"You told the officer Nick was in mid-thirties."

"Something like that. Maybe forty. It's hard for me to guess the ages of older guys."

Truscott grunted. Naomi sounded as if she was flirting. Perhaps it came naturally to her. Or maybe it was a byproduct of her job as an internet performer. "That description isn't much to go on," he said. "We need more."

Naomi shook the box. "I never really saw him stand but he seemed short. He was definitely pudgy. I saw him without his shirt." She pretended to study the box after she admitted that. "He wore glasses. Thick ones and he had a big nose."

Truscott hurriedly wrote the descriptors in his notepad. It was a lot of detail. "Why didn't you tell all this to the officer who took the initial report?"

Naomi set the cereal box back on the shelf. "I don't know. He really didn't ask and, to be honest, I was sort of freaked out by the whole thing. It's not every day I see someone get shot in the head."

Truscott knew traumatic event details often trickled back to a victim or a witness as they had time to process what they experienced. He wouldn't be surprised if Naomi recalled something else tomorrow or the next day. Those later details would need to be treated with suspicion, though. A lot of reasons could have caused them—a movie or a TV show the victim watched, a scene in a book the witness read, or media coverage of the event. Luckily, the press didn't know anything about this.

"Did you talk during your sessions?" he asked.

She started walking again. "Of course, we talked," she said over her shoulder. "Not a lot, but we talked. I told the officer that, too. Did he not tell you any of this?"

Truscott hurried up to her. "What did he sound like? Did he have a low voice? Or a high one?"

She shrugged. "It was normal, I guess. Sort of in the middle."

They left the breakfast aisle and entered another—canned goods.

"Did he have an accent?" Truscott asked.

Naomi scoffed. "Seriously? That other cop must not have told you anything."

"What do you mean?"

She stopped and grabbed a can of vegetables. "Why are they called navy beans?" Naomi turned the label so he could see them. "I've never figured that out."

He stared at her.

Naomi frowned. "Geez, fine. Whatever." She put the can back. "I told the other cop Nick sounded Russian."

Truscott cocked his head. If she told Ron Rowe and Lucas Jefferson about Nick's national origin, it never made the report. Truscott wasn't sure it would have made any difference, but it was an additional descriptor he could have given while talking to the Chicago detective.

"A white male who is mid-thirties to forty years old and speaks with a Russian accent," Truscott said aloud.

"Is that a question?"

"Does that sound like Nick?"

"You forgot he lived in Chicago." She continued walking.

Truscott hurried beside her. "The report said Nick had a tattoo, but it didn't say what kind."

Naomi shrugged a single shoulder. "At least the other cop got that right."

"Can you describe it?"

"I don't know. It was hard to see under all the hair."

Truscott lightly touched Naomi's arm to stop her. She faced him.

"Please," he said. "This is important. I need you to think. Close your eyes if you have to but try to remember it."

Naomi looked away. "I don't want to close my eyes."

Truscott nodded. Images of the murder must flood back to her whenever she shut her eyes.

"It's okay," Truscott said. "You're safe here."

It seemed a silly statement. They were in the middle of a grocery store.

Naomi lowered her head and stared at her flip-flops.

A heavyset man pushing a cart entered the aisle. He leaned his elbows on the handle and shuffled forward. His attention swept the shelves lining the aisle. Truscott stepped to the side to allow him by.

Naomi didn't look up, but she moved out of the way. After the man passed, Naomi lifted her head. "It was sort of a half-moon thing with a hammer through it."

"A hammer and sickle?" Truscott asked.

"I don't know what that is."

"A sickle? It's a cutting device. It looks like a crescent moon. Was there a star above it?"

Her face pinched. "I think so, but I'm not a hundred percent certain. There was a lot of hair."

Truscott knew the image. It was the symbol for the Soviet Union and a broader symbol of the communist movement. The Soviet Union had fallen before Truscott graduated high school, but he still remembered its flag. It was hard to forget its impact on his childhood.

"Where was this tattoo?" he asked.

She touched the area above her left breast. "Right here."

Truscott wondered if it was truly above Nick's left breast or if she mirrored what she saw on the screen, and it was on his right. Regardless, she'd just given him an identifiable tattoo.

"Okay," Truscott said. "He had a hammer through a half-moon with a star above it."

"Do you think that'll help?"

Truscott smiled. "Every bit helps. Can you describe the killer?"

Naomi looked toward the ceiling. "Not really." Her gaze dropped to him. "I mean, he was white and Russian and scary as fuck, but that's not much to go on, is it?"

"But you could pick him out of lineup if you saw him again?"

She nodded. "I'm certain of it. A thousand percent."

He motioned toward the shopping basket she carried. "I'll let you get back to it. Thank you for your time." He stepped away.

"Hey," she said.

He stopped.

"You never said if you knew why they were called navy beans."

"I have no idea."

Naomi shrugged. "I guess it's one of life's great mysteries."

Chapter 14

Morgan thought things were better before the developers and investors started their impulsive spending following the Great Recession. Back then, there was a straight line for trouble, and it ran through the heart of the city. Sprague Avenue started at the east edge of town on Havana Street, and it ran all the way through what the hipsters now call the West End.

At the start of Morgan's career, just saying Sprague brought images of corner drug deals and junkies lingering about like sucker fish. Strolling prostitutes brazenly attempted to make eye contact with drivers while their watchful pimps stood in nearby shadows. Illegal gun dealers worked from the trunks of barely operable cars. Gang members weaved in and out of this activity like unafraid sharks.

Now, Sprague Avenue had been overrun by well-heeled greed. Investors renovated old structures, and developers built new ones. Coffee shops, salons, and restaurants filled storefronts that once only sported *For Rent* signs.

Morgan disliked the change. He preferred citizens to stay in their neighborhoods so criminals could remain in theirs. Gentrification muddied the rules. Truth be told, Morgan preferred the criminals to the citizen trespassers.

He especially hated the shoppers from wealthy neighborhoods like South Hill and Liberty Lake. They dawdled on East Sprague sidewalks, unafraid of the area's history. Bored housewives bathed in the trendy flavor of a once-dangerous neighborhood as they loosely carried Gucci purses over their shoulders. They knew, as did

Morgan, no purse snatching would occur today. That time was long gone.

Morgan wouldn't find Joey Greene strolling on East Sprague anymore. Those days had disappeared surprisingly fast. Most of her work came from repeat business or by reference. When she didn't have a client, she might stroll along Riverside Avenue, a street lined with industrial buildings.

There was no need to hunt for her today. She had told him where to meet.

Morgan left Sprague at Napa, then turned west on Riverside. He saw her immediately.

About half a block away, Joey sat on the sidewalk with her legs crossed. She wore black shorts and a black T-shirt with Mike Tyson on its front. The boxer had a championship belt slung over his shoulder.

Morgan drove past her, then he pulled his Dodge Charger into an alley behind a coffee production facility. When he climbed out, the aroma from the nearby warehouse overwhelmed him.

"The smell," Joey said. "It's nice, isn't it?"

"What are you doing?"

"Taking a break."

He glanced up and down Riverside. "You all right?"

She shrugged. "Sometimes I get restless, you know? Like I feel lost. You ever get that?"

Morgan did, but he shook his head once.

"Of course, you don't." Joey smirked. "Not you. What do you need?"

"I need to know about the girl."

"Which one?"

"You know which. The one who told you about The Hempstead."

Her expression froze. "No."

Morgan shifted his stance. "Get up."

"Why?"

"Because I don't like talking down to you."

Joey rolled her eyes. "Fuck, Morgan. That's all you ever do."

He stared at her until she muttered, "Whatever." Joey languidly got to her feet. She brushed off her butt. She was several inches shorter than him and still had to look up at him. "Better?"

"Tell me this. Was she Russian?"

Joey's eyes narrowed. "Why's it matter?"

"It matters. Are they sending Russian girls into The Hempstead?"

Her jaw flexed. "What if they were?"

"I thought the Russians didn't work the stroll."

"They don't."

Morgan's brow furrowed. Years ago, she had told him where the Russian whores worked, but he never needed to work them for information. Now he did. "I need your contact."

"I can't. I promised her."

He grabbed Joey's arm and pulled her closer. She winced. "Don't screw around," Morgan said.

Joey tried to pull free, but he didn't let go. "I'm telling the truth," she said.

"I need a name," Morgan said. His grip relaxed and she yanked her arm loose.

"Why?" Joey asked. "What's going on there?"

"We don't know. That's what I want to talk to her about."

Joey cocked her head. "You're the cops. Bust in there and look around."

Morgan still didn't have enough probable cause to get into the individual apartments. Something was certainly strange but didn't rise to the level necessary for a judge to approve a warrant. If a prostitute had gone into an apartment, perhaps she had seen something he could use.

"Tell me her name," Morgan said.

"If she says it's okay." Joey crossed her arms. "But you'll hook me up again?"

"Depends on how good her info is."

"Don't be a dick. It'll be good." Joey looked away. "Hey, you hear about that gold find up in Republic?"

"Don't believe everything you read."

The Spokesman-Review had reported a Canadian mining company had located a gold deposit worth three billion near the town of Republic. The locals were ecstatic, as it might invigorate the former boom town.

"I'm thinking about moving up there," she said. "There's gonna be a lot of workers coming in, making beaucoup cash with nothing to spend it on."

"And?"

Her gaze cut back to him. "You don't care?"

"Why would I care?"

She sniffed dismissively. "Fuck you, Morgan." Joey reached down for her bag. "All I do is give and all you do is take."

"I do for you."

"Yeah?" she snapped. "What do you do for me?"

He spread his arms wide. "I don't see a pimp with his hand in your pocket."

"You got your hand in my pocket."

"But I give when I take."

Joey studied him for a moment, then she looked at her dirty white sneakers. "Yeah, I guess you do that."

"What's all this about?"

She didn't lift her eyes to him. "How come you never ask me to suck you off anymore?"

He didn't respond.

Joey finally looked up and read something in his expression. "Goddamn it, Morgan. I'm not wearing a wire. You wanna pat me down?" She dropped her purse and lifted her arms. "Go ahead."

"No."

"You want me to strip?" She reached for the hem of her shirt.

He waved for her to stop. "Don't."

"Then what is it?" She searched his eyes. "Don't tell me it was the rape. You knew I was raped before and that never stopped you."

"Enough."

"Whatever it is, I'd never rat you out. Never in a million years." She crossed her arms again. "I thought you knew me better than that."

"Get me a girl to talk with," Morgan said. "Then call me."

"Someday, you're not going to have me around."

He headed toward the Charger. For a moment, he considered saying something to give Joey comfort, but he didn't. Not only would that be wrong, it might allow her to think she had something over him.

It was the push and pull, he thought. It worked on whores just like it did girlfriends.

Chapter 15

Naomi pulled the T-shirt over her head, opened the door, and walked out of the bedroom. She was thirsty and had a Gatorade chilling in the refrigerator.

Guille reclined on the couch with his feet on the edge of the coffee table. Images of silent violence flashed across the TV screen. He must have noticed her walking because he turned the sound back on.

"Done finally?" he asked.

"Yeah."

His attention remained on the screen. "How'd it go?"

"Fine."

"The fuck does that mean? Tell me a number."

"Twenty."

He paused his game and rolled onto his knees so he could talk with her face to face. She was now in the kitchen. "Twenty exactly?"

"Something like that." She yanked open the refrigerator door and leaned in. She didn't want to face him. She heard his feet hit the floor, then the approaching footsteps.

"Yo," he said. "Look at me."

"I'm hungry."

Guille slapped the door. "Close it."

Her shoulders slumped, and she closed the refrigerator door. Naomi faced him. "What?"

"How many was it? Exactly."

"Seventeen."

His eyes bulged. "Are you fucking kidding me? Seventeen? This isn't your first day. Them perverts usually line up to jerk off to your feet."

"Don't call them that."

Guille smirked. "Why not? That's what they are." He mimed masturbating. "Just because you can't see them, you know that's what they're doing. Hell, you even saw Dirty Feet Nick doing it. He's all the proof you need that they're sickos."

"Those sickos pay our bills."

His eyes narrowed. "How much did you make?"

Naomi stared at him.

His expression hardened. "I asked you a question."

"Four hundred."

Guille inhaled sharply. "That's it?" He pointed at the bedroom. "You been in there like an hour. What the fuck you doing?"

"Making the rent."

"I don't know what you were doing, but it wasn't that."

Her lip curled. "Well, at least one of us is working."

Guille's hand shot out so fast it surprised her. It wrapped around her throat and pinned her to the refrigerator. He lifted her to her tiptoes. His face contorted in anger.

"What'd you say?" he asked.

Her hands wrapped around his wrist, but she didn't speak.

Guille's face contorted with rage. "I missed that. Say it again."

"I didn't say anything," she croaked.

"Bullshit. Say what you said."

His grip tightened, and her fingernails dug into his arm.

"My neck," she rasped.

"That's not what you said."

She didn't want to repeat the words. She knew it would only anger him further, so she said something that would get through to him. "You're going to bruise me. It'll be bad for the camera."

Guille's hand relaxed immediately, but he didn't let go of her neck. Her hands remained on his arm.

"You're lucky, bitch."

Naomi didn't feel lucky. Tears welled in her eyes.

"I love you," he said harshly. "You know what would happen if I didn't. Nobody speaks to me that way. You understand?"

She nodded.

His fingers uncurled from her neck, and she let go of his arm. "Now, get what you need and get back in there. Work on your content." His gaze traveled her length. "But clean yourself up first. You look like shit. Maybe that's why your tips are down."

Guille hopped over the couch and landed in his gaming position. In a moment, the explosions and gunfire returned. The house sounded like a war zone.

Naomi opened the refrigerator, pulled out the flavored sports drink she'd originally wanted and ran to the bathroom. She closed the door and locked it.

She flopped against the door and slid to the floor. The tears flowed freely then. Naomi dropped the plastic bottle, and it rolled away. She wrapped her arms around her knees and pulled them into herself.

Guille hadn't struck Naomi before, but now he'd laid hands on her twice in two days. He talked tough previously and said mean shit, but he never crossed the line.

The only thing that changed was the murder she witnessed. She angrily wiped the tears away. That wasn't true. The cops had been in their house. They'd never been there before.

It all went back to the murder.

Guille wasn't mad she was doing OnlyFans. It was his idea, after all—that's what she let him think. Naomi used to work at the Amazon distribution plant on the West Plains. She thought it was going to be a great job, but they wanted her to do a bunch of stuff that was never her style. Getting up early. Talking like a team member. All that garbage made no sense to her. Then her job was to move items from one bin to another so the robots could eventually drag pallets to shipping.

After she got fired for poor performance, she got hired as a bikini barista. The owners—a nice woman with a leering husband—said Naomi had the perfect qualifications for the gig. In other words, they thought Naomi had a nice body. The other baristas taught her how to work the espresso machine, but in the end, Naomi made a shitty cup of coffee. That wasn't a qualification for the job, though. Guys who bought lattes on Topless Tuesdays didn't care if the coffee was any good; they cared if the stand was open. Naomi repeatedly slept in or failed to show up on time. Even though the husband wanted to sleep with her, the couple eventually fired her. That's when she started driving for UberEATS. She liked being her own boss, driving when she was awake. Her car wasn't nice enough to drive for Uber and shuttle passengers around. Unfortunately, she didn't make much money delivering food.

That's when she manipulated Guille into suggesting she try OnlyFans.

Naomi stood and faced the mirror. Her eyes were red and puffy, and tears streaked down her cheeks. She couldn't take any pictures or film videos looking like this. Naomi pulled the plunger to stop the sink and started the cold water.

Her thoughts returned to Guille. He thought it was hilarious that guys paid to see her naked. His first comments were always about how some suckers were forking over dollars for what he was getting for free. In the beginning, she did only pictures. Then she moved to videos of her masturbating. When some fans requested she bring in a guy, Guille jumped at the opportunity to be on camera, but he wasn't comfortable with the experience. He only did it once. He never discussed it afterward, but Naomi got the impression he was freaked out by the idea of guys masturbating to them having sex.

Guille forbade her from even thinking about having sex with some other guy to make content. Naomi really didn't want to have sex with anyone else, but she would if Guille was cool with it. However, he was only fine with her masturbating in front of the camera since it paid their bills.

When the sink filled, Naomi turned off the water. She dipped her fingers in and felt the coldness. Naomi turned sideways so she could fit her head into the sink. She held her breath and dunked her face into the water. Its icy bite felt good against her skin. While she was submerged, all the other thoughts were pushed away.

She stood upright and let the water cascade down her T-shirt. It looked as if she were bawling now. Naomi felt better but dunked herself once more. She couldn't be puffy if she was going in front of the camera again.

Chapter 16

Damien Truscott parked his unmarked Chevy Impala in the parking lot west of the Public Safety building. After exiting the car, he took several steps toward the department but stopped. That wasn't the direction he wanted to go. He headed that way out of habit.

He spun on his heel and walked in the opposite direction. The Gardner Building sat across Adams Street. It was a large, mostly nondescript building.

Truscott entered the lobby and motioned toward Rebecca, the receptionist who sat behind the Plexiglas window. He couldn't recall her last name. She pressed a button underneath the counter and the lock opened with an audible click. Truscott wended his way through the building, passing cubicles and glassed-in offices as he went. Several folks nodded or waved politely. He returned their gestures.

When Truscott arrived at the closed door marked Digital Forensics, he knocked once.

The door jerked open immediately, as if the man on the other side had been waiting. Detective Mark Wickenhauser seemed surprised.

He wore a white button-up shirt, and his massive belly hid his belt. His black slacks puddled around black loafers. A lanyard hung from Wickenhauser's neck, but the ID card it held disappeared underneath the man's armpit, compressed between two wedges of fat. The detective held an empty coffee cup in his left hand. "Truscott," he said.

"Hey, man. I came by to get an update on that computer."

Wickenhauser frowned. "Which one?"

"The laptop brought in yesterday. The one the idiot boyfriend drowned."

"We're still drying it out." Wickenhauser stepped out of the office, pulled the door behind him, and walked away.

Truscott glanced around. *Was this guy for real?* He hurried to catch up with the other man. "Hey."

Wickenhauser looked over his shoulder.

"Where you going?" Truscott asked.

"To get coffee."

"We were talking."

Wickenhauser shook his head. "You were talking."

The heavyset detective passed through a series of cubicles. It wasn't wide enough for the two men to walk side by side, so Truscott followed behind.

"Hey," Truscott said again. He lowered his voice. He didn't want to make a scene.

Once again, Wickenhauser glanced back. Just like before, he didn't stop.

"Can we finish our conversation?" Truscott asked.

"Would have been better if you called ahead."

Truscott's face warmed. "Are you kidding?"

Wickenhauser entered the break room. Soda and snack machines stood next to each other on the far wall. Several small tables were clustered in the middle of the room. On the nearest wall, a refrigerator stood next to the sink. Two coffee pots and a toaster were on the counter.

A woman Truscott had never met sat alone at one of the tables. She leaned over a newspaper opened to the *Sports* section. Her hand was buried into a small bag of Doritos chips. The bag rustled as she worked for the next handful.

Wickenhauser headed toward the first coffee pot. He grabbed the carafe, saw it was empty, and shoved it back into place. His lip curled. "What's your problem, Damien?"

"My problem is you didn't give me any information."

"I said we're still drying it. What more do you want?"

Truscott didn't normally want to yell, but right then might have been an exception. "Listen," he said and noticed the sharpness in his tone. He quit talking.

The woman at the table stopped rustling in her bag of chips. She turned to watch them.

Wickenhauser pulled the second carafe from its pot and studied it. There was hardly any coffee left. He angrily jammed it back into place. His face pinched.

The heavyset detective tried to step around Truscott. Not finding an easy path, he frowned. "What do you want?"

"When will you be done with the laptop?"

"You'll get it when we get it."

"That's not good enough."

"All right." Wickenhauser pinched his pudgy lips together. "How's this for an answer? Three weeks."

"What?"

"You'll get it in three weeks. How's that rock your boat?"

The woman at the table quietly slid her chair back and stood.

"You arrogant bastard," Truscott said. "How about I stick my foot up your ass? Will that make you go any faster?"

Wickenhauser smirked. "Four weeks."

The woman hurried out of the room.

Truscott stuck his finger in the other man's face. "Listen, you fat bastard—"

"Ah, ah, ah." Wickenhauser waved his empty coffee cup back and forth. "Mustn't do that. You'll anger the computer gods."

"What are you going to do? Tack another week on to my job?"

"You should be careful is all I'm saying."

Truscott's brow furrowed. "You're threatening me?"

Wickenhauser innocently touched his chest. When he did so, he noticed the lanyard had gotten lodged underneath his armpit. He yanked it out. "I'm not threatening anything. All I'm saying is karma has a strange way of evening life out. You say something bad to me, suddenly something bad happens to you. Haven't you read *The Secret*?"

"Must I remind you that you work for the department?"

"Same as you." Wickenhauser started to lift his coffee cup, remembered it was empty, and stopped.

"Maybe you can give me an update without my needing to set an appointment."

"And maybe somebody could make coffee." Wickenhauser motioned toward the two empty pots. "We can't always get what we want."

"Why don't you make the coffee, Mark?"

Wickenhauser suddenly seemed offended. "What's your problem? We don't make coffee."

Truscott shook his head. He didn't know if Wickenhauser was referring to detectives or computer forensic investigators. Either way, it was arrogant. "Whatever," he said. "I'll take this to my sergeant and he'll talk to yours. I'll get my answer that way."

The heavyset detective laughed. "Have it your way. You already know the answer you're going to get. Four weeks."

"Stick it up your ass." Truscott turned to leave.

"Make it five," Wickenhauser said.

Truscott didn't engage in further discussion.

"Have a nice day. Too bad we couldn't be of service."

He stopped at the door to the lobby and noticed Wickenhauser had followed him. The empty coffee cup dangled in his hand.

"Instead of harassing me," Truscott said, "you could have told me what's going on with the computer."

"I told you—"

"Yeah, yeah. You're drying it out."

Wickenhauser smirked. "I'll let my sergeant know to expect a call from yours."

Truscott motioned toward the empty cup. "Enjoy your coffee."

Wickenhauser's face pinched. "Don't be a dick." He turned and headed back toward his office.

Chapter 17

Morgan parked along the curb, across from the unimaginatively named Broadway Foods.

The business was named after the road it sat on. The small convenience store had served the West Central neighborhood for years. Customers paid no attention to him as they walked through the small parking lot. Morgan and his car didn't look like the cops they normally interacted with.

Those who recognized Morgan knew better than to show it. They simply went about their business. That behavior was part of the game, and Morgan expected it. More than that, he respected them for it.

He approached a nearby four-story apartment building. The dilapidated structure was long past its prime. Its gray paint had faded, and its lower portion carried decades of dirt and grime from passing cars. All the south facing windows were blocked out with the aid of curtains, tinfoil, or cardboard.

Morgan entered the unlocked building and bounded up the stairs to the fourth floor. There was no elevator. He would have skipped it anyway in this building for a variety of reasons, the least of which he couldn't trust it to work. The hallways smelled of old cigarettes, body odor, and failure.

On the fourth floor, Morgan paused to catch his breath. He didn't remember needing to do that before. He looked both ways, hoping no one saw him pause. He slowly started walking, inhaling deeply, holding his breath longer each time.

The white paint on the walls had yellowed from time and ugly brown spots littered the ceiling—telltale signs of roof leaks.

Morgan stopped at a door with an upside-down seven. The door's red paint was chipped in several places and revealed a white coating underneath. Someone had stuck a round sticker in the middle of the door. In the middle of it was a smiling yellow face with sunglasses. Around the edge of the sticker were the words *It's Cool to be Drug Free*.

He knocked.

"What?" a man yelled.

"Open up, Laszlo."

"Not again," the man muttered.

Morgan smiled. He was glad he still had that effect on Laszlo Nagy. It had been months since he'd seen the man. Morgan kicked the base of the door. "Now."

"I'm coming, I'm coming." It was said with the enthusiasm of a man going to the dentist.

The door unlocked and slowly opened to reveal a scrawny man with long, stringy hair. He was shirtless, wearing only a pair of large basketball shorts and dirty Air Jordans. Two dragons breathed fire at each other on his unimpressive chest. Nagy stunk and his skin shone as if he hadn't bathed in days.

"Geez, Morgan, where's the fire?"

"Step back."

"Why?"

Morgan shoved Nagy into the apartment. The man stumbled backward, twisted to catch his balance, then stutter-stepped through the kitchenette. Nagy finally launched himself onto his bed. It was far more momentum and drama than the push deserved.

"What was that for?" Nagy hollered.

"You done, drama queen?" Morgan asked.

"I ain't done nothing."

"Right."

"I'm clean, Morgan." Nagy pointed toward the door. "Didn't you see the sticker?"

"That sticker proves you're clean?"

Nagy pointed again. "I got it from the clinic."

Laszlo Nagy was a user and part-time dealer. Him getting clean was as believable as the January 6th insurrection being a peaceful gathering or the Kennedy assassination being the work of just one man.

Morgan snapped his fingers. "Where is it?"

Nagy tried to create a look of innocence. It failed miserably. "Where's what?"

"The drugs. Your kit. Give them to me."

Now Nagy motioned toward the door with both hands. "But the sticker," he whined.

"I'm gonna tear this apartment apart and you know I'll find it." Morgan's expression hardened. "I always do."

"I'm clean."

"When I find them, I'm taking the drugs and booking you for possession."

Nagy's shoulders slumped. "Shit." He pointed to a hardback book on the floor.

Morgan picked it up. The title was *Everybody Lies: Big Data, New Data, and What the Internet Can Tell Us About Who We Really Are*. A dust jacket wrapped the cover and a UPC code was above the title. A marker with the Dewey Decimal reference was on the spine.

"You checked this out?" Morgan asked.

"I can't have a library card?"

That wasn't his question, but Morgan let it go. He tried to flip it open, but only the cover worked. The rest of the book remained stationary. All the pages had been glued together. The middle of the pages had been carved out with a razor blade. It was a shoddy job, something likely seen in a prison. Perhaps that's where Nagy got the idea. Inside the little compartment was a baggie of dope, a needle, and a bent spoon.

Morgan slapped the cover closed. "You ruined a library book."

"I checked it out."

"But you ruined it."

Nagy's face pinched. "It's still mine. I can do with it what I want."

Morgan shook his head. "Whatever. What do you know about Russians?"

Nagy shrugged. "They aren't so bad."

"Wrong answer." He turned for the door.

"Hey! Where you going?"

"I'm leaving."

Nagy stood. "But that's mine."

"Not anymore."

"You can't take that."

Morgan cocked his head. "Who do you think you're talking to?"

Nagy looked briefly away. "You got no right," he murmured.

"What was that?" Morgan moved toward Nagy. "Say it again."

Nagy stepped back, bumped into the edge of his bed, and sat. "What Russians do you want to know about?"

Morgan towered over him. "What Russians do you know?"

"I know a few."

"Who do you know?"

"Which ones do you want me to know?"

Morgan jammed the edge of the hardback into Nagy's bare chest. The smaller man winced.

"Quit fucking around, Laszlo."

"All right, all right. Jesus." Nagy rubbed his chest. "That hurt."

"It'll hurt a lot more if I walk out of here with this book."

Nagy's eyes widened. "You wouldn't really do that, would you?"

"I'll start walking now unless you give me some names."

Nagy extended his thumb. "Well, there's Grigori."

"Grigori who?"

"Grigori *Grigori*." Nagy shook his head. "I don't know his last name. You want me to make it up?"

"What's he do?"

"He works at the Mission."

Morgan jammed the book into Nagy's chest again and the junkie howled in pain. The man flopped to his side and curled in a ball.

"What'd you do that for?" he cried.

"No citizens," Morgan said.

"Grigori isn't a citizen."

"He's a do-gooder. Gimme another name."

Nagy's face pinched in pain. "Yuri."

"Yuri who?"

"I don't know his last name."

"What's he do?"

"He's like me."

Morgan angrily slapped the book across Nagy's knee. The junkie popped upright on the bed and grabbed his leg. "Stop doing that!"

"Why do you think a junkie can help me?"

"I don't know," Nagy said. "I don't know what you want."

"Let's try it this way. You ever hear of two thugs named Sergei Golubev and Mikhail Semyonov?"

Nagy shook his head. "No. Never."

"Too bad." The detective stepped away from the bed. "Call me when you do."

"What?"

Morgan headed for the door.

"What about my stuff?"

He waggled the book. "You'll get it back after you call."

"But I'm gonna need it soon."

Morgan grabbed the doorknob. He looked over his shoulder before stepping out. "Then I guess you better work fast."

"Wait!"

He paused.

"What were those commie names again?"

Chapter 18

Naomi Stapleton pulled her Frappuccino in tighter. The plastic cup was cool to her touch and a layer of condensation had formed on its outside. "You're not going to believe what I have to tell you," she said. "I still don't believe it."

Kennedy Bray sat across from her. She wore a tight blue T-shirt, white shorts, and sandals. Her cinnamon skin glistened. She'd just left the tanning salon, so Naomi supposed Kennedy had applied some sort of lotion. Her friend's long, dark hair was worn in a ponytail underneath a light blue baseball cap.

"All right, bitch," Kennedy said. "Spill." She sucked on the straw tucked into her own Frappuccino. As she drank, Kennedy's eyes narrowed, and she leaned slightly to study Naomi's face.

Naomi turned to hide the left side of her face. She had applied extra makeup to cover the bruising from where Guille had hit her. She thought it had worked, but maybe the lights in the small cafe revealed the truth.

They were at Starbucks on Cleveland Street. Some hipster song played over the speakers. There were no other patrons inside, probably due to the lateness of the afternoon. The baristas cleaning behind the counter chatted amongst themselves.

Naomi set down her drink, bumping her muffin to the side as she did so. "I saw someone murdered."

Kennedy wrinkled her nose. "Fuck off. No, you didn't."

"Yes, I did." Naomi widened her eyes. "Sure as shit. Guy got it in his head." She used two fingers to mime a gun to the side of her head. "Two times. Just like that."

"Where did it happen?"

"On the Fans."

Kennedy lowered her drink. Her gaze kept returning to Naomi's left cheek. "When did it happen?"

"Yesterday."

"And you're just telling me about it now?"

Naomi leaned back in her chair. She turned her head and pretended to be interested in the baristas. It was an attempt to continue hiding the side of her face. "You know how it is."

Kennedy's expression pinched. "Guille."

"He didn't want me reporting it to the cops."

"So this guy really was killed?"

Surprised, Naomi faced her. "You think I'd lie about this?"

Kennedy lifted an apologetic hand. "That's not what I meant. I thought maybe the guy was funning you or something."

"Like as a joke?"

Her friend nodded.

"It was real as shit," Naomi said. She looked toward the baristas again. "It was the most gangster thing I've ever seen. Like it was a movie or something."

"What did you do?"

"I screamed."

Kennedy sucked deeply on her straw. After she swallowed her drink, she asked, "We're you in the middle of a private bang?"

"Right in the middle."

"Christ."

Kennedy was on OnlyFans, too. She was the one who introduced Naomi to it, but Naomi had to let Guille think it was his idea. Otherwise, he probably wouldn't have let her do it. Kennedy had paved the way for her, giving her some tips and tricks. Kennedy did way more private sessions than Naomi did.

The two stared at each other for a moment, each lost in their own thoughts.

Eventually, Kennedy leaned forward. "I'm imagining the guy beating his meat, just really going at it, when someone busted into his house and popped him in the head. Like, did he freak out before they shot him?"

Naomi shrugged. "Nick never heard them enter, but it was pretty much like that."

Kennedy started to look away, but she quickly turned back. "And Guille didn't want you to tell the cops?"

She shook her head.

"Why the hell not?"

"He said they'd come looking for us."

Kennedy flicked her hand. "That's stupid. Why'd he think that?"

"Because the killer—" Naomi again mimed the gun with two fingers. "He looked at the computer and saw me."

"Because you were screaming."

"That's right."

Kennedy scoffed. "Baby, all he saw was your cooch. He's not looking for you." She paused. "Unless he saw your screen name, then maybe he's going to subscribe to your channel and ask you for some scream porn." She laughed.

Naomi didn't see the humor in the situation.

"All right," Kennedy said. "I'm just kidding. So, Guille didn't want you to report it, but you did. That's when he smacked you?" Kennedy used her drink to point at Naomi's face.

"It was an accident."

"Hitting a woman is never an accident."

Naomi slid the muffin in front of her and picked at it. "It's never happened before."

"That doesn't make it okay."

"He's under a lot of stress."

"Him?" Kennedy asked. "Did he see the murder, too? Was he in the room with you?"

Naomi stopped picking the pastry.

"See?" Kennedy said. "What'd I tell you? Guille's a piece of shit."

"Please don't say that."

"Fine. Then tell me this. Why doesn't he want us hanging out?"

She shrugged.

"I'm a bad influence," Kennedy said. "That's what he thinks."

Naomi shrugged a second time.

"What I am is someone who tells you to think for yourself."

"I do," Naomi said. "I am."

"He's still acting like your pimp."

"I'm only letting him think that."

"Uh-huh." Kennedy frowned. "Sure you are."

"I am."

"Girl, you're his hostage."

Naomi waved her hand. "I'm out here with you. I can't be his hostage."

"He's got you trapped." Kennedy tapped her temple. "In here. He takes your money. Tells you when you can work and when you can't. Says who you can hang out with. That's a pimp."

Naomi smirked. "That's a boyfriend."

"A shitty boyfriend."

"Stop."

"All right, all right." Kennedy held up an apologetic hand. "So, what's happening now?"

Naomi furrowed her brow. "With what?"

"The murder. Are the cops doing anything?"

"They're looking into it."

Kennedy grunted. "Sounds like normal cop bullshit." She lowered her voice an octave. "We're looking into it. Now, show us your hands." She sipped from her Frappuccino. "Nothing's going to happen."

Naomi turned her drink on the table. "I don't know. The detective seemed nice."

"Was he cute?"

"He was old."

Kennedy raised an eyebrow. "How old?"

"Forty, maybe."

"I've fucked older."

Naomi smirked. "No shit."

"Don't knock it until you've tried it."

"I'll pass."

Kennedy motioned toward Naomi's cheek. "All I'm saying is I bet that detective wouldn't do that to your face."

"How do you know?" Naomi asked. "Cops hit their wives, too."

"Yeah, probably." Kennedy shrugged. "Men suck."

Naomi stuck her tongue out. "But I'm not switching teams."

"Don't knock it until you've tried that, too."

"You're dirty."

Kennedy laughed. "Oh, yeah. So, are you back on the Fans?"

"Right away."

"Good girl."

Chapter 19

Damien Truscott dropped into his desk chair and pulled himself forward. He'd check his emails a final time before calling it a day. He opened Outlook and several messages populated the program. Most of them were spam. A couple were related to ongoing burglary investigations. He highlighted them with stars. They could wait until the morning.

His desk phone rang, and his eyes drifted to the caller ID screen. It showed a 312 area code. That number seemed familiar, he thought. He slowly reached for the receiver, and the phone rang again.

As he answered, the realization came to him. He had dialed that area code earlier in the morning.

"Detective Truscott," he said.

"Truscott," a gruff voice said. "Harvey Lowden. Chicago PD."

"Yeah?"

"Catch you at a bad time?"

He looked at the clock on his computer. It was almost five. What time zone was Chicago in? Central? That made it almost seven there.

Truscott felt a wave of embarrassment. Homicide investigators didn't look to break at five. They worked a case until a natural stopping point. When he was in the Special Victims Unit, what used to be called Sex Crimes in a more unenlightened time, he often worked past five. He had quickly adapted to his recent rotation back to Property Crimes and its slower pace. It wasn't a good realization.

"The time is fine," Truscott said.

"That's good." Lowden's voice moved away from the phone now. "Hey, Sully," he hollered, "get me a meatball sando if you're going and a bag of chips. I'll pay you when you get back." He returned to the conversation. "Sorry about that."

"No worries."

"Where were we?"

"We just started."

"What's the weather like out there?"

Was this guy screwing with him? Did he really call to talk about the weather? "It's fine."

"What's that mean? Fine? Is it sunny? Cold? You guys get snow, right? How long does it hang around?"

Truscott leaned back in his chair and pinched the bridge of his nose with his free hand. There had to be more to this call. "It was nice today. Warm. Mostly sunny. Just a few clouds."

"That's nice. You almost sound like a weatherman." Lowden laughed. "It's pissing rain here. Miserable fucking day. You ever get out here?"

"Chicago?"

"No, New York. Yeah, Chicago."

"Never been."

"Don't bother. Unless you're a Bears fan, and then don't bother. Watch the games on the tube." He howled with laughter.

Truscott dropped his chair forward. "You're working late."

"Overtime, baby. Cha-ching, cha-ching."

That's why Lowden wasn't in a hurry to get to the point. He was clocking pay for talking about the weather. Meanwhile, Truscott could be on his way home to his wife and sons.

"Was there something you called about?" Truscott asked.

Lowden cleared his throat. "Yeah, of course. You think I forgot?"

"No."

"I was just making nice. Throwing a little chit-chat. Don't they do that where you're from?"

"Sure."

The sergeant grunted. "Doesn't seem like it."

"I apologize. It's just that I got a date tonight."

"Girlfriend?" Lowden's voice raised with curiosity.

"My wife."

"Oh." The curiosity fizzled.

"And kids."

"You going to church tonight, too?" He chuckled. "I'm teasing. That's nice."

He was killing time again, Truscott thought. "Sergeant."

"Yeah?"

"Does this have something to do with the homicide I called about this morning?"

The chuckling stopped. "Yeah." A piece of paper rustled on the other end of the phone. "We found your guy."

"You're shitting me."

"Why would I do that?"

A moment of silence passed on the line.

"Anyway," Lowden said, "you're never going to guess his first name."

"Nick?"

"Bzzt. Wrong."

"Why don't you tell me?"

"Jesus, you Spokane guys don't get how to do overtime, do you?"

Truscott knew plenty of officers and detectives who milked the system. They probably would have loved to have had a conversation with Sergeant Lowden, but Truscott wasn't one of them.

"His name was Alexei."

"So Nick was a screen name?"

Lowden chuckled. "Nah. The guy was Alexei Nikolaev."

Truscott's lip curled. The guy couldn't have led with that? "What happened to him?"

"He was shot twice in the head. We found him naked on the floor in front of his desk."

"Makes sense. He was masturbating in front of his computer."

"That's the strange part."

"What is?"

"The computer was missing."

The news caused Truscott to bolt from his seat. He stood and looked around the Property Crimes section. There was no one in the area. "That means the killer took the computer."

"Look at you, Detective. Connecting dots and everything." Lowden laughed. "Maybe you Spokane guys are sharper than I'm giving you credit for."

"Who was Nikolaev?"

"That's the question, isn't it? As far as we can figure it, he was an accountant. He had a degree on his wall from Illinois State. Go Redbirds."

"You don't know where he worked?"

"We don't know," Lowden said, "but maybe the FBI will tell you. They wouldn't tell us shit."

Truscott cocked his head. "The FBI?"

"That got your attention, huh?" Lowden chuckled again.

"What's the FBI got to do with this?"

"What do you think? Our patrol boys got a call about a red spot on a ceiling. Seems like old Nikolaev bled through to the apartment below. An apartment manager lets our boys in and, what do you know, we've got a homicide. Not unusual in our city. How many bodies you catch a year, Truscott?"

"I don't know."

"C'mon, take a guess. Humor me."

"Maybe twenty."

"Twenty!" He guffawed. "Shit. How small is your city? We have almost seven hundred every year. Probably not a fair comparison. Like trying to measure your dick against Shaquille O'Neal."

Truscott grimaced at the comparison. "So, the Feds?"

"Right. Well, the uniforms locked down the scene, and my boys started processing it. Even had the evidence techs out and everything. You know the drill."

Truscott wasn't a homicide investigator, but he'd been on plenty of crime scenes to know how they went.

"Anyway," Lowden said, "that's when the suits arrived with their fancy badges and Quantico attitudes. You ever met those pricks?"

He hadn't.

"Consider yourself lucky," Lowden said. "Arrogant pricks to a man." He cleared his throat again. "Or woman. One of each, if you must know."

"What'd they want?"

"To snatch the case from us." The sergeant snapped his fingers. "Just like that. Not that we give a damn. Let 'em.

Although if they can't solve it, they'll hand it back to us and let it pollute our numbers."

Truscott furrowed his brow. "Did they tell you why they wanted the case?"

"Does a dog tell you why it wants a bone?"

"Huh?"

Lowden grunted. "Listen, the Feds take what the Feds want. They didn't say why they took it, or what they were going to do with it. I don't even bother to ask anymore. They sure as fuck didn't give two shits about our feelings. They're like my ex-wife in that regard." The sergeant laughed.

"Basically, my witness told the truth—a guy was murdered."

"It's no longer your worry, Detective. Expect a call from the feebs. Meantime, write your report and close your file. Consider the whole affair handled. I know we are."

Once again, the sergeant hung up without saying goodbye.

Chapter 20

Detective James Morgan leaned back against his Dodge Charger and crossed his arms. He was underneath the freeway. To the south sat Lewis & Clark High School. To the north lay downtown in all its illuminated glory. To the east was the UTF skatepark.

For years, Under the Freeway Park was the city's only haven for skateboarders. The city paid tepid support to it with an occasional cleaning. When Spokane finally realized the importance of the sport to its younger citizens, the city built a couple of parks in the suburbs. That allowed the city to turn a blind eye to the UTF and its urban youth. It was now overrun with homeless tents and junkies.

Night had fallen, and the freaks were out. The citizens had gone home. Drunken zombies and half-dead souls moved among the shadows of the underpass. This was their time. They could freely roam about downtown without fear of reprisal.

Traffic on the freeway zoomed above, clattering loudly whenever a vehicle passed over a connection joint. Cars and trucks raced down Washington Street, none of them bothering to slow as they went by Morgan. All were unaware they were speeding past an off-duty cop.

A woman approached through the UTF. She dodged junkies and walked around ramshackle homeless tents. She wore a light blue jean jacket, camouflage pants, and combat boots. Her arms swayed confidently as she moved. This was a woman who had walked through the worst this city had to offer and feared little of it.

Her eyes locked on to Morgan's and he stopped surveying the neighborhood. He was confident this was who he was to meet.

When she neared the edge of the park, she placed one hand on the small concrete wall and leaped it in a single bound.

"You Morgan?" she asked in a heavy Eastern European accent.

"Yes."

She extended her hand. "Svetlana."

He didn't bother asking if that was her real name or not. If this was an official interview, it would have been different. Morgan would have handled it like any other cop. Name, birthday, and address. Right now, Morgan needed information, and he didn't care who provided it as long as it panned out.

His hand slid into hers. "Thank you for meeting."

"I do this for me."

Morgan cocked his head. "How so?"

She looked around. "Let's go for a ride."

"Why?"

"Too many eyes."

He thought about it. "Put your hands on the car."

Svetlana moved to the trunk. She put her hands on the edge of the car and spread her feet wide.

Morgan patted her down, searching for a weapon or anything foreign. Right now, he was suspicious anyone might be wearing a wire.

"Get in," he said.

She moved toward the front door.

"No," Morgan said. "The back."

Svetlana nodded. "Yes. That's the right way." She opened the back door and climbed in.

Morgan slid behind the steering wheel and started the engine. He pulled into traffic. "Where to?"

"Your choice." Her head swiveled about, checking for something. "Someplace private. Someplace safe."

"This better be worth it."

Svetlana slid down the back seat. "I will make it worth your while."

Morgan headed west on Second Avenue, checking his rearview mirror as he went. The woman's cautiousness spooked him. Could she have been followed? He made occasional turns and double-backs but never saw anyone behind him.

Eventually, he made it to Sunset Boulevard, and the Charger climbed the hill.

The entire time he drove, Svetlana remained quiet. She never looked at her phone—Morgan tried to recall feeling one during his pat-down. He didn't think she had one. Perhaps she left it somewhere. Was she afraid of being traced?

She didn't carry a purse either. Not that it was a requirement, but Morgan had not felt anything in her pockets. That seemed unusual for a woman in her profession. Usually, they carried all sorts of items, never knowing where they might end up.

He pulled off on Assembly Road and wound along the way until he found a turnoff in a wooded area. About a hundred yards off the road, Morgan located a small turnaround and backed in. He flicked off his lights.

"Okay," he said. "This is about as private and safe as we can get."

Svetlana sat upright and looked around. "This is good." She climbed over the middle console and plopped into the passenger seat.

"Why all the secrecy?" Morgan asked.

Svetlana twisted in her seat to face him. "Because I am not a stupid woman. If I tell you certain things, my life will be in danger."

"How will they know it came from you?"

She shrugged. "The man above it all is former FSB. Do you know what this is?"

Morgan shook his head.

"They replaced the KGB when the Soviet Union dissolved."

That surprised Morgan. He figured the KGB was still around. If what Svetlana said was true, the man running The Hempstead was a former counterintelligence spy. It sounded like bullshit.

"What's this guy doing in Spokane?" Morgan asked.

"No," Svetlana said. "This is not how this is going to be." She pushed back against the door. "I need assurances."

"What assurances?"

"I need what Joey has."

Morgan's jaw tightened. "Nobody gets that."

"Then drive me back."

He stared at her for a moment. If that's how she wanted to negotiate, Morgan understood the rules. Slowly, he nodded. "Fine."

"You must prove it."

He lifted the steering wheel and pushed his seat back a little further. Morgan reached for his zipper.

Svetlana reached out to stop him. "No. I will do it. Let me show you I am better than her." She shifted in her seat and bent over the console. Her eyes darkened with fake lust as she looked up at him.

With his left hand, Morgan grabbed her by the hair and yanked her head up. He violently twisted his hand. Svetlana flipped onto her back over the console, and she stared up at the car's ceiling. Morgan's right hand crimped down on her throat, a vise closing fast but stopping short of death.

Svetlana's hands clamped around his wrist. Her eyes widened in terror and her feet kicked at the door.

"No one gets what Joey has," Morgan said. "Understand?"

She nodded and her feet stopped moving.

"Tell me what you know, or I dump you here. A hiker will find your body in a couple days."

Her fingers dug into Morgan's arm and her legs kicked wildly again.

His hand tightened around her throat. "Are we clear?"

Morgan pulled her hair and yanked her by the throat until she was deeper in his lap. Svetlana's back arched higher over the console. Her hands didn't leave his wrists and her feet were on the ceiling of the car now. Her eyes never left his.

"Nod if you understand," Morgan commanded.

She nodded several times.

He held her for a moment longer before relaxing his hand. Morgan didn't remove it from her throat, however.

"We're going to start over," he said. "If I don't believe what you're saying—"

"I'm sorry," she whispered.

"It's too late for that."

Tears streamed down her cheeks.

"Only the truth will save you now."

Chapter 21

The doorbell rang.

"Hey!" Guille hollered. "Pizza dude's here."

Synthetic gunshots and explosions came from the living room.

Naomi rolled her eyes. "Can't you get it?" she asked from the bathroom.

The door was open. She stood in front of the mirror, checking her face. It wasn't like she couldn't answer the bell, but Guille was in the same room.

"I'm in the middle of something," he called. "'Sides, you got the money."

Naomi stared at herself in the mirror. Maybe she should yell back she was pooping. That would get him off his dead ass. She knew he had money. She gave him three hundred at the beginning of the week. He couldn't have spent all that by now, could he?

The doorbell rang again.

Guille shouted, "You gettin' that or what?"

Naomi sighed. It wasn't like she was doing anything.

She left the bathroom.

When she opened the door, the Lunar Pizza delivery guy's eyes widened. He held a large pizza in his right hand like a waiter balancing a tray.

The sounds of Guille's video game continued. Someone yelled, "Grenade!" right before an eruption occurred.

The driver was a skinny white guy with short hair. Two thin lines were cut into his left eyebrow. Faded blue jeans fell below his waist and the legs puddled around his white Adidas. Several gold chains hung outside his T-shirt, which displayed an image of Biggie Smalls wearing a crown. Behind him, at curbside, sat a souped-up, cherry red Toyota Corolla.

The delivery guy quickly recovered. His eyes narrowed and a sly smile formed. "What up?" he said as if he had just approached her at a club. "How you doin'?"

Naomi shoved her hand into her pocket and pulled out a wad of cash. "How much was it?"

"How come a fine girl like you isn't out right now?" The driver leaned slightly to see into the house. "Got a kid or something?"

Naomi lifted her hand to display the cash. "How much?"

The driver touched his chest with his free hand. "C'mon, girl. Why you gotta be that way? I'm just a working man trying to get to know you."

She thought it was about twenty bucks. The guy wasn't getting a tip now. Naomi pulled a twenty from the wad and handed it to the driver.

The video game noises stopped.

"You're short," the driver said. "By eighty-seven cents."

Guille approached, then. "Problem?" He wasn't wearing a shirt and puffed his chest, trying to look gangster hard.

Naomi resisted rolling her eyes. "I'm paying the man."

"Sounded like he was trying to make time with you," Guille said.

"He wasn't doing that."

Guille's lip curled. "Is that true?"

The driver shrugged. "I asked how her night was."

"Why'd you ask if she had a kid?" Guille said.

Naomi handed the driver a one-dollar bill. He took it.

"I heard someone playing a game."

The driver extended the pizza. Guille snatched the box from him and handed it to Naomi.

"Motherfucker," Guille said. "I was playing. Men play games, too." He slammed the door shut.

"No tip?" The driver shouted from the other side of the door.

Guille faced Naomi. "Why do you let them talk to you like that?"

"Like what?"

"I heard what he said."

She carried the pizza to the coffee table. She pushed some empty Big Gulp cups out of the way before setting the box down. "He was being an idiot."

Guille grabbed her arm and spun her around. "He did that shit because you encouraged it."

Naomi threw her hands into the air. "How'd I do that?"

"Look at how you're dressed." Guille waved his hand at her. "Shorty shorts and a hoochie shirt."

"You used to like how I dressed."

"You look like a whore."

Her mouth dropped open. "Excuse me?"

Guille pointed to the back room. "You're letting that job go to your head. All those men telling you how hot you are—" He tapped the side of his head. "It's messing with your mind."

"You're an asshole."

"I'm an asshole? I'm not the one getting guys to hit on me in front of my boyfriend."

Naomi's face pinched. "That doesn't even make sense. You saw what I did."

"That's right. I saw."

Her face warmed. "No, you didn't. You didn't see shit because you were playing that stupid game. That's all you ever do anymore."

"That's not all I do."

Naomi pointed toward the front door. "At least that guy has a job."

"Pizza boy?"

"At least he could afford to take me out on a date."

"I take you out."

"With my money!"

Guille raised his hand, and Naomi flinched. "Whose money?"

"Our money."

He laughed. "That's right. *Our* money." Guille lowered his hand. "Don't forget that. All those men saying you're something special—where are they now?"

Naomi lowered her head.

"They're out there, in make-believe." He poked her in the chest. "Look at me."

She lifted her gaze to him.

"I'm right here. I know the real you. The person you were before you got to be famous."

Naomi didn't consider herself famous. She wasn't even in the top tier of performers on OnlyFans. She had a small group of followers who liked her content. Still, it made her feel special.

"That's the person I loved," Guille said.

Naomi straightened.

He waved at the front door. "Not this girl who's trying to get every guy's attention."

She hadn't thought she did that with the delivery driver, but maybe she had. Perhaps she had sent some signal.

Maybe Guille was watching instead of playing the game. She didn't know. She didn't actually see him.

Guille flipped open the pizza box. "Why don't you get us some plates?"

Naomi headed toward the kitchen.

"Maybe we could watch a movie or something," Guille called. "Then you can show me some of those moves those guys pay premium for."

She didn't know if he was flirting with her or cutting her down, but she smiled anyway, in case he was watching. "Okay, baby."

Naomi carried a couple of plates and some paper towels with her when she returned to the living room. "Can we watch a comedy tonight?"

Guille flopped onto the couch. "A comedy?"

"Yeah. You know? Something to take my mind off all the crazy shit that's been going on the past couple days."

"Fuck that noise." Guille reached for the remote. "Let's watch an action movie."

Chapter 22

"What about an action movie?" Damien Truscott asked.

Tessa looked at their sons, Jace and Cole. They were teenagers now, sixteen and fifteen, respectively. Both boys were using their cell phones. "Guys?"

"Mmm?" they replied in unison.

"Dad asked if you wanted to watch an action movie."

Jace stood. His attention remained firmly affixed to his phone's screen. "I've got homework." He wandered off toward his bedroom.

"Me, too." Cole stood now. He, at least, looked away from his phone. "But a movie sounded fun." He trotted after his brother.

Tessa leaned from her position on the couch to watch the boys disappear into their rooms. "It's just the two of us."

"Like that old song."

She sat upright. "What old song?"

"'Just the Two of Us.'" Truscott sang the chorus. "Don't you remember it?"

"It was before my time."

He chuckled. "We were kids. Our parents listened to it."

"Not my parents."

Truscott handed her the remote. "What would you like to watch?"

"Shall we journey to England and see what's up with the Old Dogs?"

He settled onto the couch next to his wife. "Start it up."

Tessa found the latest BBC show they'd been watching, New Tricks. It was about a group of retired detectives brought together to solve cold cases.

"Work was okay?" she asked.

"It was fine," he said. He didn't feel like talking about the job tonight. "How was your day?"

"Same as always." Tessa was a dental hygienist.

She started the show, then snuggled into him. Truscott put his arm around his wife and felt her warmth along his side.

Prior to the attack she suffered, Tessa never cared for many foreign shows. Since then, though, she watched them almost exclusively. Truscott wondered if watching shows based in England meant Tessa could compartmentalize her feelings. If witnessing a traumatic event on a foreign show felt different because it was so far away, as opposed to it being set on American soil.

If they watched a movie with the boys, it was usually a big budget American flick. Tessa always wanted to know what the movie was about. If there were triggering images for her, she'd look away or go into the kitchen for a snack. She did her best to hide her discomfort, and the boys never seemed to notice.

Truscott didn't suggest they watch anything other than the BBC cop shows. He enjoyed them even if there were elements he found unbelievable. He found the same issues in American shows portraying the police, too. Whenever that happened, he watched for the story and tried to ignore the technical elements they got wrong.

Besides, the shows they'd been watching were easy to follow, and they allowed his mind to wander.

Truscott's thoughts often drifted to his wife and her attacker. He frequently contemplated what he'd do if the two ever met. In fact, it plagued his sleep. He only had a vague description of the man, but he understood where and how the attack took place. It was enough to start looking—if Tessa allowed him to.

While still in the Special Victims Unit, Truscott fantasized about investigating a case and discovering the identity of Tessa's attacker in the process. What would he do then, since Tessa didn't want the man arrested? She wanted the memory of the attack to sink into an abyss like a capsized boat at sea.

Truscott knew what he'd do if he found her attacker. There was never any doubt.

As a police officer, Truscott had certain duties to uphold the law. One of those meant respecting the rights of those in custody. If Truscott found and arrested his wife's attacker, he would be responsible for the man's safety until jail booking.

If Truscott came face-to-face with his wife's rapist, he knew for certain he would kill the man without hesitation. He'd lose his freedom as a result and likely his family. By killing Tessa's attacker, Truscott would selfishly betray his wife because she wanted the assault to fade away in her memory. That was the real reason he left the Special Victims Unit. He had a higher likelihood of running across the man in that position. It was less likely he'd ever find her rapist while assigned to Property Crimes.

Tessa's breathing deepened. Truscott bent slightly to see her eyes were closed. He let her sleep through the rest of the episode.

Chapter 23

James Morgan crossed the parking lot and climbed the steps to his apartment. He carried a bag of groceries in the crook of his left arm. He'd stopped on the way home to get a few essentials. It had been some time since he'd stocked up with anything more than that. He'd have to do it soon, but tonight wasn't the time.

He unlocked the door, stepped through, and shut it with his foot. Morgan had taken a couple of steps and paused. He returned to the door and flipped the lock closed. He also secured the deadbolt.

Morgan lost count of how many months had passed since his last girlfriend. There were always stretches of time when he had no woman in his life, but he couldn't remember a period as long as this.

He set the groceries on the kitchen counter. Then he removed his gun, badge, extra clip, and handcuffs. He set them on the counter as well. He slipped off his jacket and threw it over the living room couch.

Morgan pulled a can of beer from the fridge and cracked it open. He was hungry, but priorities had to be maintained. After a second gulp, he put the beer aside.

He sprayed cooking grease in a pan and set it on the stove. Morgan removed a carton of eggs from the bag of groceries. He selected two and cracked them in the pan. Next, he pulled a loaf of bread and put four slices into his toaster. It was at moments like this he was glad he splurged on the bigger appliance.

While he continued to prepare dinner, his thoughts drifted back to Svetlana, the Russian prostitute.

"Shit," he muttered.

He grabbed the beer and kicked it back. The third healthy swallow nearly finished the can. Morgan shook it before polishing off the remaining amount. He tossed the empty can into the garbage. He opened the refrigerator and grabbed a second beer.

Svetlana had provided information about The Hempstead, but it came at a violent cost. He wasn't upset by it. The application of physical pressure often elicited the truth. It was an effective tool while on the street, but most cops didn't know how to wield it correctly. He was mad he needed to choke Svetlana at all. It showed the street how much he was exposed by his relationship to Joey.

Morgan flipped the eggs in the pan before setting half a piece of cheese on each. When the toast popped, he put them onto a plate. He squirted ketchup on two pieces. On the other two, he slathered some mayonnaise.

He sipped the beer and waited for the eggs to finish and the cheese to melt. Svetlana filled his thoughts again.

When the prostitute said she wanted what Joey Greene had, Morgan had only himself to blame. For years, he ran a tight ship. Never taking anything from the street that he didn't give back in exchange for information.

Morgan wasn't corrupt—he told himself that repeatedly. He knew about the downfall of officers in other departments, and he realized how the slippery slope often started. Those cops first broke the law with an idea of doing what was right. Then they enriched themselves. Morgan never did that. He never once took anything for himself.

Until he met Joey.

Morgan turned off the stove. He grabbed a spatula and lifted the eggs onto two pieces of toast. He carried the plate and his beer out of the kitchen.

In the living room, a large black-and-white photo hung on the back wall. Mickey Mantle, twisted like a corkscrew, had just hit a homerun. A color photo hung on the neighboring wall. Ken Griffey Jr. jumped above the outfield wall to rob a hitter of a dinger.

Morgan sat in his recliner and brought the footrest up. He turned on the television and went directly to ESPN. At this time of night, there were no games on. The broadcasters droned on about the day's events, but Morgan's thoughts remained on Joey.

He shouldn't have taken advantage of the situation with her. It created too many problems. Nothing stayed secret on the streets. He knew the rule, and he violated it. Beyond that, he also developed feelings for Joey.

It wasn't love. She was a whore, and Morgan wasn't that stupid. He felt something akin to her guardian, even while he continued to take advantage of her. Morgan could blame Joey all he wanted, but he knew everything was his responsibility. He shouldn't have gotten involved with her in the first place.

Morgan swallowed a bite of his sandwich and washed it down with a swallow of beer. The meal was less satisfying than he hoped. He would finish it, though. Just because it wasn't gratifying didn't mean he should throw it out.

The sportscasters began talking about the Mariner's game. Morgan's worries drifted away amid the report of four homeruns that night. The sandwich's lackluster taste faded, and Morgan smiled. The M's had pounded the Texas Rangers 11-2. The team was off to a good start this year, but the season was long. There was still plenty of time for them to screw it up.

When the show cut to commercial, Morgan stuffed the last bite of the first sandwich in his mouth. All the toast required an extra swig of beer to get it down.

Morgan lifted the second sandwich and paused. He thought about Joey again and put it down, deciding to wait until *SportsCenter* returned to the air.

He no longer took advantage of Joey. Well, not in a way the streets could misconstrue. He continued to trade for information, but he did that with everyone. Morgan never thought making their relationship strictly business would bother Joey. He thought she'd be happy about it. At worst, she wouldn't care. Her earlier statement had given him pause. He could never return to that scenario. Not since Internal Affairs became aware of her.

He knew for sure he needed to keep his eye on the Russian prostitute. He put his hand around her throat, and it was likely to bruise. If she went to Internal Affairs, there was evidence of an assault.

It would be her word against his, but Svetlana knew Joey. IA could use those connections to tie Morgan up. He needed to be smarter, or he needed to get out of the game. Perhaps he'd pushed his luck for too long.

Morgan could have retired long ago. Maybe he should take his chips off the table and get out before he made a mistake that cost him his freedom.

SportsCenter came back on, but Morgan ignored most of it.

Jesus, he wished he had a girlfriend. A woman would help quiet the noise in his head.

Images of Vivian Basler entered his mind. It was too late to call her, but she would only make matters worse for him tonight. He loved the game with her—the push and pull—but he was already on edge. Talking with her would give him more frustration tonight. That wouldn't help.

He set his plate to the side and stared up at the ceiling.

Morgan knew what he wanted right then, and it wasn't a woman. He wanted to get back on the street. He wanted to get back in the mix and work on the problem of The Hempstead.

He knew if he didn't get some sleep, he'd be worthless tomorrow.

Morgan lay in the recliner as the sportscasters droned on. Next to him, the Mick and the Kid played their eternal game of baseball.

His eyes eventually grew heavy.

DAY 3

Chapter 24

The banging on the door caused Naomi Stapleton to jump awake. She looked to where Guille should be sleeping but the bed was empty.

"Guille?" she said, but there was no answer.

Naomi grabbed her phone to check the time. It was shortly after six. There were several missed phone calls from a blocked phone number.

The same blocked number had texted her. She opened the text application and found three text messages.

The first came in at 5:23 a.m. NAOMI STAPLETON, THIS IS SPECIAL AGENT SMITH WITH THE SPOKANE OFFICE OF THE FBI. WHEN YOU HAVE A MOMENT, PLEASE RETURN MY CALL. THIS IS URGENT.

A number was provided.

The second message came nine minutes later. MS. STAPLETON, THIS IS SPECIAL AGENT SMITH AGAIN. THIS IS IMPORTANT.

The third message arrived six minutes after the second. PLEASE CALL.

The banging at the front door intensified.

Naomi slid out of bed. She wore a light T-shirt and a pair of loose-fitting shorts. She padded out to the living room.

Guille crouched near the large window. He wore only a pair of plaid boxers. "It's the cops," he whispered. He frantically motioned for her to get down. "I told you not to call."

Naomi considered her phone.

"What are you doing?" Guille hissed.

"Asking a question."

Her thumbs bounced across the screen. ARE YOU AT MY HOUSE? she texted.

The banging stopped.

"Naomi," a male voice said from the other side of the door. "This is Special Agent Smith."

"Who?" Guille asked.

She moved closer to the door. "What do you want?"

"You reported a murder."

Her hand started for the doorknob, but she hesitated. She'd seen the movies where the bad guys impersonated the police to gain access to a house. "The cops were already here. How do I know you're for real?"

"We found the victim you reported," Smith said through the door.

Guille bear-crawled toward her now, keeping himself below the window. "Don't open the door," he whispered.

"You're in trouble," Smith continued. "Your life is in danger."

Naomi glanced at Guille. He shook his head. "He's lying. All cops do it."

"Why would he do that?" she asked.

"To trick us."

"For what?"

"How the fuck should I know?" Guille rolled back on his heels. "That's how the cops do. There's not an honest one in the bunch."

"Naomi," Agent Smith said, "the clock is ticking. We need to get you some place safe."

"What's going on?" she called through the door.

"Please, open the door."

"Tell me."

"The man you saw murdered," Smith said. "He was an informant."

"A rat," Guille whispered.

"We believe the men who killed him," Smith continued, "took his computer and are attempting to track their way back to you."

Guille waved a dismissive hand. "They can't find us. That's why we drowned the computer."

"I'm going to hear them out," she said.

Guille pointed at her. "Bitch, if you do that—"

She grabbed the doorknob. "He said we're in danger."

"You're gonna be in danger all right."

"What if he's telling the truth?" Naomi unlocked the door and pulled it open.

A man in a dark suit stood on the landing. He wore a white shirt and a black tie. His brown hair was cut in a businessman's style. Flecks of gray peppered the sides. He held a wallet in the air with his left hand. In it were an FBI badge and an ID card.

Agent Smith nodded at Naomi, then leaned slightly. "Guillermo Messi?"

The color faded from Guille's face. "What'd I do?"

"May I come in?"

Naomi stepped back. "Yes."

"No," Guille said. He hopped closer to the door and puffed his chest. "You can't come in."

Smith stepped inside. He stood several inches taller than Guille. His shoulders were broader, and it appeared the agent spent his free time at the gym instead of playing video games.

Guille moved backward.

"Please, put some clothes on," Smith said to Naomi. "We need to get you someplace safe." His attention moved to Guille. "You, too."

Guille shook his head. "I ain't going nowhere."

"For how long?" Naomi asked.

Agent Smith shrugged. "At this time, we don't know, but you need to hurry."

"Should I take my computer?"

"Leave anything traceable. Your computer, your phone, even a tablet if you have one."

"She can't take her phone?" Guille whined. "How's she gonna talk with me?" He looked at Naomi. "You ain't going nowhere. You don't know this shit is real."

"It's a credible threat," Smith said.

"How do you know?" Guille snapped. "You show up here, bossing my girl around, and she's supposed to believe you?"

Naomi did believe the lawman, but it was a good question.

Smith pulled his phone from the inside of his jacket. He spoke while he talked. "The victim was Alexei Nikolaev."

"Nick," Naomi whispered.

"He was an enforcer for the Novy Brat Nation." Novy Brat rhymed with cozy caught.

Guille's lip curled. "Never heard of them."

Smith briefly looked up from his phone. "Why would you?" His gaze swept up and down her boyfriend's frame. "You have nothing to offer them, Mr. Messi."

Guille clucked. "I can offer plenty," he said defensively.

Smith held up his phone. "Is this the man you saw murdered?"

It was a mug shot, those pictures jail staff take after the cops book people in on bullshit charges. Naomi had been arrested while in high school, but never went to jail as an adult. She'd had her photo taken a couple of times.

"That's Nick," she said.

"When we get you someplace safe, we'd like to have you look at some photographs to see if you can identify his killer."

"Do it here," Guille said. "She ain't leaving."

Smith slipped his phone into his pocket. "Mr. Messi, it's obvious you don't grasp the severity of the situation."

Guille crossed his arms over his bare chest and pinched his lips.

"If the NBN can determine where Naomi is," Smith said, "they'll send someone to kill her. They'll kill whoever is with her. It's their way. It's why they killed Mr. Nikolaev."

The image of Nick's killer flashed through Naomi's mind. "I'll go get changed," she said.

Guille lifted his chin. "I ain't going nowhere."

Agent Smith shrugged a single shoulder. "Suit yourself. If you don't come with me now, we can't protect you if they show up later."

"I can protect myself."

"How?" Naomi asked.

"Bitch." Guille's face pickled, and he flicked his hand at her. "Take your ass on." He walked over to the couch and flopped into it. "How'm I gonna protect myself?" he muttered to himself. "Like I need some rent-a-cops to do that for me."

Agent Smith leaned into Naomi. "Get dressed. Don't bring a bag. We'll get you everything you need. Time is of the essence."

Naomi took a final glance at Guille before running into her bedroom.

Chapter 25

Early morning traffic cruised westbound on Spokane Falls Boulevard. No one paid notice to the man standing near the entrance to Riverfront Park. The fact he leaned against the hood of a Dodge Charger didn't seem to matter. Most folks were likely headed to work and had other things to worry about.

Over the past year, this same strip of downtown had seen a man shot by the police after firing his AK-47 in the air, another man arrested for assaulting homeless people sleeping in the park, and a woman's self-immolation as a protest for abortion rights.

Detective James Morgan checked his watch. Laszlo Nagy was late. The junkie had called earlier in the morning with information. Morgan tried to get him to cough up his intel right then, but Laszlo was cagey—he wanted the book Morgan had taken.

The part-time dealer and relapsing junkie was careful not to say drugs on the phone. Morgan was thankful for that.

Laszlo Nagy came into view now. He approached along Howard Street, about a block away from the park. His arms were crossed as he shuffled, and his head was down.

Morgan pushed off the car and stretched his back, pulling his shoulder blades together. He wanted Nagy to hurry up, but the junkie looked worse for wear. It must have been a long night without his medicine.

Nagy walked too close to a signpost and bumped it with his shoulder. It spun the man, but he didn't lose his footing. He pirouetted, wobbled for a moment, then regained his path. His arms never uncrossed, and his gaze remained on the sidewalk.

Traffic paused at the intersection of Howard when the light turned red. Morgan lost sight of Nagy for a moment due to a jackass in a lifted pickup. The detective walked a couple of paces to get a better view. As soon as he got a decent view of Nagy again, the light changed, and the vehicles started moving.

Nagy was almost at the intersection now, and Morgan got a decent look at him. He wore a Spokane Chiefs sweatshirt, gray sweatpants, and high-top basketball shoes. His stringy gray hair looked the worst it had in years—unwashed, uncombed, and thinning beyond recovery.

It was then Nagy lifted his eyes and noticed the detective. There was no emotional reaction—no anger, no happiness, and there wasn't any physical manifestation—no wave or nod. Nagy simply saw Morgan and stepped into the street without pausing for oncoming traffic.

A horn blared. A Honda Accord locked its brakes and its tires skidded as it tried to come to a sudden stop. Behind it, a Kia Sorrento whipped into the neighboring lane. It locked its brakes and honked its horn when Laszlo Nagy stepped in front of it.

Soon, a cacophony of horns trumpeted the man's successful arrival at Riverfront Park. As traffic began to flow again, drivers extended their arms from car windows and saluted Nagy with their middle fingers.

The part-time dealer stepped onto the sidewalk. "Sorry, I'm late."

"You're lucky you're not dead," Morgan said.

"Tell me about it. I guess I'm jonesin' harder than I thought."

Beads of sweat formed on Nagy's forehead.

"What'd you find out?" Morgan asked.

"You bring the stuff?"

"You first."

Nagy danced impatiently. "C'mon, Morgan. I just need to know it's here."

"It's here."

"For real?" Nagy's gaze hardened.

"Have I ever lied to you?"

The small-time dealer thought about it. "No, man, you haven't." This seemed to bring him a little peace, but he didn't relax. Nagy looked at the Charger. "You want to sit inside?"

"You stink, Laszlo. You're not getting in my car."

Nagy hugged himself tighter. "All right. Geez."

"Get on with it. Tell me about Golubev and Semyonov."

"They're muscle."

Morgan grunted. "No shit. Who are they protecting?"

"From what I heard, they're protecting a roof."

"A roof?"

Nagy shrugged. "I don't get it either."

"Tell me about this roof," Morgan said.

"What do you mean?"

"What building is it on?"

Nagy's face pinched. "I didn't ask."

Morgan's lip curled. "Who told you about it?"

"A friend."

"Which friend?"

"A friend of a friend," Nagy said. He held out his hands as if begging for a cup of water. "You got to believe me, Morgan. I worked all night on this."

"And all you got is they're protecting a roof?"

Nagy looked down at his shoes. "Maybe it was lost in translation."

"What do you mean?"

"English is their second language."

"It's your second language."

Nagy's brow furrowed. "The fuck is that supposed to mean?"

"Is there something special about this roof?"

"You know, I tried really hard."

"Not hard enough to get your dope back."

Nagy licked his lips and his eyes refocused on Morgan.

"Now," the detective said. "Think. Was there something special about this roof?"

"I guess it stops a house from getting wet or something."

"It stops a house..." Morgan leaned in. "Did you even ask a follow-up question?"

Nagy feigned offense. "Of course, I did."

"What question did you ask?"

Nagy looked away. "I don't remember."

Morgan's cell phone rang, but he ignored it.

"You better remember if you want your medicine."

"I asked what a roof was."

"You did?" Morgan said. His cell phone rang again. "And what did your friend of a friend say?"

Nagy glanced away.

"Well?"

The phone rang a third time. Morgan pulled it from his pocket but didn't check the ID screen.

Nagy's head bobbled. "He said a roof protected a house."

Morgan glared at Nagy. "You didn't ask any questions."

"I did!"

The phone rang a fourth time. The ID screen read Sergeant Bynum. Morgan answered the call.

"Where you at?" the sergeant asked.

"Following up on a lead."

"I need specifics. How far out are you?"

"I can be back in ten minutes. Why? What's going on?"

"Meeting with the chief. Fifteen minutes."

Morgan's stomach tightened. His mind immediately returned to the incident the previous evening. Would the Russian prostitute have already called Internal Affairs? Morgan doubted it, but he steeled himself just in case.

Bynum continued. "CTF just got an assignment. Sounds like something big, but that's all I know. If we're not here when you get back, meet Senai and me over in the chief's conference room."

"I'm on my way."

Morgan hung up and slipped the phone back into his pocket.

"Gotta go?" Nagy said hopefully.

"Last chance."

"What do you mean last chance?"

Morgan walked to the driver's door.

Nagy hurried to him. "I did my part."

"You did shit, Laszlo."

"Hold on." Nagy grabbed Morgan by the arm. "You can't go yet."

The detective shoved Nagy away. "Don't ever touch me."

"You got my stuff."

"You didn't earn it back."

Nagy's eyes watered and his lips trembled. "I tried."

"You don't get for trying, Laszlo. You get for doing. That's how the world works."

The small-time dealer stared as if someone had stolen his puppy.

Morgan pointed downtown. "If you want your stuff back, get me some intel I can use."

Nagy's gaze dropped to the ground.

"Or fuck off," the detective said. "Either way, you'll get what you deserve."

Morgan dropped into the car. The engine fired up, and he drove away.

Chapter 26

Damien Truscott poured a cup of coffee and leaned against the counter. He was in no hurry to return to his desk. There were burglaries and vehicle thefts he could work on, but his heart wasn't in any of them. He had called his sergeant last night after getting the Chicago call.

"Call Brand," was the advice Sergeant Yager gave him.

Truscott did as instructed and called Lieutenant George Brand. However, the man didn't answer the call. Damien left a message. The night passed without a return call.

He sipped his coffee and listened to the chatter occurring in the nearby cubicles. Some of it focused on a Mariners game last night—they won big. A couple of other guys complained about the union's lack of response to the city's attempt to give more power to the police ombudsman.

Truscott pushed off the counter and headed toward the Major Crimes section. He'd already left one message for Lieutenant Brand this morning. Perhaps the man had returned the call while Truscott stood there sipping his coffee.

What harm would there be in stopping by the lieutenant's office?

He wandered through the Major Crimes office. Most of the detectives were at their desks, which was surprising. He figured they would have been out in the field, either at fresh crime scenes or following up on old leads. The detectives were too busy to notice him, or they pretended not to care he was there. Either way was fine with Truscott.

Lieutenant Brand hurried out of his office as Truscott approached.

Truscott held up a hand. "Can I get a minute--"

"No time," Brand said and rushed by. The lieutenant's arms swung wide, and he almost bumped into Truscott's coffee cup.

Truscott hurried after the tall man. "I can walk with you wherever you're going."

The lieutenant glanced over his shoulder. The glare he flashed said more than any words could.

Truscott slowed and turned in the other direction.

He passed through the coffee section and topped off his coffee mug. The nearby detectives were still chattering about the Mariners and the union. Truscott had no interest in getting involved in either discussion.

He returned to his desk, settled into his seat, and put his coffee down. He tapped the space bar on the keyboard and called his computer to life. The monitor brightened and he entered his password.

The phone rang.

Truscott's eyes cut to the ID screen at the top. It was an intra-department number, but he couldn't place it. He answered it on the second ring. "Detective Truscott," he said.

"What kind of shit did you get me involved in?" a harried male voice asked.

Truscott pulled the receiver from his head and considered it. When he put it back to his ear, he said, "Who is this?"

"It's Wickenhauser, you ass."

Digital Forensics, Truscott thought.

"I'm waiting for my supervisor to call me back, but I thought I'd call you to say thanks for siccing the Feds on me."

"What Feds?"

"The FBI. They're here for the computer."

"Did you get anything off it?" Truscott asked.

"Are you kidding? It was wet when you brought it in. It's been under a heat lamp since then. If I plug it in while it's wet, it might do more damage. Are you coming over here or not? I need some backup."

"On the way."

"Dude, I really appreciate—"

Truscott hung up without letting the man finish. He ran out of the Property Crimes section, down the hallway, and burst through the west doors. He hopped down the stairs.

He sprinted through the parking lot shared by the Public Safety Building, the County Jail, and the Spokane County Juvenile Court. Truscott raced across Adams Street and ran toward the front door of the Gardner Building.

He hesitated long enough to see a black Jeep Cherokee parked along Gardner Avenue. It had blue government plates.

Truscott yanked open the door and stepped inside. The woman behind the Plexiglas barrier buzzed him through the security door without hesitation. He trotted toward the back.

A group of employees surrounded the doorway to the Digital Forensics office. A late twenties man with shaggy brown hair, an untucked white shirt, blue jeans, and Doc Martens stood before Wickenhauser. The interloper held a white folder.

Truscott forced his way to the front of the group. "What's going on?"

Wickenhauser waved at the man in the untucked shirt. "This mope thinks he's taking the computer."

"This warrant says it's mine." He held up a folder.

"Who are you?"

"Brandon Krell. Digital forensic examiner."

Wickenhauser's face pinched. "Big whoop. That's my title, too."

Krell's eyebrows raised. "Does your title also say Federal Bureau of Investigations? I didn't think so."

Truscott held out his. "Let me see the warrant."

Krell moved the folder further away. "You the supervisor?"

"He's the detective investigating the murder," Wickenhauser said.

"You were supposed to call your supervisor."

"I did." Wickenhauser shrugged. "I called him, too."

Krell considered Truscott before handing him the folder.

Truscott opened the file and skimmed the warrant.

A superior court judge authorized the seizure of a laptop taken pursuant to Naomi Stapleton's claim she saw Alexei Nikolaev murdered. The FBI had the Spokane Police case number—how they had gotten it so fast, Truscott didn't know.

Truscott read on. The FBI's investigation concerned the murder of an informant. Second, it was an ongoing case, none of which could be divulged in the warrant due to the sensitive nature of their inquiry.

"Who's leading your investigation?" Truscott asked Krell.

"Agent Walker."

He closed the file and handed it back. "Where can I find Walker?"

"He's meeting with your chief right now."

Truscott thought about Lieutenant Brand's hasty exit from Major Crimes. Was he on the way to meet with Agent Walker?

He turned to leave.

"Hey," Krell said.

Truscott looked back over his shoulder.

"Can I get the computer now?"

He motioned toward Wickenhauser. "Don't ask me. I'm just a detective."

Truscott pushed through the crowd and headed back toward the Public Safety Building.

Chapter 27

"Everything will be fine," Special Agent Smith said.

Naomi Stapleton didn't respond. He'd said something similar two other times on their drive. Smith had done almost all the talking so far. She realized at some point he wasn't trying to interview her like the cops from the other day.

Naomi studied him. He had intense eyes and a firm jawline. He probably wasn't trying to interview her because he was focused on protecting her.

Regardless, Smith jabbered on about the safe house. She muttered the occasional "uh-huh" or "okay" to let him know she was listening, but her mind whirred.

She'd asked to know what was going on when they first got into the car, but Smith told her he'd "bring her up to speed" as soon as he got her secure. Naomi figured she had to be patient now. She'd seen those movies where the FBI whisks a person to safety. She had an idea of what would happen. Smith would fill her in on the Novy Brat Nation and the FBI would keep her safe if she testified against Nick's killer—if she could identify him.

The government might want to take away her identity and give her a new one. Would she agree to that? Did she have a choice?

She had no idea where they were going; Smith wouldn't tell her. He never drove in a straight line for very long. He frequently took lefts or rights, doubling back. The agent's head constantly swiveled. Smith didn't tell her what he was searching for, but she knew—she wasn't stupid.

If the killer figured out she lived in Spokane, perhaps he could be following them right now.

Even though Smith spun the car around multiple times, Naomi wasn't lost. She knew her way around the city from her time driving for UberEATS. Delivering food and groceries for folks wasn't the best money she ever earned, but it certainly helped her learn about Spokane.

"Can I ask a question?" she asked.

Smith glanced at her before leaving Kiernan to turn back onto Monroe Street. He'd taken a detour through the neighborhood, no doubt to make sure no one was following them. "Ask away."

"How long do I have to hide?"

He shrugged a single shoulder. "Hard to tell. Could be only a day or two. Might be longer."

Naomi leaned her head against the passenger door's window. The agent's words sounded hollow. She guessed she might be hiding for some time.

Eventually, Smith turned onto Rosewood Avenue. Naomi noticed the street sign as they entered the neighborhood. She straightened and glanced around.

Smith glanced at her. "Everything all right?"

"Yeah," she muttered.

It was a nice neighborhood, far better than the one she grew up in or the one in which she currently lived. The houses were all single level with attached garages. Some had chain-link fences around their front yards. All had fences around their backyards. Each was nicely maintained. Most had new vehicles in their driveways. A couple had RVs.

"Been here before?" Smith asked. He sounded concerned.

"No," Naomi lied.

"Do you know anyone who lives in this neighborhood?"

"Just wondering where we're going." She glanced over her shoulder. "Are we near the mall?" Naomi knew they weren't since they were driving in the opposite direction from it.

Smith eyed her for a second longer, then returned his attention to the road. "No," he said. "We're not near the mall."

Naomi pretended to be disappointed as she watched the houses pass by. She'd already seen the one she was interested in. Naomi once had a boyfriend whose grandmother lived in this neighborhood. The guy took Naomi there many times for no other reason than he liked visiting his grandmother.

Evelyn was her name, but her friends and family called her Pinkie. Her grandkids called her Grandma Pinkie. Agent Smith had driven by the house and didn't seem to notice the gaggle of plastic pink flamingos gathered on the front lawn.

"We're down here," he said.

The second house from the west end of the block was a yellow rancher. White trim highlighted the house. A two-car garage was attached. The lawn was neatly cut, and flowers bloomed in pots placed on the exterior stairs.

Smith pulled into the driveway and removed a remote control from the center console. He pressed a button and the garage door rolled up.

Black blocky numbers on the house caught Naomi's eye—4321. It seemed a silly number, like a kid had made it up.

When the path was clear, Smith pulled the car inside. When Naomi got out, she noticed how clean the garage was. Nothing was inside except Agent Smith's car.

He opened the connecting door to the house. "I need to get your sizes. Shirt, pants, shoes. We'll have an agent bring you some clothes later today."

She followed him inside.

"We'll try to make you as comfortable as possible," he added.

The living room had a flat screen television, full-sized couch, coffee table, and recliner.

Smith pointed off to the right. "The kitchen is fully stocked. If there's something not there you want to eat, let me know and we'll get it. Okay?"

A laptop sat on the dining room table. Smith moved toward it. "Take a look around. I'm going to get us set up here."

Naomi wandered toward the back of the house. She passed a couple of bedrooms. Each had a bed and a dresser, but that was it. The bathroom had a new shower curtain—the crease lines were still in the plastic. It felt like a hotel, as if the cleaning staff had just turned it over for the next guest.

She stared at the bathtub and thought about her drowned laptop, which led her to think about Guille. Naomi wondered if he regretted not coming with her. She missed him and wished he had come.

"Any questions?" Agent Smith called from down the hall.

Naomi returned to the dining room table. "I want to know what's going on."

"Have a seat." Smith turned the computer to show a photo of Nick. He tapped the monitor. "Alexei Nikolaev was an informer for our Chicago office."

"Was Nick in witness protection?"

"No. He was providing us with intelligence, living his life as if nothing changed."

"Why was he doing that—providing intelligence?"

"His sister was facing prosecution for murdering her boyfriend. He was trying to lighten her sentence."

Naomi sat at the table. "He could do that?"

"For information on the NBN, our Chicago office would make a lot of deals. Besides, the dead boyfriend was abusive. No one was sorry to see him gone. I doubt even his mother was broken up."

She considered Nick's picture. "They killed him for a reason. Do you think the people he worked for found out he was a rat?"

Smith shrugged. "I don't know the details of that. The Chicago office was lead. All I know is I need to keep you safe. While we're doing that, would you look through some photographs?" The lawman tapped a key, and another program came to life. "Here are all the known associates of the Novy Brat Nation. Go through them slowly and see if you can find someone that looks familiar."

"If no one does?"

Smith stood. "Then we'll look at affiliates. Are you hungry?"

She nodded.

"How about a sandwich and chips? It's hard for me to screw that up."

"Thank you."

Smith headed for the kitchen. "Holler if you find someone."

Naomi slid the laptop closer to her. She studied the first picture. It was of a bald man with dead eyes. If all of them looked like him, it was going to be a long morning.

She tapped the arrow for the next picture.

Chapter 28

Morgan was cutting it close, but he still parked at the Monroe Court Building. It wasn't expedient for the meeting in the chief's conference room, but he wouldn't have to move his car later. He walked across the campus and entered the Public Safety Building's front doors.

The blocky building housed the municipal court as well as the administrative functions for both the Spokane Police Department and the Spokane County Sheriff's Office.

As usual for this time of day, activity and noise overwhelmed the lobby. A line of citizens waited at the metal detectors. Beyond that, citizens lingered at the counters to schedule court hearings and pay fines.

Attorneys and clients moved about like fish in an aquarium. Those on their way to a hearing hurried up the stairs to the second level. Those who were finished came down. It was easy to tell the winners from the losers. Some hung their heads and heavily trudged with each step. Others held their heads high and wore broad smiles—they had beaten the system.

The lobby, like the building's architecture, carried 1970s styling. Dark brown tile covered the floor. Thick wood railings protected the stairwells and lined every counter. Plexiglas elements were scattered about with an eye toward modernity before the concept of a cell phone, personal computer, or the internet ever existed.

Morgan walked to the foremost security checkpoint. A guard moved to intercept him. The heavyset woman wore the uniform of the latest security firm to win the county's bidding process. Her face strained, and she held up a hand.

The detective opened his jacket to expose the badge and gun on his belt. The guard nodded and jerked her head for him to proceed.

He pressed his ID card against a security reader to unlock the double doors and entered the east hallway. Fluorescent lights reflected off highly polished white vinyl flooring. It was a stark contrast to the PSB's lobby.

The chief's conference room was at the end of the hallway. The door was open and there were already people seated at the table. He wasn't late, so there was no reason to hurry. He'd likely never hurry to an administrative meeting, anyway. He'd been with an informant when his sergeant called. He responded almost immediately. If they didn't like how quickly he got there, they could pound sand.

When Morgan entered the room, he paused and assessed those attending. He immediately sensed something was off.

At the head of the table sat Chief Liam Dillon. To his right were Lieutenant George Brand and Detective Damien Truscott.

The absence of Captain Gary Ackerman was the first inkling something was amiss. Ackerman oversaw the Investigations Division and was attached to the chief's hip like a Siamese twin. Morgan knew the captain was working this week, so him not being in the room felt wrong.

The second clue was the presence of Truscott. Lieutenant Brand ran Major Crimes, so Truscott had no business being there. He was a Property Crimes reject. He wasn't one of the Golden Children.

All detectives cut their teeth in Property Crimes or what was once called the general detectives pool. Even Morgan did. But only Truscott got bounced back there after ascending to the Special Victims Unit. Rumors abounded about his demotion, but Morgan believed he had found the truth. He hadn't told anyone or even spoken to Truscott about it. Morgan only traded in rumors if it served a purpose.

To the chief's left sat an unknown white man in a dark suit. He had stopped talking when Morgan entered the room.

Seated next to him were Sergeant Bynum and Detective Nayla Senai.

"Shut the door," Chief Dillon said, "and grab a seat."

Morgan pushed the door closed. It banged louder than he expected.

There were two chairs remaining—one next to Truscott and one at the opposite end of the table from the chief. He took the latter because it put him next to Senai.

"Is this everyone?" the man in the suit asked.

Dillon nodded.

"Some of you have met me, but for those who haven't, I'm Special Agent Brendan Walker, Federal Bureau of Investigation."

Walker scanned the table. When his gaze met Morgan's, the detective kept his expression flat. He'd met Feds before and was always unimpressed. All of them could shove their jurisdictional interdiction up their collective asses.

"We're taking over Detective Truscott's investigation," Walker said, "but we need your help."

Morgan was already lost. Why would the FBI care about a property crime?

Truscott shifted in his seat but didn't speak up.

Senai glanced at Morgan and raised an eyebrow. He shrugged.

Chief Dillon said, "A woman here in Spokane observed a man murdered during an online sex act. She called 911 and the resulting report landed in Truscott's lap."

Morgan eyed Lieutenant Brand, then he studied Truscott. Now he understood the play. The Major Crimes supervisor didn't deem the report a worthy enough case for one of his golden children to investigate, so he kicked it down to Property Crimes. It was an overflow case. Unfortunately for Brand, he misjudged it and now it had come back to bite him in his fat ass.

"Who was the victim?" Morgan asked.

"Alexei Nikolaev," Agent Walker said. "An accountant for the Novy Brat Nation."

Morgan straightened. From the corner of his eye, he noticed Senai doing the same.

"Novy Brat?" Dillon asked.

"Officially, they're the *Novobratskiye Narod*," Walker clarified. "New Brother Nation, although I'm probably mangling it. According to our Russian language experts, so is the gang. Apparently, no one in the old country would say it that way. Seems America and the English language have influenced the new generation or something. Anyway, it's a mouthful. That's why everyone—including the gang itself—has bastardized it to the Novy Brat. Nikolaev was our informant. He provided information to us about his employer, Viktor Kuznetsov. Our Chicago office has been after Kuznetsov for years but hasn't been able to get anything on him."

"What's he into?" Morgan asked.

"Fraud."

The answer surprised Morgan. He expected a variety of standard responses—drugs, guns, extortion, or prostitution. Fraud wouldn't have cracked Morgan's top five.

Walker continued. "From what I understand, and I'm getting this information secondhand mind you, Kuznetsov established identity theft rings around the greater Chicago area. He's got hackers clacking away on their computers day and night trying to steal identities." The agent's fingers mimed typing on a keyboard.

Morgan leaned in. Something the Russian prostitute had told him last night made sense now.

"Why can't your team bust this Kuznetsov?" Lieutenant Brand asked.

"That's a good question," Walker said. "I don't know the answer. It's a Chicago case, but I worked with some of the Russian gangs while assigned to the L.A. office. What I was told about Kuznetsov is he sets the teams up like cells. Groups of hackers sprinkled about the city, independent of one another. If one goes down, it doesn't take the other with it. No site knows the other. Kuznetsov gets a piece of all the action."

Senai bumped Morgan's arm. "Do you think?" she whispered.

He waved her off so he could continue to listen to the agent.

Walker continued. "There was an analysis done by one of the credit reporting agencies a couple years back that said more than thirty thousand fraud rings are operating worldwide. As an agency, we don't disagree with that risk assessment. Our only question is how many are operating on US soil?"

"*Oliver Twist*," Truscott said.

Everyone at the table turned their attention to him.

"It's a movie about pickpockets. Their leader—"

"Fagin," Brand offered. "I read the book."

"Anyway," Truscott said, "Fagin teaches these homeless kids how to steal. He then fences their stolen goods. That's what Kuznetsov is doing."

Walker smirked. "Don't give them too much credit. Kuznetsov is former FSB, what we once knew as the KGB."

Morgan's eyes narrowed. The Russian prostitute's words rang true in his ears.

"He's not a nice guy," Walker said. "The guy is a killer. He surrounds himself with killers and he knows how to manipulate people."

Morgan looked around the room at the others in attendance before raising his hand.

"Yes?"

"If you're investigating Truscott's case," Morgan asked, "why are we here?"

Walker tapped the table as if considering his answer. "We've taken Detective Truscott's witness into protective custody. Alexei Nikolaev's computer was missing from his apartment and we believe his killer took it. If Kuznetsov is involved, it's likely his team is working to backtrack the communications to our witness."

Lieutenant Brand leaned forward. "Is that possible?"

Walker interlaced his fingers. "It's unlikely. Tracking a URL through a closed platform like OnlyFans is impossible. However…" The agent let the last word hang in the air for a moment. "Kuznetsov's people are creative. Maybe they'll find something on Alexei Nikolaev's computer that leads them to the girl. Perhaps he had a fascination with her we didn't know about."

"And what do you want from us?" Sergeant Bynum asked.

Chief Dillon motioned toward the FBI agent. "The CTF will support Agent Walker's team."

"We're short on personnel," Walker said. "Our team is dealing with an issue in Ellensburg right now. All we need is outside surveillance. If our man inside needs to be relieved, we'll ask Detective Truscott to handle it because he's already familiar with the witness."

Babysitters, Morgan thought. *Classic.*

"Why aren't the marshals providing support?" Lieutenant Brand asked. "Isn't protection usually their bailiwick?"

Morgan cocked his head. It was a good question.

"You're correct," Walker said. "However, the local office is supporting Tri-Cities contingent with a task-force situation."

"Everyone's stretched thin," Brand said. His comment had more bite to it than Morgan expected. Even Chief Dillon raised his eyebrows. Maybe the lieutenant was embarrassed now that his case assignment error was being passed up to the FBI.

Walker said, "If your department can't lend a hand, Lieutenant, we understand. We'll ask the sheriff's office for support. With how much help we've provided over the years, we thought the city would be happy to help."

"We're helping," Dillon said flatly. "End of discussion."

Walker nodded his appreciation.

Chief Dillon said, "Brand and Bynum stay behind. We'll work out the details with Agent Walker. The rest of you are free to go."

Truscott and Senai stood, but Morgan leaned forward.

"Excuse me," he said to Agent Walker. He motioned at Senai. "Nayla and I, along with the rest of the CTF, are watching The Hempstead."

The FBI man glanced questioningly at the chief.

"It's a downtown apartment building," Dillon said. "Low-income housing. What's the point, Morgan?"

"We're not sure it's low-income housing anymore, Chief," Morgan said. "It sold a few years back to an LLC. We tried to do some research on the ownership group, but their registered agent is an attorney out of Chicago. We dead-ended there."

The mention of the Midwest city seemed to catch the agent's attention. "Okay."

Truscott and Senai returned to their seats.

"The Hempstead's locked down," Morgan said, "but the units appear occupied. However, no residents come out."

"Like a roach motel," Chief Dillon said.

"Except no one ever goes in," Senai added. "Deliveries from a Russian grocery have been made and prostitutes have been sent to the building."

"Prostitutes?" Walker asked.

"They serviced the workers," Morgan said. "I interviewed one of them last night and confirmed that."

Senai watched him with suspicious eyes. He hadn't briefed anyone on the team yet about his conversation with Svetlana.

Chief Dillon rested his forearms on the edge of the table. "Workers? What do you mean by that?"

"According to my source," Morgan said, "it's a digital sweatshop. Each with their own apartment. The prostitutes were hired to service the men and women in the building, and they were bonused for their discretion."

Walker's gaze passed over Senai and Bynum. "Anything else?"

"One more question," Morgan said. "What's a roof?"

The chief and lieutenant grunted. Truscott cocked his head. Even Senai seemed confused by his question. It was so simple a child could answer.

Only Agent Walker seemed to grasp the complexity it really held. "How'd you hear it used?"

"Another source said two thugs connected to the Hempstead were protecting a roof." Morgan noticed Senai studying him and he whispered, "Laszlo Nagy."

Her face pinched. "For real?"

He shrugged. "That's what he said."

"*Krysha*," Walker muttered.

Everyone faced the FBI man.

"It's a Russian concept," Walker continued. "A roof is a shield, private protection, if you will, against criminals."

"A protection racket," Chief Dillon said.

"In a way, but corruption is rampant in Russia. A *krysha* protects businesses, wealthy individuals, even high-level state employees if the money flows in. When the cash stops, the protection stops."

Dillon leaned back in his chair. "The mob has done that for years."

"In Russia, the concept is so prevalent it's discussed in the mainstream papers, on the nightly news. *Krysha* is an important function for maintaining order in a corrupt society."

"Does *krysha* apply here?" Morgan asked. "If The Hempstead is linked to your guy in Chicago—" He snapped his fingers as he struggled to recall the name.

"Viktor Kuznetsov," Agent Walker said.

"Viktor," Morgan said. He wasn't going to try to pronounce the last name. "If The Hempstead is linked to Viktor, how is it *krysha*? Isn't it just part of his organization?"

Walker shrugged. "Maybe this apartment building you mentioned is set up like a franchise and whoever is running it kicks up to Viktor. Or maybe your source didn't understand how *krysha* was used. There are a lot of maybes to consider."

Morgan inhaled deeply. Right now, he felt the intel he'd gotten from Laszlo Nagy and the Russian prostitute had proven valuable.

Agent Walker turned to Chief Dillon. "This news about The Hempstead creates a problem."

"You want them to continue watching that building as well as the witness?"

"That's correct."

Dillon eyed Sergeant Bynum. "Can your team divide its resources?"

"We'll be thin."

"Everyone's stretched thin," Brand whispered, but everyone pretended not to hear him.

Sergeant Bynum turned to Morgan and Senai. "What do you guys think?"

Morgan didn't want to let either assignment go. If the cases were connected, it was an opportunity to take a bite out of a Russian crime syndicate. He eyed Senai. "We can make it work."

She tilted her head. "I don't know."

Bynum faced the chief. "Let us figure it out. If we can't cover it all, we'll talk with SIU."

Walker raised a hand to interrupt. "Actually, the fewer people who know about this, the better. The NBN uses technology as a weapon. If they know they're being monitored, they'll start monitoring us back. Do you understand?"

"In that case," Bynum said, "We'll make it work. What's the address where the witness is? We'll get one of our people up there right now."

Walker glanced at Chief Dillon and rattled off the address.

Sergeant Bynum turned to Morgan and Senai. "Got that?"

They nodded.

"What's the witness's name?" Bynum asked.

"Naomi Stapleton."

Senai wrote it in her notebook. Morgan knew he wouldn't forget the name.

"All right, Detectives," Dillon said. "You're dismissed. Brand and Bynum, stay behind."

Chapter 29

Naomi Stapleton tapped the right arrow key and called a new picture to the screen. This man appeared to be in his late fifties. He had graying hair cropped close to his head. A five o'clock shadow darkened his thin face. Fading tattoos wrapped around his neck. Dead eyes stared back into the camera.

This wasn't the man who had killed Nick.

She lost track long ago of how many scary looking white men glared back from the monitor. At first, she counted the booking photos. *One, two, three.* Somewhere around eleven, she stopped counting. The evil faces were no longer fun to add up. If she had to guess, she was somewhere in the fifties now. Maybe sixties.

Agent Smith stood at the kitchen counter, slowly making sandwiches. If she didn't know better, Naomi would think he was purposefully dragging his feet to give her time to look at the photographs.

He didn't fill the silence with chatter, though, and she appreciated that. Whenever there was quiet at home, Guille talked. Naomi loved him and wanted to hear what her boyfriend had to say, but sometimes she just wanted to sit in peace and let her thoughts sort themselves out.

Next to the computer was Agent Smith's cell phone. Naomi wanted to call Guille and let him know she was okay, but she knew better than to ask. If the house had a phone like her grandmother's did, the type that hung on the wall, she would have used that. Reluctantly, she pulled her attention away from the cell phone and returned it to the computer.

She flicked to the next photo. This man was in his mid-twenties. He had a handsome face, and she lingered on the picture for a moment. After so many thuggish men, it was nice to see a good-looking guy.

According to Agent Smith, all the men in the photos were known affiliates of Novy Brat Nation. Could they all be killers? Naomi didn't want to think the handsome man was a murderer. Surely, a mob had to have guys around who did tasks other than kill. Perhaps some guys did low-level crimes like selling drugs or running blackmail schemes—the mob did that, right? She certainly hoped so for the handsome man's sake.

"You like mayonnaise and mustard?" Smith asked.

Naomi looked up. Was he really just applying the condiments now? "Got ketchup?" she asked.

Smith glanced over his shoulder. "For a sandwich?"

She nodded.

"It's ham and cheese," he said.

"I know."

"Ketchup it is." He went to the refrigerator and retrieved a small bottle of the condiment.

Naomi tapped the arrow key and called up the next photo. This photo was of a heavyset man. His eyes were too close together and his cheeks resembled a squirrel with nuts stuffed inside them.

Smith squeezed ketchup onto her sandwich. "I appreciate you looking through those photos."

"No problem." She leaned back in her chair and her hand slipped away from the computer. It rested on the edge of the table now.

The FBI man set the ketchup bottle to the side. "You're what we call a golden witness."

Naomi immediately thought of her hair color, but that didn't seem right. Otherwise, what would they call a brunette witness or one with red hair?

"I don't know if everyone uses that term," Smith said, "but my boss does, which means our office does." Smith reached into a cabinet and removed two plates. "A golden witness is someone who saw an event clearly. Not the victim because their perspective is skewed."

"Nick's dead."

"There's that." Smith put the sandwiches on separate plates. "But a golden witness can identify the parties involved in the incident—"

"I haven't identified the shooter yet."

"You will." Smith opened a lower cabinet door and removed a bag of potato chips. "You like these?"

She nodded.

He pulled the bag open and put a handful of chips on each plate. "I guess most importantly, a golden witness is an independent and disinterested party."

"I'm not independent," Naomi said. "And I'm certainly not disinterested. I want this guy caught for what he did."

Smith rolled the potato chip bag closed and put it back in the cabinet. "In the eyes of the court, you're independent. Although I'm sure some attorney will argue otherwise. You want a Coke or something? We got Sprite, too."

"Coke," she said. "Thank you."

The agent turned to the refrigerator.

Naomi leaned toward the computer and tapped the right arrow button. The next photo appeared, and she stiffened. Staring back at her was a white male in his early thirties. Naomi immediately recalled those intense, blue eyes studying her from the opposite end of the Zoom call.

"Agent Smith," she said.

"Call me Tyler." Smith walked over to the table. He carried a plate and a can of Coca-Cola.

Naomi pointed at the computer. "That's him. That's the guy who killed Nick."

Smith set the items on to the table in front of Naomi. He reached over her shoulder and tapped a function key. A small window popped over the lower portion of the photograph. It contained a variety of information.

"Vadim Savin," Smith said. "You're sure?"

"I'll never forget that face."

Smith grabbed his cell phone. "Excuse me." He sat at the table and turned the laptop toward himself. After finding a contact on the phone, he placed a call. "This is Smith," he said. "Yeah, that's right. The witness just identified the shooter. Right. It's Vadim Savin. You know him? No shit."

Naomi picked a potato chip from the plate and slipped it into her mouth. She crunched while Smith continued to talk. For several minutes, the agent only said "uh-huh" and "yeah."

Finally, Smith nodded. "All right. Yeah, I'll get her statement and email it as soon as we're done. Happy hunting." He hung up and set his phone on the table. "That was our Chicago office."

"I figured."

"Vadim Savin is a phantom."

"What's that mean?"

"He's suspected of killing many people, but no one's ever proved it. Rumor has it the guy can pass through walls."

Naomi shivered. "Like a ghost."

"A phantom. You're the only one who's ever seen him kill."

She stared at the agent.

"Our Chicago office has chased Savin and his boss for years. You really are the golden witness."

Her thoughts went back to the moment when Vadim Savin leaned into the camera. *We will find you.*

"Do you think they'll come after me?"

Smith shrugged. "Hard to say. We're treating it like they are. Don't worry. You're safe. We've got you."

She did worry, though. Not about herself, but about Guille. She thought about asking Agent Smith if she could use his phone, but she believed he would tell her no. He had talked about all sorts of safety precautions while on the drive to the safe house. She didn't want to ask him to call Guille because she knew how her boyfriend would respond. He didn't trust cops and would figure it was a trick of some kind.

No, she would have to call and warn him.

"We need to get your statement," Smith said. "That way Chicago can locate and arrest Savin. If they can grab him, that'll be the first crack in Viktor Kuznetsov's armor."

Naomi nodded because that's what the agent expected her to do. She didn't look at his cell phone either because she didn't want him to become suspicious of her intentions.

"All right," he said. His fingers danced across the keyboard. "Let's get a word processor ready for you."

The first chance Naomi had, she would warn Guille to leave the house.

He would do it for her; she was sure of it.

Chapter 30

Damien Truscott left the chief's conference room and headed toward his office. The door closed behind him a moment later.

He hated that he had to wait around longer so the Criminal Task Force could get the address to the safe house. It felt like the department was rubbing his nose in this whole debacle. He'd been handed the Naomi Stapleton case by Lieutenant Brand because the man thought it wouldn't go anywhere. Then Truscott linked it to a murder in Chicago and the FBI showed up to take it away. Now, CTF would be involved, and Truscott would get to sit around spinning his wheels.

He probably shouldn't have even been in the meeting, but he crashed it after leaving Digital Forensics. Brand seemed surprised to see him standing outside the conference room. Chief Dillon had waved him in and introduced him to Agent Walker.

"Hey," James Morgan whispered. He lightly grabbed Truscott's elbow, then glanced up and down the hallway. "Let's chat."

Nayla Senai stood next to Morgan, but she seemed unaware of what the brutish detective had planned. Truscott let himself be led further away from the conference room.

"Tell me something," Morgan said. "How's your witness linked to a Russian enforcer in Chicago?"

Senai moved closer to hear Truscott's answer.

"She's an online sex worker," Truscott said. "She witnessed a murder."

Morgan glanced up and down the hall before saying, "Yeah? So?"

"The killer got a good look at her."

"Right." Morgan snapped his fingers. "Cameras. The guy probably realized he'd been seen doing the deed."

Truscott nodded. "It didn't help that she screamed."

"Were they recording?" Senai asked.

"No," Truscott said. "It was a private, one-on-one session. She definitely wasn't recording."

Morgan nodded slowly. "Which explains why the FBI swooped in. Their organized crime team is watching the Chicago crew. Somehow, they found out there was a witness in Spokane."

"A sergeant I talked with at Chicago PD informed them, or maybe one of his detectives did."

"They swooped in and picked her up," Morgan said. "How would they get to her so fast?"

Truscott shrugged. "Everything is entered directly into the system. Why couldn't they find her?"

"Fucking computers," Morgan muttered.

"Speaking of computers." Truscott motioned over his shoulder. "They also snatched her laptop from Digital Forensics before our meeting."

Morgan and Senai exchanged glances.

"Not sure they're going to get anything. Her boyfriend beat it up pretty bad then dunked it in the bathtub. Wickenhauser didn't even have a chance to work on it before the Feds showed up."

"They're playing this heavy-handed," Morgan said.

Truscott shrugged. "I've never dealt with them, so I have no frame of reference."

"Don't you know what getting railroaded feels like?" Morgan turned and walked away.

Senai glanced at her departing partner. "Sorry," she said to Truscott. She trotted after her partner.

"Good talk," Truscott said. "You're welcome."

He continued back toward his cubicle where he dropped into his chair. Truscott thought about Naomi Stapleton and her jackass boyfriend. He wished he could have helped more, but the murder occurred so far out of his jurisdiction there was no way for him to get involved.

It felt good to work on a case that mattered more than stolen property. This was his lot now, and he accepted it for the person he loved the most in life.

He opened a folder and reviewed the case notes. A burglary had occurred a couple of nights ago at a construction office. He would work it, and maybe even solve it. Then he'd go home and hold his wife.

If that's what mattered most, why did he feel so hollow?

Chapter 31

Guillermo Messi rolled off the broken coffee table and pushed himself to his hands and knees. Tears welled in his eyes and blood drooled to the floor when he opened his mouth. He ran his tongue over his teeth and winced. Some were broken and jagged.

Two men had forced their way into his house a moment ago. He'd been in the middle of an epic run on the latest *Call of Duty* when someone playfully knocked. He thought it might be one of his friends since he'd texted them after the bullshit with the FBI agent.

Messi paused the game and hurried to the door. The video game continued to loudly play its background music.

He answered the knocking without thinking. Messi blamed the distraction of the game. He also could've pointed to the several bong rips he'd done earlier. The truth was, he hadn't taken the whole threat to Naomi's life seriously. Had he really thought trouble might be headed their way, he would have gone along with the FBI man.

Messi never really considered Naomi's initial worries. He only destroyed the laptop because Messi knew she could afford to buy a new one. The girl was getting so popular with the feet freaks she could afford to buy a new computer every month if she wanted.

So when Messi yanked open the door, he expected one of his buddies to be there with some Taco Bell or a new strain from Locals, his favorite weed store. He hadn't expected to see two hip white dudes.

Messi wasn't even worried since they seemed old-school chill. One wore a red tracksuit while the other was in green. Each sported a Kangol hat and wraparound sunglasses. Time seemed to pause as he assessed the situation.

He cracked a smile and said, "Yo. Wotcha?"

That's when Messi's world erupted. The man in the green tracksuit punched Messi in the face, exploding his nose.

Messi stumbled backward and Green followed him into the house, where he slugged him in the gut.

The sound of the game vanished, and Messi's vision narrowed onto that single man before him.

Messi fought several times in his life. No one who had met him before would ever consider him a pussy.

This other man, though, was a straight brawler. Green threw punches and kicks in several brutal combinations. Messi bounced about the living room before he finally flopped onto the coffee table. The legs collapsed underneath Messi's weight, and it sounded like a small detonation had occurred.

While Green beat him, Messi kept expecting Red to join in, but the other man had vanished into the remainder of the house.

Now Messi was on his hands and knees with blood spilling out of his mouth. He inhaled deeply and felt a sharp pain in his side. Had the man in the green tracksuit cracked Messi's rib?

Footsteps returned to the living room. Messi looked back to see Red approaching with a gun in his right hand. The man muttered something that sounded Russian. Messi had watched enough spy movies and played enough war games to know what Russian sounded like.

Shit, Messi thought. He knew what this was about.

"You." Red kicked Messi in the butt. "Look at me."

Messi rolled over and stared up at the two men.

The man in the green tracksuit now held a gun, too. He must have had it in his pocket when he entered the house.

The two watched Messi the way visitors at a farm might watch a dying lamb—with no fear and little pity.

"Where is the girl?" Red asked.

"They took her." Messi's voice sounded slurred because of the blood in his mouth and the broken teeth.

"Who took her?"

Messi turned his head and spat blood onto the floor. "The FBI."

Green scoffed. "You do not protect her. Is good for you." The man then said something in Russian to his partner.

Messi felt ashamed. He hadn't even thought about protecting Naomi. What good would it have done? He didn't know where she was, anyway. Besides, she was the one who got him into this mess.

"Who is this girl to you?" Red asked.

"My girlfriend."

"When did the FBI take your girlfriend?"

"A couple hours ago."

Messi winced after speaking. He'd have to go to the dental clinic now to get his teeth fixed. Messi hated the dentist.

Red snapped his fingers. "Call her."

"It won't do any good."

"Call!" Green angrily kicked his foot.

"Listen, man!" Yelling hurt Messi's mouth, and he covered it with a hand. "Her phone is over there," Messi mumbled. He pointed at the kitchen counter with his elbow. "They wouldn't let her take it."

Red picked up Naomi's phone and examined it. "Why did the FBI take your girlfriend?"

"They wanted to protect her because she saw some guy murdered."

"What is the name of this man who was murdered?"

Messi shrugged. "He called himself Nick."

Red glanced at his partner before asking, "That is it. Only Nick?"

"That's it. Nothing else."

"How did she see this murder?"

"She saw it on the internet."

Red smirked. "What was she doing with Nick on the internet?"

Messi wiped blood from his chin. "She was putting on a show."

Red said something in Russian and jerked his head toward the back bedroom.

Green tilted his head and mimed jerking off.

Red nodded, and both men laughed. He turned to Messi. "Your girlfriend, she is a whore."

Messi didn't take the bait. He'd already lost one fight with an intruder. Why let the other one provoke him so he could lose a second?

"Why did you not go with her?" Red asked. "To wherever the FBI took her?"

Messi lowered his head. "I didn't think anyone would come look for her."

Red chuckled. "Too bad for you."

The two men spoke in Russian for a couple of minutes. Messi thought about running, but they were both armed. He'd have to get to his feet first before he could even scramble to the front door.

What if Red had locked it before searching the house? Messi might pull the door and discover it locked. That would waste a valuable millisecond. He'd have to look for a different opportunity to escape.

Red faced him. "You have five minutes."

Messi stiffened. "For what?"

"We want to find your girlfriend. If you do not give us help in five minutes, we will shoot you and leave. If you give us help, you will live."

"Is simple," Green added.

"Yeah," Messi said. "Is simple."

Except he didn't think it was. He had no way of reaching out to Naomi. His brain raced for ways to get in touch with her. If the FBI wouldn't let Naomi take her phone, they wouldn't let her check in with her mom.

Maybe that would buy Messi some time. If he could point these Russians to Naomi's mom, perhaps they'd let him live. He'd get out of town and run down to Kennewick to visit his cousin. No one would find him there.

Messi's phone rang.

"Who is that?" Red asked.

"I don't know," Messi said. He couldn't find his phone.

It had been on the coffee table before it collapsed. It rang a second time.

"There," Red said and pointed at the floor, next to the couch.

Messi scooped up the phone. The display showed a 509 number he'd never seen before. "I don't know who it is."

The phone rang a third time.

"Answer it," Red said. "Put it on speaker. Be careful what you say."

Green lifted his gun. "Be smart."

Messi swiped his thumb across the screen. "Hello?"

"Hey baby," Naomi whispered. "It's me. I can't talk long." She spoke quickly. "Are you okay?"

Green stepped menacingly forward. The barrel of the gun looked as if it could swallow Messi whole.

"I'm fine," he said.

"You don't sound fine. Your voice sounds weird."

"I'm sucking on a jawbreaker." It was the only lie he could think of, and Red nodded his approval. "What are you calling me on?"

"It's Tyler's phone."

"Who?"

"The FBI guy."

Jealousy flashed through Guille. It was a strange emotion at this moment, but he knew all of Naomi's exes were white boys. She probably thought that Fed was handsome. Messi's face hardened.

Naomi continued. "He's in the bathroom, so I gotta talk fast. I just want you to know where I am in case you decide you want to join me. Okay?"

Green pressed his gun against the side of Messi's temple.

"Yeah," he muttered. "Where you at?"

"Four three two one West Rosewood. You got that?"

"Four three two one," Messi repeated.

She giggled. "That's hard to forget, huh? Like a countdown."

Messi looked up into Red's eyes. "Yeah, hard to forget."

"Okay, baby. Don't forget. I gotta go. I love you."

"I love you, too." He said robotically and hung up.

Green didn't lower his gun.

Messi frowned. "You guys aren't going to let me live, are you?"

Red shook his head. "Why would you ever think we would?"

Chapter 32

Morgan slammed his hip against the push bar and the door burst open. It swung wide and banged loudly against the outside wall of the Public Safety Building. Morgan burst through the side exit with Nayla Senai on his heels.

"Hey," she said, "slow down."

Morgan called over his shoulder. "Keep up."

Senai trotted to his side. "What's wrong?"

He spun now and walked backward. Morgan motioned toward the PSB. "This whole thing is bullshit."

"What thing?"

"You don't think so?"

For a moment, her gaze drifted away. When it returned, Senai asked, "I'm not seeing it."

He eyed her as they passed the fence separating the Monroe Court Building from the PSB. Since it was privately owned, the MCB wasn't considered a part of the Public Safety Complex.

"They're gonna make us babysit. It's not what we do." He tapped his chest. "We're bird dogs. We go after the bad guys. We don't sit around with our thumbs up our butts."

When they passed the Monroe Court Building's corner, Senai started toward the front door. Morgan continued into the parking lot. She hurried back over.

"That's not true," she said. "We do that plenty." Morgan furrowed his brow, and she waved him off. "Not the thumb part."

"What're you talking about?" Morgan asked.

"We run surveillance. Doc and Adrian are watching The Hempstead now. And we've set up buys where the bad guys come to us. So, we've sat around plenty."

"But we don't use a witness as bait." Morgan stopped at the driver's door of his car.

"They're not doing that."

"You don't think so?" He pointed in the direction of downtown now. "Some Russian asshole is running digital sweatshops around Chicago. He's a modern-day Capone and the Chicago branch of the FBI wants him bad. You heard Walker say that, right?"

She nodded.

Morgan slapped the roof of his car. "Damn right, he did. If this digital Capone is affiliated with The Hempstead like we think, we've got a serious problem."

Senai cocked her head.

"How many of those crooked hackers will Viktor Khrushchev—"

"Kuznetsov," she interrupted.

Morgan waved her off. "Whatever."

"You can't pronounce it."

"I can pronounce it fine." He glared at her. "What I'm trying to say without your interruptions is how many hackers will Viktor have looking for this Naomi woman?"

Senai shrugged. "It won't matter. Whatever agent is assigned to her will make sure she stays off the network. They'll disable her cell phone. They'll make sure she's not connected to any wi-fi. I'm sure of it."

"The agents? What about them? Can you guarantee they won't make a mistake? They won't post something stupid to their Facebook pages."

Senai rested her forearms on the roof of the car. "Relax, Morgan. No agent is going to post a status update about protecting a federal witness. It won't happen."

He yanked open the car door. "I wouldn't put it past them. Remember, this is the same group that shot and killed a kidnapping victim." He dropped into his seat.

Senai opened the door but didn't get in. She squatted so she could see him better. "Where are you going?"

Morgan stuck the key in the ignition. "I'm going to run up to Rosewood and check on the girl."

"I'll go with."

"I need you to rally the boys." He started the engine.

"Why me?"

"Because you're second in command."

Senai's brow furrowed. "How do you figure? You're the one on the hot seat."

"I'm older and wiser."

Her face flattened. "You're also fatter and slower. Those arguments won't win with me."

"You fight dirty."

She started to say something, but Morgan interrupted.

"That's a compliment, Senai."

"Didn't sound like it."

"Trust me. It was. Rally the boys. Bring them up to speed, then figure how we can divide the team between two locations."

Senai frowned. "That's the sergeant's job."

"We let him pretend it is," he said. "You know what he'll do. He'll over think it before concluding we can't do it."

"And bring in SIU."

"Exactly. Let's keep this in house."

Morgan dropped the gearshift into Drive and accelerated out of the parking stall. The door latched shut.

In the rearview mirror, Senai stood in the middle of the parking lot, watching him leave her behind.

Morgan entered the traffic on Monroe Street.

Chapter 33

Naomi Stapleton lay on the bed in the backroom. She put her hands behind her head and stared at the ceiling. There wasn't anything in the room except a dresser and a small chair. It wasn't quite jail, but it was close.

She'd been locked up before, each time occurring while she was a juvenile. That's when she was completely off the rails according to her mother. Once she turned eighteen, she knew she had to stop that behavior or the charges became real.

Naomi used to break into homes with Spyder, a crazy ex-boyfriend. He was twenty-two when she was sixteen. That relationship drove her mother insane, but it produced some of the best times of Naomi's life.

According to her friend, Kennedy, Naomi had daddy issues. She called bullshit on Kennedy, and said she was with Spyder because he was good in bed.

That was a lie, though. Spyder was terrible in the sack. Even at sixteen, Naomi knew a lousy lay when she was under one. However, Spyder was good at making her feel safe whenever situations felt out of control. When he went to prison, Naomi moved onto the next boyfriend. Other boyfriends might have given her orgasms, but no one made her feel as protected as Spyder.

Until Guillermo.

She felt anxious now and sat up on the side of the bed. She wished she had her cell phone to text Guille. The short phone call with him only settled her for a few minutes.

Naomi knew she should be worried; the FBI told her as much. Right now, boredom was a more pressing issue. She stood and paced the room.

Perhaps she should go into the living room and watch some TV. She shook her head. That sounded boring as hell. There was never anything good on.

Earlier, when she had come back to the bedroom, Agent Smith remained in the kitchen, working on his laptop. Maybe she should join him and chat him up. He said she could call him Tyler. At first, she thought he did that to develop some sort of rapport. What if it was for another reason?

He was handsome, even if he dressed like a defense attorney—not a public defender, but one of the good ones.

Flirting wasn't cheating, she rationalized. She would only do it to break the monotony. She'd do it to goof around and have some fun. He'd understand.

Naomi wondered if Smith had a girlfriend. A guy his age probably had a wife. There was no harm in asking.

Unfortunately, the bedroom didn't have a mirror to check how she looked. She left the room and tiptoed into the bathroom.

A mirror check revealed she looked like crap. Her hair was messy and the light makeup she applied earlier needed a touch-up. The bruising on her cheek was still there, but it wasn't bad.

Naomi sniffed her armpits and crinkled her nose in response. She'd only washed her face that morning. Naomi planned to shower after she and Guille had an afternoon roll, but that never happened because of the FBI's interruption.

She should take a shower now, but a change of clothes hadn't arrived for her yet. Naomi ran her fingers through her hair and flashed a practiced smile. She'd charmed guys while looking worse.

Besides, she wasn't trying to screw the lawman; she was only trying to stave off boredom. Naomi cupped her hand near her mouth and blew her breath into it. She scrunched her nose again.

Naomi opened a drawer and found an unopened toothbrush and a new tube of paste. She ripped apart the package, removed the brush, and applied some paste. She quickly brushed her teeth. After rinsing, she smiled at the mirror.

Better, Naomi thought.

In the dining room, Agent Smith leaned an elbow on the table. He rested his chin in his hand as he studied something on the computer. Now that she was prepared to flirt, Naomi thought he looked more handsome than she previously recalled. He had broad shoulders, and his face carried a relaxed confidence.

Smith's suit jacket hung over the back of his chair. She expected him to wear a shoulder holster like the agents in movies, but Smith didn't.

His eyes cut to Naomi as she entered the room. "No nap?"

"Too anxious. My brain won't settle down." She sat at the table and smiled. "What're you doing?"

Smith motioned to the laptop. "Reading case notes."

His left hand rested on the table. No rings adorned any finger.

She widened her eyes. Guys liked it when she did that. A previous boyfriend called it her 'doe eyes.' Naomi opened her mouth slightly. "Want me to leave?"

"You're fine." He leaned back in his chair. "The notes are dry, anyway." Smith lifted his chin in the direction of the living room. "Why don't you watch some TV?"

Naomi shrugged. "I'm not interested."

"You hungry? I'd be happy to make another sandwich. That's about the extent of my cooking skills."

She saw her opening. Naomi cocked her head and locked eyes with him. "Does your wife cook for you?"

"I'm not married," Smith said. His eyes drifted away from her toward the front window.

"Girlfriend?"

"No," he said absently and stood. A gun rode on Smith's right hip.

"How does that happen?" she said. "A good-looking guy like you?"

His attention remained on the window, but he slowly reached for her. Naomi pulled back.

She hadn't expected the flirting to move so quickly.

Guillermo had cheated on her before and she retaliated by giving his friend a blowjob. Guille never found out about it, so it's not like she couldn't keep a secret. This seemed too much. Naomi was just playing around. She never wanted it to amount to anything more than some harmless flirting.

Smith's attention remained on the window. She turned to see what he was looking at.

Outside, two men in tracksuits climbed out of a black SUV. Their gazes swept to the house.

"Get out of sight," Smith said. "Now."

He turned to the table and grabbed his cell phone.

Naomi bolted from her chair and moved down the hallway. She glanced back in time to see Smith remove his gun from his holster.

His voice was low and hurried as he spoke with someone on the telephone.

The doorbell rang.

Smith entered the hallway but stopped at the corner. He motioned for Naomi to get into the bedroom. She stepped in and closed the door behind her.

Someone playfully knocked on the front door. Why did they knock that way? That didn't seem to be the announcement of someone looking to do her harm.

Agent Smith seemed to think it was. If those men came inside, it would be two against one. The FBI man had a gun, but what if those men in tracksuits were armed as well?

Naomi looked around. The bedroom had two windows. One on the side. Another on the back. Naomi moved toward the rear window to see if she could open it.

Just in case, she thought.

A head moved by the window, and she ducked. The guy in the green tracksuit was in the backyard. He wore a Kangol hat and wraparound sunglasses.

She should warn Agent Smith.

Naomi started toward the bedroom door when there was a large crash and a gunshot. Someone had entered the house.

"FBI!" Agent Smith shouted. "Put your weapon down!"

There was another crash and more gunshots followed. It sounded like a war zone inside the house now.

Naomi scrambled toward the side window. It was chest high, and she opened it fully. A screen to keep out the bugs remained. She didn't know how to remove it properly, so she banged her palm against it. The screen popped free, and it floated to the ground.

The gunshots continued, and Agent Smith screamed.

Naomi jumped at the window and her shoes scrambled against the wall. When she wriggled enough of her body through the opening, her weight shifted like a teetertotter.

Her head dropped toward the ground and her feet sailed toward the ceiling.

Naomi twisted as she slid through. The window's sliding track tore her skin. Naomi flopped onto the ground.

Inside, a final shot rang out and Agent Smith's screaming stopped.

She stood and saw the open gate nearby. Naomi sprinted through it and was soon on the sidewalk, paralleling Rosewood Avenue. As she ran, she looked over her shoulder.

The men in tracksuits hadn't emerged from the safe house yet.

Naomi faced forward and ran harder. She knew where she was going. All she had to do was make it to the house with the pink flamingos. If she could make it there, she'd call the police. She'd call Guille.

She would be safe again.

Chapter 34

Detective James Morgan pulled into the drive-thru lane of Zip's Hamburgers on Monroe. He waited patiently as a rusty pickup idled in front of him. Its driver leaned an arm on his door and seemed almost in a playful conversation with the employee speaking through the intercom. Several vehicles waited before the truck, so Morgan didn't get upset. Zip's was a popular local chain and usually busy.

He decided to detour from checking on the FBI agent and the witness for a quick bite. It was a long-standing rule of police work not to work on an empty stomach. He hadn't eaten much of a breakfast, and hunger was now starting to niggle him.

Morgan leaned his head back against his seat and listened to the chatter emanating from the radio hanging underneath the dashboard.

An officer initiated a traffic stop on Market Street and immediately said, "Code 4," a signal to dispatch and others he didn't need backup.

Almost instantly afterward, a second officer advised she had a subject in custody for Second Degree Assault and requested a dispatcher notify a supervisor.

Morgan smiled. He loved the radio's patter. He'd been a cop for so many years. The sounds associated with the job were second nature.

Another officer called dispatch to request an additional unit start toward his position. He needed help with an uncooperative subject.

Being a detective with SPD felt special to Morgan. He was a member of an exclusive club—the department, not the rank. Morgan had experienced something similar when he was in the Marines. He liked the fraternal nature of both organizations.

The pickup moved, and Morgan eased his Dodge Charger forward.

He glanced at the order board, but he already knew what he wanted.

"Welcome to Zip's," a tinny, female voice said. "*Go ahead and order when you're ready.*"

"A Papa Joe," Morgan said. He could already taste the greasy goodness of the beef, ham, and cheese combination.

"*Anything else?*"

"That'll do it."

The cashier said, "*I'll have your total for you at the window. Please pull forward.*"

Morgan couldn't move, however. The truck was still right in front of him. The line was slow today. It usually moved much quicker than this. Someone had probably ordered a fish sandwich.

If Senai knew Morgan had stopped at Zip's for a sandwich, she would give him an earful. She preached clean eating. He knew she was right, and he should make better food selections. Morgan had a stubborn streak when it came to food, which was not good for a man who'd passed fifty a couple of years ago.

It had become much harder for him to manage his weight. Morgan worked out and still did cardio, but the pounds wouldn't stay off. He hated to admit it, but he couldn't eat the same way he could when he was younger.

A Chrysler 300 drove by the waiting cars and stopped, blocking the exit for anyone not in the drive-thru lane. A chunky white woman hopped out of the sedan and stalked over to the passenger side of a parked Toyota. She swung her arms as she went.

"What's this bullshit?" Morgan murmured.

The plump woman pounded on the roof of the Toyota. "Get out!"

A skinny white man with a sheepish look climbed from the sedan. He wore a blue button-up shirt and tan slacks. He held a hamburger in his right hand. The man appeared to apologize.

The woman slapped him, and the man collapsed into the car. His burger flew into the air and flopped onto the ground.

From the opposite side of the car, a heavyset black woman climbed out. She pointed at the stout white woman and screamed something.

"Oh, this is great," Morgan said to himself.

The two women charged each other.

Morgan didn't want to deal with a lover's quarrel. He was hungry and wanted to get up to the safe house. He reached for the microphone clipped to the side of the police radio but paused when a dispatcher started a new broadcast.

"*Adam one-fifteen, Baker one-twelve, and other available units to back.*" It was never a good sign when an operator called for that many officers.

The two big women collided behind the Toyota. They each grabbed the other's hair and yanked. They spun and bounced off the side of the Chrysler, which continued to block the egress for anyone wanting to leave the parking lot.

Morgan considered breaking up the fight, but neither woman had produced a weapon yet. It seemed the two were evenly matched. At the very least, letting them tire themselves out before he approached seemed a decent strategy.

The dispatcher continued. *"A report of multiple gunshots at four three two one Rosewood."*

Morgan stiffened when he heard the address. That was the safe house.

He might have been there now had he not given into his stomach. He shouted in frustration.

Morgan grabbed the steering wheel to leave the drive-thru lane but immediately realized his dilemma. The vehicles waiting for their food orders blocked him in. He couldn't turn the car to the right because the Chrysler 300 barred his escape route.

Were fish sandwiches on special today? Had everyone but him ordered one?

The dispatcher repeated the address. *"Four three two one Rosewood. Caller reports two men entered the residence prior to shots being fired. Shooters wore running suits—one green, the other red. They arrived in a black SUV. Unknown make and model. No more information."*

Adam-115 and Baker-112 responded they were enroute to the call.

The two heavyset women continued their struggle. They slapped each other now. The skinny white man stood next to the passenger door of the Toyota with a pleased look on his face.

Morgan briefly flipped on the siren and emergency lights. The squawk paused the brawl, and the women looked in the Charger's direction. The skinny man took two stutter steps before sprinting into the nearby neighborhood.

Morgan grabbed the microphone and flipped the radio to PA mode. He keyed the microphone. "Move your car."

The sturdy white woman flipped him off. Morgan had no trouble reading her lips.

He turned the Charger toward her car, then keyed the microphone once more. "Move your car or you're both under arrest."

The black woman yelled at her adversary. "Do it, bitch!"

Reluctantly, the white woman shuffled back to the Chrysler. She dropped into the driver's seat, closed the door, and pulled the car forward. It didn't move far enough, so Morgan blared his horn. When that didn't get the desired result, he flicked on the emergency lights and siren again.

The Chrysler left the parking lot.

Morgan jammed the accelerator to the floor, and the Dodge Charger bolted out of the parking lot and shot north.

He pulled his cell phone from his pocket. The first call he made was to Courtney Earley.

"You hear the broadcast?" Morgan asked.

"I did. You think it's the same guys?"

"I do."

Morgan slowed as he approached the Garland intersection. The light was red. The cars ahead couldn't get out of his way. He pulled into oncoming traffic. It was an inadvisable move, and if something bad happened, he would be completely responsible. However, he saw a break long enough to sneak into the intersection, then he turned westbound on Garland.

"Watch for those two commie bastards," Morgan said. "They might be headed your way."

"Copy."

"Is Nayla there?"

"No."

"She should be there soon. Brief her if she didn't hear the broadcast."

Morgan hung up.

He was about to drop his phone into a cup holder so he could focus all his attention on driving, but another thought occurred to him. He dialed dispatch. Morgan could have called them on the radio, but he wanted to stay off in case one of the responding units to the safe house needed the airwaves.

The call was answered on the first ring. "Police radio. This is Juan."

"This is Morgan. I'm headed to that shooting on Rosewood."

"We'll show you enroute."

"Call Detective Truscott," Morgan said. "It's related to his case."

Morgan hung up and now dropped his phone into a cup holder.

He didn't really care if Truscott showed up, but there was always a long game to be played in the department. It only took a moment for Morgan to be nice. Maybe Truscott would remember that kindness down the road.

That was Morgan's way of paying it forward.

He pressed the accelerator harder to the floor.

Chapter 35

Officer Ron Rowe spun the steering wheel and his patrol car turned onto Rosewood Avenue. His gaze flicked to the rearview mirror. Lucas Jefferson followed closely behind in a black and white Ford Interceptor. Emergency lights flicked back and forth above his SUV.

"Adam one-fifteen and one-sixteen on scene," Jefferson called. He used Rowe's call sign since they arrived on scene at the same time.

"One-fifteen and One-sixteen on scene," a dispatcher responded. *"Caller advises the shooters have fled westbound in a black Chevy Suburban, unknown license plate."*

"Copy," Jefferson replied.

Rowe pulled the patrol car to the curb, well short of the target house. He jammed the transmission into Park, clicked off the engine, and jumped out. By the time he had his Glock out of its holster, Jefferson was out of his car and running up.

Jefferson patted Rowe's shoulder. "Ready."

The two men moved forward. Rowe led the way with his gun held in the low-ready position. He imagined Jefferson did the same, but he didn't look back to confirm. He had to trust his BUM—back-up man.

There was no discussion about waiting for additional officers to arrive. The two men were members of the department's SWAT team. The only other SWAT guy on the clock right now was at jail booking a mope who fought over an outstanding domestic violence warrant. Rowe made it a habit to know where his SWAT brethren were for moments like this.

That meant the rest of the officers showing up were regular Joes. They'd do in a pinch, but Rowe wasn't waiting for them to make entry, especially after a neighbor reported a shooting.

Jefferson was the only guy Rowe needed. He knew his friend felt the same way.

An elderly man stood outside a brown rancher across the street. He wore a dirty white T-shirt and brown slacks. He held a cell phone to his ear and waved at the uniformed officers. He anxiously pointed to a house a couple of lots away from Rowe.

An older woman emerged from the house the officers trotted by now. Plastic pink flamingos gathered in her yard. She wore a pink sweater and blue slacks and she also held a cell phone. She looked across the street at the elderly man.

Rowe noticed both senior citizens but didn't acknowledge either. He needed to stay aware of threats. Dispatch reported the shooters had fled the scene, but it wouldn't be the first time they were given bad information or had miscommunicated what they had learned.

He hurried up the driveway of the target house. Jefferson's footsteps were comforting behind him.

Rowe noticed the numbers on the edge of the garage— 4321. They were at the right location.

The front door stood open. Rowe hurried to the left side of the door frame. Jefferson took up a position on the right. On closer examination, it appeared the door had been kicked in. The jamb had splintered near the lock.

"Spokane Police Department," Rowe yelled. "Anyone in the house, make yourself known!"

There was no response.

Rowe shouted again, "Spokane Police Department. Answer now, or we're coming in."

He glanced at Jefferson, who pointed at the ground. Rowe followed his gaze. Blood spatter was on the transom and the stairs.

Jefferson keyed his radio. "Adam-116, we're making entry."

A dispatcher responded immediately. *"Channel is restricted for Adam One-sixteen and One-fifteen."*

Rowe moved into the house and Jefferson followed, button-hooking to the right.

The living room was clear. However, spent shell casings were everywhere. A trail of blood went out the door.

"Moving," Rowe whispered.

Jefferson repeated, "Moving."

Rowe shuffled deeper into the room, near a hallway, and paused. On the floor lay a dead man. He wore a white shirt and black slacks. Most of his face was gone and blood seeped through his clothing. An empty holster was on the dead man's right hip, but Rowe couldn't find a gun. Perhaps it was under the body.

He stepped carefully over the fallen man and continued toward the end of the hallway. There were two bedrooms. Rowe covered one bedroom and motioned for Jefferson to search the other.

His partner disappeared from his sight for several moments. Rowe kept his attention on the remaining bedroom and the hallway. His job was to protect his partner while he searched.

"Clear," Jefferson said. He returned to cover Rowe.

Now, Rowe entered the second bedroom. The first thing he noticed was an open window. He didn't approach it, though. He needed to check the hiding places. He looked underneath the bed and in the closet. He found no one.

Rowe went to the window and stuck his head out of the opening. A screen lay on the ground.

He returned to his partner. "Clear," he said.

The two officers continued to search the rest of the house, the basement, and the garage and found no one. A Jeep Cherokee was parked inside the garage.

Rowe grabbed his shoulder microphone and keyed it. "Adam-115, the house is clear. Also."

"*Copy One-fifteen,*" a male dispatcher said. "*Channel is unrestricted. All units, slow your response. Go ahead with your also.*"

"One-fifteen," Rowe said. "Start a supervisor and keep additional units coming for scene control." He didn't announce the discovery of the body over the radio. Citizens often listened to scanners and could decipher whatever codes or euphemisms officers created. Rowe figured the dispatcher and other officers could put two and two together.

The two officers returned to the living room.

"The back door was kicked in, too," Jefferson said. "Shell casings are everywhere."

"Uh-huh," Rowe said. His eyes bounced around the living room.

Rowe grunted. He moved to the kitchen. The house was too clean. Like it had just been moved into or maybe it was staged for a sale. He turned and looked through the front window. It didn't contain a For Sale sign.

Something wasn't right, Rowe thought. "Did you see any moving boxes?" he asked.

Jefferson headed for the front door. "Say again?"

"Moving boxes," Rowe said. "You know. Cardboard boxes and packing materials. That kind of shit."

Jefferson shook his head. "Why?"

"Isn't this place too clean? Doesn't it bother you?"

"There's a dead guy over there with a holster on his hip." Jefferson pointed to the body on the floor. "We need to get out of here before the Nut Crusher shows up."

Rowe waved him off. He spun around and saw it then. In the kitchen, a suit jacket hung over the back of the dining table chair. A power cord was plugged into the wall, but no device was attached to the opposite end.

"C'mon, man," Jefferson said. "We need to go."

"Inna minute."

Rowe approached the body now. He wouldn't disturb it; he knew the rules against that. But he hoped to find an answer in the suit jacket.

"What're you doing?" Jefferson hissed.

"Watch the door."

"Ledbetter's going to hammer us if she finds us standing around in the middle of a homicide scene."

In the left inside pocket, Rowe found a wallet. He pulled it out and flipped it open. "Holy shit."

"What?"

Rowe faced his partner.

Jefferson almost shouted, "*What?*"

He opened the wallet wider and showed it to his partner.

"Are you fucking kidding?" Jefferson glanced outside. When he turned back, he whispered. "What's the FBI doing here?"

Rowe tucked the wallet back into the jacket pocket. He then considered the power chord. "The shooters stole this guy's laptop."

"The sergeant will crucify us now that we know this. We gotta get out here."

Rowe nodded. "Okay, I hear you. Let's go."

The two men hurried from the crime scene.

Chapter 36

Damien Truscott's desk phone rang, and his fingers hovered over the keyboard. He was in the middle of typing an update on a report. He'd just gotten off the phone with a suspected burglar. The guy had agreed to come in for an interview tomorrow. Truscott almost couldn't believe his good fortune. Although, the guy still had to show up for the interview. Whether that happened was still up for debate.

Truscott's gaze drifted to the phone's ID—*Dispatch.*

He languidly reached for the receiver. "Truscott," he said.

"Detective, this is Juan in radio."

"Hey, Juan." Truscott grabbed his coffee and leaned back. "What can I do for you?"

"There's a report of shots fired."

The cup hovered at Truscott's lips. Property Crimes detectives didn't usually get notified about active shots fired calls. Those were the responsibility of patrol officers. Afterward, if someone was hurt, those calls went to Major Crimes. If gang members were involved, maybe the Special Investigations Unit got involved.

Adrenaline surged through Truscott's system. This was personal, Truscott thought. Perhaps something happened with the boys or Tessa.

Truscott lowered his coffee.

"Detective Morgan asked that I call you."

"Morgan?"

"That's correct," Juan said. "He's enroute to the shooting now."

Truscott lowered his coffee and reached for a pen. "All right. Gimme the details."

"It's at four three two one—"

"Rosewood," Truscott interrupted, recalling Agent Walker's words.

"How'd you know?"

He flipped the pen onto this desk. "Show me enroute."

Truscott slammed the receiver into place and stood. He didn't bother letting his sergeant know where he was headed. If the man really needed to know, he would eventually check with dispatch and find out.

He ran from the Public Safety Building. Several county detectives milled about in the parking lot. Truscott had worked with them previously while in SVU.

"Everything okay?" one of the county detectives yelled.

Truscott didn't respond. Instead, he sprinted to his car, climbed in, and started the engine. The tires chirped as he dropped the transmission into Reverse. They squealed after he slammed the gearshift into Drive.

He activated the emergency lights and siren. His car rocketed up Monroe Street, weaving in and out of traffic.

The siren's wailing drowned out the police radio since it was usually kept low. He flicked the volume higher.

"*Copy One-fifteen*," a dispatcher responded. "*Channel is unrestricted. All units, slow your response. Go ahead with your also.*"

"*One-fifteen*," an officer said. "*Start a supervisor and keep additional units coming for scene control.*"

Truscott read between the lines. A supervisor and additional officers were needed because a body was discovered. Truscott smacked his hand on the steering wheel. He thought about cursing, but that would offer little help at this moment. He grabbed the microphone and keyed it. "Ida-47 to One-fifteen."

He didn't know the officer's sector designation, whether he was an Adam or Baker, so he didn't try to guess.

"*One-fifteen,*" the officer answered.

"Is the victim female?" Truscott asked. He cringed as soon as the words came from his mouth. The responding officers hadn't announced the discovery of a body over the radio likely due to citizens listening on scanners. They wouldn't want a bunch of looky-loos showing up at the scene.

There was a pause on the radio. "*Negative,*" the officer eventually said. "*The victim is male.*"

That answer should have given Truscott relief, but it didn't.

A slow-moving minivan struggled to get up Monroe Street hill, yet it stayed in the left lane. Truscott jerked the steering wheel to the right and stomped on the accelerator again. As he passed the van, he noticed its driver was an older white male with a long ponytail. The man glared at Truscott and stuck his tongue out.

Truscott drove too fast and too recklessly, and he knew it. There was no longer a need for him to drive at this speed. Officers were on the scene and had secured it. A supervisor was likely on the way. If Truscott collided with a civilian now, he'd have no excuse for his behavior.

He still didn't ease off the accelerator.

He caught the green light at Wellesley Avenue and turned westbound.

The case felt too important to him, and he knew why. He wasn't chasing stolen bicycles anymore. For a moment, he got to handle something important. When he left SVU, he handled one important case involving a string of burglaries that morphed into a homicide case. He wasn't the lead investigator on the murder investigation, but he helped tangentially.

Since then, it had been a string of property crimes and his work felt almost meaningless. That wasn't fair to the victims of those crimes, but that's how Truscott felt. He hadn't shared those thoughts with anyone, not even his wife.

He tapped the brakes, spun the steering wheel, and turned onto Rosewood.

Several patrol cars were already parked on the double block. Morgan's Dodge Charger was there, too.

Truscott pulled to the curb and grabbed the microphone. "Ida-47, show me on scene."

A dispatcher responded, *"Copy. Ida forty-seven, on scene."*

He stepped onto the sidewalk and surveyed the neighborhood. Officers had already strung crime scene tape around the exterior of the target house. Truscott started in that direction until he heard his name called. He searched for it and saw Morgan waving him across the street to a brown rancher. The other detective stood on the front steps and talked with an elderly man.

Truscott trotted over to them.

Morgan said, "Philo Costas, meet my friend, Detective Truscott."

Costas wore brown slacks cinched tight with a black belt and a sweat-stained white T-shirt. Scuff marks covered his brown loafers. The old man held out his hand, and Truscott shook it. On his forearm was a Marine Corps tattoo.

"Pleased," Costas said. His voice was frail.

Morgan studied the old man. "Philo said two men entered the house behind us. Isn't that right, Philo?"

Costas nodded. "That's right. I saw it happen. Right from my living room."

"Then a bunch of shooting starting?"

"Uh-huh. That's true, too."

Truscott noticed Morgan didn't have a notebook out.

"They killed a man," Morgan said. "Did you know your neighbor?"

Costas frowned. "Never did. Work crews showed up over there now and again. Mowed the lawn in the summer. Shoveled the snow in the winter. Occasionally, someone went inside, but they never stayed long. I checked the assessor's records." The old man glanced at Truscott and smiled. "You can do that on the computer. Did you know that?"

Truscott nodded.

"It's owned by a trust. I figured it was going to be a rental, but no one ever stayed. That's when I figured it was a tax shelter or something. You know how those rich people are." Costas smirked. "Sneaky."

"What happened to the girl?" Morgan asked.

The old man stiffened. "What girl?"

"Listen, Philo," Morgan said, "we're the cops. We're not the bad guys."

"I know that, but I don't know nothing about no girl."

"You want to see our badges?" Morgan pulled his coat to the side to show his badge and gun.

Costas waved him off. "I believe you. Him, too." He lifted his chin toward Truscott.

Morgan glanced back at the target house. "Sergeant is on scene."

Truscott turned to look. Sergeant Megan Ledbetter climbed out of her patrol car and moved toward the crime scene tape. Officer Ron Rowe approached her.

"Lady police," Costas said with amazement. "You boys sure are lucky."

"Here's what's going to happen now," Morgan said. "The sergeant is going to order the uniforms go door to door to find a witness to the shooting."

"But we're already talking," Costas said. "Doesn't that count?"

"It doesn't." Morgan waved a hand. "Since you're holding out on the girl. We know it. If you were watching that house, then you saw her leave, Philo."

The old man swallowed with some difficulty.

"I'm gonna level with you," Morgan said. "Marine to marine."

Costas's brow furrowed. "You're a devil dog?"

"Oorah."

The old man's gaze flicked to Truscott. "What about him?"

Morgan clapped Truscott's shoulder. "This man was a squid."

Costas shrugged. "That's all right. We like the Navy. They gave us rides."

"I'm gonna let you in a secret," Morgan said. He glanced over his shoulder. "That was a safe house."

The old man's eye widened. "Like in the books?"

"And the missing girl is a material witness to a murder."

Costas leaned in conspiratorially. "Those guys tried to kill her?"

Morgan nodded. "That's the way it looks. They killed an FBI man."

The old man whistled. "The FBI." He leaned to look past the detectives. Satisfied with whatever he saw, Costas straightened. "Okay, but you can't tell Pinkie I told you."

"You have my word," Morgan said. "We won't tell Pinkie."

Costas lifted his chin. "The girl is at the house with all the flamingos in front."

Truscott started to look over his shoulder, but Morgan slapped his arm.

"Do it slyly," Morgan said.

Costas smirked. "Navy men."

Truscott surreptitiously glanced across the street. Two houses down the block was a blue rancher. A flock of plastic pink flamingos gathered on the front lawn.

The old man continued. "When the shooting started, the girl came out of the side gate over there like her hair was on fire. She ran straight to Pinkie's house like she knew where to go. I watched her the whole time. She went inside without knocking."

Morgan asked, "Why didn't you tell us this right away?"

"Pinkie called and told me to keep my big mouth shut." He cocked his head. "We got a good thing going, and I don't want to screw it up, especially by talking with you fellas."

"Why did you tell us now?"

"Because you're a Marine and you said the girl was in trouble." Costas shrugged a single shoulder. "Been a long time since I got to do something good for someone. If I gotta do damage control with Pinkie, I guess it'll be worth it."

"Do me a favor," Morgan said. "Keep this between us. If the uniforms ask if you saw the girl, play dumb."

Costas frowned. "Why?"

"We need to get the girl to another safe house. The fewer people who know, the safer she's going to be."

The old man nodded. "Loose lips sink ships." His eyes slid to Truscott. "Right, Navy?"

"Right," Truscott said. "Thanks for your help."

The two detectives started toward the street. When they neared the sidewalk, Morgan stopped him.

"Are you willing to keep the girl safe?" he asked.

Truscott thought about how he felt driving to the crime scene. "What are you thinking?"

Morgan pulled his notebook from his pocket. He wrote something down, then tore out the page. "Get the girl and take her to that address."

"What's there?"

"A friend. She'll understand the girl. We can trust her."

Truscott glanced toward the crime scene. Sergeant Ledbetter directed officers to conduct various tasks. "We're not going to tell anyone what we're doing?" he asked.

Morgan shook his head. "There's a dead federal agent in that house. Somehow, those Russian pricks found her. We know they use technology. Are you willing to bet every cop over there will put down his phone until we get her safe? I'm not."

"What are you going to do?"

"I'm going after the shooters."

"You know where they are?" Truscott asked.

"No, but I'm going to ask some folks who might have an idea." Morgan headed for his car. "Good luck," he called over his shoulder.

Truscott turned and started toward the flamingos.

Chapter 37

"What's going on now?" Naomi asked.

Evelyn "Pinkie" Harstad stood next to the side of the large front window. Long, amaranth-colored curtains hung closed, but Pinkie pulled the furthest edge back for a peek. "More police keep showing up. They're everywhere."

Naomi crouched behind a carnation-colored sofa. She rested her chin on the back of her hands and remained silent. Her thoughts were a jumble.

How did those bad guys find her? Wasn't she supposed to be at an FBI safe house? Didn't that mean the location was secret?

And why hadn't Guille called her back? She called him a few minutes ago with Pinkie's cell phone, but he didn't answer. He was probably playing that stupid game again. She glanced at the phone resting on the couch's armrest. Maybe she should call him once more.

She shook her head. No, if he saw a bunch of frantic calls, he'd be mad.

Pinkie craned her neck for a better view from behind the curtains. She was a large woman, both in stature and weight. She wore a ruby-colored muumuu. "Good Lord, girl. It's like a movie out there, but I'm pretty sure you can stop worrying. Ain't nobody gonna hurt you with so many cops around."

When Naomi first visited Pinkie's house years ago, her then-boyfriend warned it looked like a cotton candy machine exploded inside his grandmother's house. Naomi believed it had gotten worse since her previous visits.

Pinkie pulled the curtain open a bit more. "Two detectives are talking with Philo. What's that old coot saying?"

She was in her late sixties with long black hair someone obviously colored for her. A single streak of silver ran down the middle of her head. Naomi thought she resembled a skunk except she smelled like cinnamon, just like her house. Something baked in the kitchen; its aroma wafted through the place.

After she fled the safe house, Naomi ran through the neighboring yards. A dog barked at her from behind a fence. Before she turned toward Pinkie's house, Naomi stole a glance over her shoulder. No one followed.

She sprinted by the flock of plastic flamingos, jumped up the concrete stairs, and burst into her house. Pinkie never locked her front door when she was home. She wanted her family to always feel welcome to "walk right in" as she once explained to Naomi.

"That old bastard better keep his big mouth shut," Pinkie said, "if he ever wants to see my lady parts again. I'll tell you what."

Naomi stood. "Thank you."

"For?"

"Letting me come here."

Pinkie waved her off, but she didn't look away from the street. "It's what we do. You're family."

She wasn't, though. After her boyfriend dumped her for some South Hill brat—trading up, he actually called it—Naomi stopped coming around. At most, Pinkie was an acquaintance.

The older abruptly woman pulled the curtain's edge tighter to the wall. "A detective is heading this way."

"How do you know he's a detective?"

Pinkie clucked. "I've seen the shows."

Naomi moved around the couch. "What's he look like?"

"Like a cowboy."

"Lemme see."

Pinkie stepped out of the way and Naomi peeked through the curtains.

"I know him," Naomi said.

Detective Truscott approached the house. Hope burst inside her chest. Maybe everything would be okay. She rushed to the front door, unlocked it, and pulled it open as he ascended the top stair. Naomi frantically waved him inside. "Hurry."

Truscott moved by her, and Naomi closed the door. She locked it again.

His gaze swept the room, and he briefly considered Pinkie before turning his attention back to Naomi. "You okay?"

She was so happy to see the cop she wanted to hug him, but she held back. Naomi didn't answer, though. Her words dammed up inside her. She felt like she might cry, but no tears came.

Concern filled Truscott's eyes, and he studied her. "What happened?" he asked.

Those simple words caused everything to flow.

"Two men showed up and started shooting." Naomi's words tumbled out as tears welled in her eyes. "I freaked the fuck out and ran. I was so scared. I'd never been so scared in my life." She clapped a hand over her mouth to stop the words. What was wrong with her? Naomi hadn't spoken in that frightened manner to Pinkie.

The older woman watched her with mild curiosity.

"Did you get a good look at them?" Truscott asked.

Naomi shook her head. "They were in jogging suits with those funny hats," she said through her fingers. "That's all I saw."

"How do you know there were two of them?"

"I saw them get out of a black SUV."

"How did you know to run here?"

Naomi motioned to the older woman. "That's Grandma Pinkie."

"Evelyn Harstad." Pinkie stepped forward with an extended hand, which Truscott accepted.

"Mr. Costas spoke highly of you," he said.

Pinkie's expression darkened, and she dropped the detective's hand. "Did that old coot tell you the girl was here?"

"No, ma'am."

"Uh-huh." Pinkie crossed her arms under her breasts. "Here I thought you cops were supposed to be better liars."

Truscott smiled. "If it makes any difference, I'm here to protect Naomi."

Pinkie's cell phone rang, and she picked it up from the armrest of the couch. "I don't recognize the number."

Naomi reached for it. "Here. Lemme look. It might be Guille." She took the phone and flipped it open. "Hey, baby."

"Do not make this more difficult on yourself," a Russian man said. His voice was deep and his accent thick.

She stiffened. "Who is this? Where is Guille?"

Truscott moved closer, and he put his ear to the phone.

The Russian man continued. "Stop talking to the police, and maybe we will let you live."

"Where is Guille?" Naomi asked. "Put him on."

"You talk, you die."

The call ended. She stared at the blinking screen.

Truscott motioned to the phone. "Is that yours?"

When the cell phone's screen reset, the background picture returned. It was a picture of a girl blowing a massive bubblegum bubble. Naomi stared at it.

"It's mine," Pinkie said. "She used it to call her boyfriend."

Naomi struggled to make sense of that conversation. How did some Russian guys have Guille's phone? Guille didn't know any Russians. At least, she didn't think he did.

"Naomi," Truscott said.

Could the caller have found Guille's phone? No, Naomi thought, that didn't make sense. The guy told her to stop talking to the cops. If the caller knew about her, he wasn't a stranger to Guille. Naomi gripped the phone.

Truscott touched her arm, and she looked up. That's when she knew the truth.

"Oh my God," she whispered.

The detective took the phone from her and set it on the couch. "We need to get you out of here."

Tears again clouded Naomi's eyes, but this time, she struggled to breathe.

"Do you have a car?" Truscott asked Pinkie.

"In the garage. Yes."

Naomi inhaled jagged breaths and collapsed into the detective's arms. He caught her but did not hold on to her for long. Truscott propped her up on her feet, then looked directly into Naomi's face. "We don't have time for this. Do you understand?"

She sniffled as tears rained down her cheeks.

"We have to get you to safety," he said. "There will be time for tears later."

Naomi nodded.

Truscott let go of her and she wiped the wetness away from her cheeks.

"Get your keys," Truscott said to Pinkie, "and take us to the garage."

The older woman led the way. The detective lightly grabbed Naomi's elbow, and they followed.

A Pepto Bismol-colored Pontiac Grand Prix stood proudly in the middle of the garage.

"You gotta be kidding," Truscott muttered.

"She may be old, but she runs fine." Pinkie opened the passenger door. "Just like me."

Naomi paused. "Where are we going?"

"Around the corner," Truscott said. He looked at Pinkie. "Meet me at the Five Mile Shopping Center."

"Five Mile?" Naomi said.

"Go with Pinkie until I can pick you up."

She pulled back. "I don't understand."

Truscott nodded. "Here's the situation. The guys who want to harm you are tapped into the internet in ways we don't understand. That means everyone we contact is a potential liability. Everyone has to stay off their phones, their computers. No technology. If you want, we'll walk outside right now, and I'll let the on-duty supervisor decide how to protect you. We can't account for those officers out there and their phones. We don't know what they'll say and do with them. Understand?"

"Do you think some of them are working with the bad guys?" Naomi asked.

"No. I don't. But some will gossip. Others will text their spouses. If the men who want to hurt you can tap into that, maybe they'll be able to find you. I don't want to take the risk."

Naomi glanced at Pinkie.

"Do you trust me?" Truscott asked.

Her gaze returned to the detective. "Do you think that guy on the phone hurt Guille?"

The detective's eyes softened. "I won't lie to you."

She bowed her head. Tears ran down her nose. "What do you want me to do?"

"Lie on the backseat until I tell you to get out." Truscott turned to Pinkie. "Open the garage, but don't leave until you see my car outside. When you do, drive to the shopping center. It'll take me a couple minutes to turn around. Got it?"

Pinkie nodded.

"Give me two minutes." Truscott hurried back into the house.

Naomi climbed into the back of the car and lay across the seat. All she could think about was Guille. Had her earlier phone call gotten him hurt? Was she responsible somehow? She buried her face in the crook of her arm and let the tears overwhelm her.

Chapter 38

Morgan hung up the phone. He'd just finished a call with his friend, Vivian Basler. He'd taken great liberty by telling Truscott to take the girl to her apartment. He figured Vivian would be okay with the suggestion, and she was. With that problem resolved, Morgan focused his energy on the next problem.

He raced southbound on Monroe toward The Hempstead. He wasn't running code—with emergency lights flicking and sirens wailing. Morgan's unmarked Dodge Charger was already difficult for civilians to spot. The less stress he added to inattentive drivers, the better. He drove ten miles per hour over the posted speed limit and weaved around slow-moving vehicles whenever he could.

Ahead, a transit bus stopped to pick up waiting riders. Several cars slowed behind them. Morgan moved into the middle turn lane and accelerated past them. He flicked on the emergency lights now. The last thing he needed was some overeager State Patrol trooper to stop him for improper operation of an emergency vehicle. Once he cleared the bus, Morgan whipped back into the southbound lane.

Morgan's phone rang. He lifted it so he could see the display screen without taking his eyes off the road. It was Nayla Senai. He swiped his thumb across the screen.

"Morgan," he said.

"Something's going on down here. They're leaving."

"Who's leaving?"

"Everyone," Senai said. "I think."

"Like rats leaving a ship," Courtney Earley called from the background.

"The Hempstead residents?" Morgan asked.

"Yeah," Senai said.

"I'm on my way."

Morgan activated his lights and siren now. A warbling wail filled his car. Ahead, a pickup's brake lights flashed, but the truck didn't pull to the side. Morgan jerked the steering wheel to the left and entered the middle turn lane again. The Charger raced southbound.

"Have you seen the Jersey knockoffs?" Morgan asked.

"The who?"

"Golubev and Semyonov. The tracksuits."

Senai spoke to Earley. "Have you seen Golubev and Semyonov?"

"The thugs?" the big man asked. Senai must have nodded. "I haven't seen them all day."

"Hey," Morgan said. "Put me on speaker."

He slowed as he neared Indiana Avenue. Its traffic signal just turned red. In an emergency, the five-way intersection was funky to traverse. A concrete median would block him with the stacking cars if he didn't make an immediate decision.

Morgan spun the steering wheel and cut across oncoming traffic to Shannon Avenue. He drove east now.

"Gimme an update," Morgan said.

"It's like they're running for their lives," Earley said.

"Are Doc and Adrian still on the street?"

"Yeah."

"Have them stop a runner," Morgan said. "Find out what's going on."

Morgan would rip Senai and Earley at another time for not thinking of that themselves. Right now, he had to get down there. Morgan stomped the brake, turned the steering wheel, and headed south.

Senai asked, "Where are you?"

"On Lincoln," he said. "Turning onto Indiana."

The Charger's engine revved as Morgan blew past the stop sign and entered Indiana Avenue, heading eastbound. He narrowly missed an oncoming Lexus. The driver of the other car honked, but Morgan paid them no mind. The car's siren continued to screech.

"Oh my God," Senai said.

"Holy shit," Earley added.

"What?" Morgan asked.

He hammered the brakes and turned the Charger southbound onto Washington.

Morgan heard a loud boom on the other end of the call.

"The hell was that?" Earley asked.

"What's going on?" Morgan hollered at the cell phone.

Senai's voice became clearer. She must have leaned closer to the phone. "The top floor of The Hempstead just exploded."

Morgan eased off the accelerator as he passed North Central High School. "What?"

In the background, Courtney Earley announced his call sign and asked a dispatcher to start the fire department.

Morgan's in-car radio was turned low, so he could barely hear any communications. He thought about increasing the volume, but he was already driving one handed. He'd have to take the phone away from his ear to do that. He'd turn up the radio after he ended this call.

A second explosion occurred.

"Was that another?" Morgan asked.

"The second floor," Senai said. "The whole building is in flames now."

Morgan stopped for the red light at Maxwell Avenue. Right now, there might not be any reason for him to hurry to The Hempstead. With the building burning, he couldn't get into it. His biggest priority was finding the two Russians in tracksuits.

"Listen," he said. "Keep an eye out for Golubev and Semyonov."

"You still coming down here?" Senai asked.

"In a bit."

"What are you going to do?"

"Work some sources." He hung up.

The traffic started and Morgan turned westbound. He drove slowly now, figuring out his next course of action.

He first called Crime Analysis. When Debbie Wallette answered, he said, "This is Morgan. Remember those two Russian jackals Senai sent you?"

"That wasn't me."

"Someone on your team, then. Find the info and send it to radio for a BOLO." A dispatcher would broadcast a *Be On the Look Out* alert to the entire department.

"Yeah, fine," Debbie said. "What's it regarding?"

"The homicide up on Rosewood."

"You got it."

Morgan ended that call and placed another. When it got to the fourth ring, he was about to hang up, but Laszlo Nagy answered.

"Hello?" The man sounded like crap.

"Laszlo."

"I ain't got nothing, Morgan."

"I want your contact."

"Huh?"

Morgan pulled into the high school's parking lot and stopped. "Yuri."

"Oh, come on, Morgan. Yuri's good people. Don't make him hate me."

"You want your junk back?"

There was a pause on the other end of the line. If Morgan was honest with himself, it was longer than he expected.

"Okay, but we gotta meet," Laszlo said. "I'm dying right now."

Chapter 39

Damien Truscott pulled his car to the curb in front of Pinkie's house. As he did so, the Pepto Bismol-colored Pontiac Grand Prix slowly drove out of the garage.

Pinkie drifted to the edge of the driveway and paused. She and Truscott briefly made eye contact.

Truscott's gaze lifted to the rearview mirror. He wanted to see if any officers on scene had noticed the massive pink car pulling out. No one seemed to care. The assembled men and women were focused on protecting the crime scene. They still hadn't developed a plan to canvass the neighborhood yet.

The older woman turned the car away from the crime scene. Pinkie drove with the coolness of a getaway driver. Not too fast, as if she was trying to flee the area and not too slow, like she was trying to slink away. Pinkie simply drove as if she were headed to the grocery store.

After another check of the rearview mirror, Truscott accelerated away from the curb.

Truscott reached for his radio microphone but stopped. If he announced his departure from the crime scene, some officers might question why.

He pulled his cell phone from his pocket.

A call came over the radio. *"Nora-81."*

Truscott wasn't sure who the officer was, but he thought it was one of the Criminal Task Force guys.

"Eighty-one, go ahead," a dispatcher responded.

"Eighty-one, start fire to our location. There's been an explosion."

Another detonation went off on the radio.

Truscott's eyes went to the black box underneath the dash, even though the speakers were hidden throughout the car.

"*Better hurry*," the officer said. "*The building is up in flames now.*"

Truscott's attention returned to the road.

The pink Grand Prix turned westbound on Francis Avenue. Truscott waited for an oncoming semi to pass, and he pulled out behind it. He accelerated by the large truck. Once he settled in behind the Pontiac, he relaxed. It was a straight shot to the Five Mile Shopping Center now.

It didn't take a detective to understand why The Hempstead was burning. The Chicago kingpin—the roof, Morgan had called him in their meeting with the chief—must have ordered its destruction. If he had built a franchised network of digital sweatshops, then eradicating one for the safety of the others made sense.

But how did the roof know the department was watching The Hempstead? That was a question he could worry about later. Right now, Truscott had only one mission—protect Naomi Stapleton.

He placed the call he had started a moment ago.

"Radio," a dispatcher said. "This is Juan."

"Hey, Juan. This is Detective Truscott."

Harried voices filled the background, and a nearby keyboard clattered in Truscott's ear.

"Yeah, Detective. What can I do for you?"

"I need an officer to do a welfare check."

Juan scoffed. "We're a little slammed right now. Can it wait?"

"This is related to the homicide I'm on." Truscott was glad he hadn't called it on radio. He hoped it didn't sound as if he was driving.

"Okay," Juan said. "I'll get someone over there as soon as I can. What's the name?"

"Guillermo Messi."

The clacking on the keyboard increased. "And what are you expecting officers to find?"

"A body."

There was a pause before Juan answered. "All right. We can push that higher up the list."

"I don't think anyone else will be there but have the patrol guys be careful all the same. I think we're being monitored by the Rosewood shooters."

"Copy.

"If the officers find anything, keep it off the radio."

"Will do." Juan ended the call.

The pink land yacht left Francis Avenue and pulled into the Five Mile Shopping Center. It slowly cruised through the parking lot.

"C'mon, Pinkie," Truscott mumbled. "Just pull over."

The Grand Prix aimlessly wound through the parking lot. Truscott was about to yell when he realized what Pinkie was doing. She was trying to find a secluded spot. Unfortunately, that was impossible in the busy center. The best she could have done was act like everything was normal.

Eventually, the car sped up and headed westbound. It stopped at the furthest edge of the shopping center. The Pontiac pulled nose first to a concrete retaining wall. Truscott's car came alongside.

Naomi scrambled out of the back seat and climbed into his car. She slid down into the passenger seat.

"Act normal," he said. "Sit up."

She eyed him questioningly.

"It's all right. Put your seatbelt on."

Truscott waved once to Pinkie, then backed his car out of its stall. He slipped the car into gear and headed east through the sprawling parking lot.

"Where are we going?" Naomi asked.

"Someplace safe."

"The last place was supposed to be safe."

He glanced at her but remained quiet.

"You think I did that?" she asked. Her question was filled with remorse and the knowledge she already knew its answer.

"You're going to be okay," Truscott said.

The car bounced over a speed bump and jostled them. Truscott slowed for customers exiting the supermarket.

"Do you think Guille is alive?" Naomi asked.

"I've asked for some officers to check on him."

She didn't look away. "What do you think?"

When the pathway cleared, Truscott accelerated. He didn't want to speculate about Guillermo Messi's situation, but he imagined the worst had happened to the man. A killer wouldn't leave a witness alive after extracting information from them.

Tears filled Naomi's eyes, and she turned toward the passenger window. "Why are they doing this?"

Truscott suspected she knew why, and he let her sit with the question.

At the shopping center's edge, Truscott paused for traffic to clear. When it did, he sped across southbound Ash Street so he could get to the one-way Maple Street. He turned northbound.

Naomi looked at him again. "I never would have called the police if I'd known this could happen."

Truscott shrugged. "They were coming for you even if you hadn't called. The only difference is you would have been there when they arrived. At least you have a chance now."

"But Guille..." She let the thought hang in the air.

"Why didn't he come with you?"

She turned away from him again. "I didn't want any of this," Naomi muttered. She rubbed her hands together. "It's not fair. I didn't do nothing to them."

Truscott thought about telling her about his wife's secret to ease her pain, but it wasn't his to share. Revealing it would be disloyal to the person he loved the most. He gripped the steering wheel tighter and said, "Life isn't fair."

It was a hollow platitude, but it didn't make it any less true.

Naomi curled up in the seat and rested her head on the edge of the door panel. She stared out the front window, looking like a lost little girl.

Chapter 40

Morgan pulled his car to the curb and parked in a Commercial Loading Zone. The Western Bank Building towered above him. Before getting out, he tossed a business card on the dash.

He calmly walked to the trunk, glanced around, then opened it. Morgan flipped up the floorboard and removed Laszlo Nagy's modified library book. He opened it to make sure the junk was still inside. Satisfied, he closed the lid and stepped back.

Nagy approached from down the block. His hands were in his pockets, and he looked as if he'd been dancing with death for the past twenty-four hours.

"Okay," Morgan said. "I'm here. Where's Yuri?"

"Gimme my book." Nagy held out his hand.

"That's not how this works."

Nagy reached for the hardcover and Morgan pulled it back. "I'll beat you with this again if I have to. I'm not fucking around."

"Please, Morgan," Nagy said. "I need my medicine."

"A cop is dead, Laszlo. If you think you're getting any slack—"

"He's in the basement," Nagy interrupted.

"What basement?"

Nagy jerked his head to the towering bank building. "He works for them. He's the lead janitor. Third door off the elevator in the basement."

"You're shitting me."

"I wouldn't do that." Nagy put his hands together, begging for his book. "Please, Morgan."

"If I find out you're lying…"

"You can kill me. I'm already dead inside."

Morgan set the library book in Nagy's cupped hands. "Remember those words, Laszlo."

The part-time dealer, full-time junkie scuttled away.

The detective entered the building and headed for the elevators. To his left was the Western Bank lobby. Several clerks stood behind thick Plexiglas partitions as they helped customers.

On his right was a coffee stand. The barista looked up from her phone, considered Morgan's appearance, and returned to whatever she was reading.

At the bay of elevators, Morgan pressed the down button.

The more he considered it, the less assured Morgan became Nagy told the truth about his source. The Russian thugs, Golubev and Semyonov, killed a federal agent. Soon, the FBI would arrive if they hadn't already. Once that happened, the Feds, with the help of all neighboring law enforcement agencies, would turn the city upside-down until they found the two men. If Yuri had any connection to them, he'd be found, dragged in, and interrogated.

Maybe Nagy sent Morgan on this snipe hunt to give his friend time to escape. Nagy knew better than to lie to the detective on something as important as this. Morgan would ensure Nagy landed back in prison. The man's hurt would go longer than a few days without junk.

No, Morgan thought, Nagy told the truth. Prison was a hell Nagy needed to avoid, especially now that he was older and no longer the handsome man he'd been in his youth. Nagy no longer had anything to trade for drugs.

Morgan's phone rang just as the elevator doors opened. It was Sergeant Bynum calling. He'd call his supervisor back after interviewing Yuri. Morgan stepped into the elevator and pressed the Down button. A syrupy Muzak song played. His eyes flicked to the ceiling. Morgan disliked music; he always had. But he sort of enjoyed whatever drifted from the speakers. Must be age creeping in. He didn't like that thought.

When the elevator doors opened again, Morgan stepped into the basement. Fluorescent lights glared down from the ceiling and reflected off recently shined linoleum tiles. A low hum emanated from somewhere. Morgan imagined the noise came from the building's heating system.

He turned down the first hallway and passed a closed door marked *Mail Room*. The next door he passed was marked *Storeroom 1*. The third door had a sign hanging on it that read *Lilac City Janitorial*—just where Nagy said it would be.

A voice came from behind the door. It didn't sound hurried or concerned. Morgan leaned in closer to hear it better. The voice was male and Russian. No amount of eavesdropping was going to help his understanding.

Morgan tested the knob, and it turned slightly. He spun it the rest of the way and shoved the door open.

Only one man was in the room, and he reclined in a swivel desk chair. He was white with wavy brown hair—cut too nicely for a janitor. His tan uniform appeared ironed and unblemished. He rested his black boots on the edge of his desk, crossed at the ankles. A long carrot dangled from the man's fingertips like a cigar. His eyes cut to Morgan, and he raised his eyebrows.

The second voice Morgan had heard continued to chatter from the telephone's speaker.

Morgan stepped forward and swung the door closed behind him.

Cabinets lined each wall. Some held manuals and binders. Others held supplies. It was a typical maintenance room, filled with stuff to keep an office building running.

A lunch box sat open on the desk. A bag of carrots lay opened next to a sandwich. A small package of cookies remained unopened. A nameplate on the desk read Yuri Belova.

From where he stood, Morgan could read the name tag on the uniform—Yuri.

Laszlo Nagy had told the truth.

Yuri Belova leaned toward the desk phone and interrupted the man speaking. Belova said a few words in Russian, none of which Morgan understood, then ended the call. Belova dropped back into his chair. He didn't seem concerned by Morgan's interruption.

"Yes?" the janitor said.

"Where are Golubev and Semyonov?" Morgan pulled his jacket to the side to reveal his gun and badge.

"Those names mean nothing." Belova bit into his carrot and ate with his mouth open. "They do not work here."

"Cut that bullshit, comrade. You know them."

The janitor dropped his feet to the floor and sat upright. "I am not your comrade. I am American citizen."

"You could be the Queen of England for all I care."

"I would rather be the King." Belova grinned.

Morgan moved closer. "Listen, pal. You're gonna tell me what I want to know."

"We grew up with your kind." Belova tossed the last bite of carrot into his mouth. "You do not intimidate me. America has rules."

The detective moved quickly around the desk, and Belova stood. The janitor lifted his hands to protect himself, but Morgan batted them out of the way. He grabbed Belova by the shirt, pivoted, and tossed the janitor across the room. Belova crashed into a cabinet and fell to the floor.

"We can do this the hard way or the easy way," Morgan said.

"Wait," Belova groaned. He lay on the ground, face down. He lifted a hand in the air, pleading for mercy.

"In case you didn't realize it—" Morgan grabbed the man by the fingers. He twisted and pulled, which put extreme pressure on Belova's wrist. The janitor screamed in pain and abruptly rose to his feet. "This is the easy way."

Morgan lifted his hand higher, which further torqued Belova's arm. The janitor rose to his tiptoes.

"All right," Belova cried. "All right!"

The detective released his grip and the janitor sunk to his regular height. Morgan immediately latched onto Belova's shirt, spun him around, and shoved the janitor into the desk chair, which slid back until it crashed into the wall. Belova stared back with awe.

"Keep your hands where I can see them," Morgan said.

The janitor rubbed his injured hand.

"Where are Golubev and Semyonov?"

"How should I know? I do not work with them."

"You told Laszlo about their roof."

Belova's eyes narrowed, and his face hardened. "Laszlo sent you here."

Morgan kicked the janitor in the shin. Belova howled.

"Stay focused," Morgan said. "Where can I find them?"

"I do not know!" Belova frantically rubbed his lower leg. "I do not know!"

"How'd you know them in the first place?"

The janitor looked up. "I trade information."

"From here?"

Belova leaned back. He held his hand against his chest. "It is a very good place. Nobody looks for me here."

Morgan considered that. Working as a janitor would provide him with a certain amount of anonymity. "Can you find Golubev and Semyonov?"

"Maybe." Belova's head bobbled. A sly smile appeared on his lips. "What is it worth to you?"

Morgan kicked the janitor in the other shin. Belova yowled a second time.

"Why!" The janitor bent and rubbed the second leg now.

"Those two killed an FBI agent today," Morgan said.

"FBI?"

"That's right. Big trouble is headed their way. Maybe your way, too."

A knock came from the door, and Morgan pointed at Belova. "Keep quiet."

The janitor nodded as he rubbed his shins.

Morgan approached the door and opened it.

An older woman in the same tan uniform as Belova's stood there. A plastic clip held her salt and pepper hair away from her face. Her name tag read *Georgeen.* "Everything all right in there?" she asked. "I heard yelling."

"He banged his leg," Morgan said. He turned slightly to eye Belova.

Georgeen leaned to look past the detective. "You okay, Yuri?"

Belova continued rubbing his shins. "I hurt my leg. All is good. Nothing to worry about."

"Thanks for checking." Morgan smiled and began closing the door.

"And who are you?" Georgeen asked.

"Health inspector."

Morgan pushed the door shut and locked it. He returned to Belova. "Now, can you find those two?"

The janitor slowly nodded. "It will take some calls."

"Better get started."

Belova reached for the phone. "You're not leaving?"

"I'll wait to make sure you're properly motivated."

The janitor slumped his shoulders. "Of course."

"One final question."

Belova looked up. "What's that?"

"Who's the roof they're protecting?"

The janitor shook his head. "If I tell you, he could kill me."

Morgan curled his hand into a fist. "I'm gonna remind you we've been doing this the easy way."

Belova swallowed with some difficulty. "This is America. Why do you ask questions like a Russian?"

Chapter 41

Naomi straightened in her seat and glanced around when Detective Truscott pulled into an apartment complex off Magnesium Road. Large gray buildings loomed ahead.

"Why'd we pull in here?" she asked.

"This is our destination."

Naomi studied him as he leaned left and right, searching the buildings for something. On the side of each was a single, large letter.

"You know where you're going?" Naomi asked.

He glanced at her. "Yeah."

But he continued to look left and right as their car slowly crept through the parking lot.

"If you tell me where we're going—"

"I've got it," he muttered.

Truscott shifted in his seat, then glanced over his shoulder. His expression wasn't hard to read. He was worried he might be lost.

Naomi raised her eyebrows. "I've delivered food here before."

He studied her.

"UberEATS," she said. "I was a driver." She rolled her hand. "Before the other stuff."

Truscott turned a corner and started down a new row. "Building D," he said.

Naomi didn't know where that was, but now she was looking, too. At least she felt involved. A sign displaying a map of the community stood near a curb. She pointed at it. "Maybe that'll help."

The detective pulled alongside it.

She quickly located Building D. "We drove by it."

“Yeah. I see that.”

He didn’t sound irritated. Rather, Truscott sounded embarrassed. Guille would have snapped at her. So would several of her previous boyfriends. They hated showing any weakness or admitting they made a mistake.

The detective spun the steering wheel and headed back in the direction they had come in.

“Is this another safe house?” Naomi asked.

“Not exactly.”

“Then what?”

Truscott shrugged. “A friend of a detective.”

Naomi’s brow furrowed. “Which one?” She didn’t remember meeting another detective.

“Someone helping the investigation.”

“Can we trust him?”

She blurted the question and immediately felt bad for it. She didn’t distrust the cops as badly as Guille did, but Naomi still had healthy misgivings about them. Regardless, she felt safe with Detective Truscott. Not only did he have a protective quality, but he also carried himself in a fatherly way. Naomi couldn’t describe it better than that.

Truscott slowed as he neared Building D and searched for a parking stall. His head swiveled back and forth.

“Well?” Naomi asked. “Can we trust him?”

Even though she felt bad for asking, she still wanted an answer.

“I think so.”

She narrowed her eyes. “That doesn’t sound good.”

Truscott found a parking spot and pulled into it. “Morgan’s got a reputation for being rough with suspects.”

Naomi cocked her head. “Morgan?”

The detective nodded. "The administration keeps him around because he delivers when the chips are down."

She studied the gray building in front of her. "The chips are down right now."

"We don't have many left. That's for sure."

They climbed out of the car.

Truscott scanned the apartment community as they walked up the sidewalk.

Naomi followed behind him but kept her thoughts to herself. Did she want an untrustworthy detective helping her right now? Who could she trust?

Truscott climbed a set of stairs, and Naomi dutifully followed. She crossed her arms as dread crept into her thinking. She wished she had access to a computer. She wanted to know more about Morgan. Could they trust him not to work with the Russians?

"It'll be okay," Truscott said. "I'll stay here until this gets sorted out."

His assurance felt slightly better, but an FBI agent couldn't protect her. However, she might have been the one who set that chain of events in motion with her call to Guille.

Naomi shivered. She hoped Guille was okay, even though she suspected he wasn't. Tears welled again in her eyes. She'd just gotten control of herself, too.

Truscott stopped on the third floor. There were two doors. He knocked on the left one, and it opened immediately.

A tall, blond woman in her early forties stood in the doorway. Naomi thought she belonged on the cover of *Forbes* or one of those magazines successful people read. She wore her hair almost like a man would. Or a lesbian, Naomi thought. The woman's outfit looked new—white shirt, blue slacks, and blue shoes. Had she been at an office earlier?

"Come in," she said with a polite wave.

Naomi hesitated to move. Confidence was in the woman's eyes and stance. Naomi felt it immediately. It was a quality she hoped to develop in herself someday. How did a woman grow it so extreme that it resonated?

Truscott motioned Naomi to enter the apartment before him.

When she stepped by the woman, Naomi sensed determination radiating from her. Is that why the other detective—Morgan—sent them there?

The woman shut the door after Truscott stepped inside and locked it. The three of them gathered in the living room.

Two chairs triangulated a couch. In the middle stood a coffee table on which burned a candle. Potted plants of various sizes decorated the room. Strange paintings adorned the wall; none of them resembled anything but splotches of color. Jazz played through wireless speakers in opposite corners.

It took Naomi a moment to realize there was no television in the room. How could someone live without a TV? Naomi wondered. Maybe the woman watched her shows on a laptop or an iPad. Still, no television seemed weird.

"I'm Vivian Basler," the woman said.

She extended her hand to Naomi first. Her skin was cool to the touch and her fingernails were manicured. When they broke their grip, Vivian shook hands with Truscott. "Jimmy told me about your situation."

Jimmy Morgan, Naomi thought.

"We're sorry to barge in," Truscott said.

Vivian dismissed his apology, and her gaze returned to Naomi. "You poor girl. Is there anything I can get you?"

Naomi shook her head.

Detective Truscott's phone rang, and he removed it from his pocket. "Excuse me," he said and stepped away.

Vivian motioned toward the kitchen. "If you're hungry, I've got plenty of options."

"No, thank you."

"Something to drink?"

"I'm fine. Really."

Naomi's gaze drifted to Truscott. The detective nodded repeatedly and grunted several times. Finally, he said, "Text me Agent Walker's phone number. That's right. FBI." There was a pause, and Truscott added, "If he's not at the Rosewood crime scene, he should be. Alert the chief, too."

He hung up. Truscott stared at his phone for a moment with a grave expression.

"Is everything okay?" Vivian asked.

The detective looked at her, then shifted his gaze to Naomi. His eyes softened.

"Why don't we sit down?" he suggested.

Naomi covered her mouth with a hand. "Oh, no," she said through her fingers.

Vivian moved toward Naomi and wrapped an arm around her shoulders. Vivian nudged Naomi onto the couch and the two sat side by side.

The detective kneeled before Naomi.

Naomi knew the words before Truscott spoke them.

"Officers responded to your house," he said.

Naomi tried to inhale deeply, but her breath caught. She shuddered.

"I'm sorry," Truscott said.

She let out a wail and turned in to Vivian's neck. The woman hugged Naomi as tears for Guille flowed.

Vivian rubbed Naomi's back. "It's okay," she cooed. "It's okay."

Chapter 42

Morgan's Dodge Charger zipped up Sunset Hill. He drove westbound toward a veterinary clinic, supposedly near the Waste-to-Energy Plant. After he moved around a furniture delivery van, Morgan dialed Sergeant Ken Bynum.

The sergeant skipped the pleasantries when they connected. "Answer your fucking phone."

"I'm calling you back."

In addition to Bynum's call to Morgan right before the detective entered the elevator to go speak with Yuri, there was a second missed call from the sergeant that was likely cut off because of a weak single in the basement. That's why Morgan reached out to Bynum first, before anyone else.

"Where are you now?" the sergeant asked.

"West of town," Morgan said.

"Doing what?"

"Going after the safe house shooters."

"By yourself?" The sergeant sounded exasperated. He smacked something. "Goddamn it."

"What?"

"You can't go off half-cocked."

Debris fluttered off the back of a slow-moving garbage truck when it left Sunset Highway at the Geiger Boulevard exit. Morgan followed it and impatiently tapped his steering wheel as the Dodge's speed decreased to a crawl. Once the two vehicles cleared the off-ramp, Morgan stomped the accelerator and passed the lumbering truck. The driver stuck his hand out the window and flipped off Morgan.

"I'm up here at Rosewood," Bynum said. His exasperation remained.

Morgan pulled back into the appropriate lane, checked his rearview mirror, and flipped off the driver behind him. The garbage truck honked its horn.

The sergeant continued. "It's like a law enforcement convention. FBI. Marshals. County and state patrol, too."

"Marshals finally showed up?"

"Now's not the time. You hear about The Hempstead?"

"Senai told me." Before Morgan could add some information he learned from Yuri, Bynum smacked something again.

If the sergeant was at the Rosewood crime scene, was he hitting the roof of his car?

"You know about The Hempstead," Bynum said, "and you were at Rosewood, but you're still going off by yourself?"

"What more could I do at either location, Ken?"

"It's sergeant." He smacked the roof of his car a third time. Morgan was convinced it was a car now. "You could have helped the officers up here. Or you could have helped the team at The Hempstead. This is why the administration is always after our—"

Morgan interrupted. "I found them."

Bynum hesitated before asking, "You found the shooters?"

"I did."

Morgan said it with more confidence than he should have, but Bynum's ass-chewing bothered him. Had the officers really needed Morgan's help at the Rosewood crime scene, he would have stayed and pitched in. The patrol guys had it under control.

Once The Hempstead residents fled the building, there was no reason for him to run down there. What more could he have done besides stand around and watch the structure burn?

So, Morgan did what he always did—he acted and got results. At least, that was the story he could tell the administration now.

There was another pause on the line. "Do you have eyes on them?" Bynum asked.

"Not yet. That's where I'm headed."

"Which is where?"

"The vet clinic near the Waste-to-Energy plant."

The sergeant scoffed. "The VA isn't out there. It's in Airway Heights."

"Not veterans. Animals. Dogs and cats."

"Why didn't you say that to start?" Bynum hollered to someone, "Where the hell is he going?" His voice returned to the phone. "Listen, I gotta go. Call radio and report your location."

"I will."

"I mean it. Do it now. We're on the budgetary hotseat again. CTF, I mean, and I've been trying to keep us off. So, we need to do it by the book. Understand? If you find the bastards, call that in, too. Get SWAT out there and have them make contact. Don't be a hero."

"I'm no hero."

Bynum sighed heavily. "Don't be an asshole. Do what I'm saying and be a team player."

"I got it."

"Nothing stupid, all right?"

Morgan waved his hand in frustration. "Enough, Ken. Why are you up at Rosewood, anyway?"

"Why do you think?"

Morgan's thoughts flipped through all the possibilities until he landed on one. "Because backing the agent up was our responsibility?"

"That's right. No one cares the shit went down before we could get up here. The chief is only going to remember he tasked us with overwatch."

Morgan didn't believe that. This was something else. "What aren't you telling me?"

The sergeant lowered his voice. "The girl," Bynum said. "The witness. She's still missing."

Morgan winced, but he kept his mouth shut. Now wasn't the time to admit what he and Truscott had done. The time to fall on his sword was later—once the shooters were found.

Bynum continued. "The neighbor who reported the shooting said the suspects drove off alone, but he didn't see the girl leave the house. It's like she vanished."

"We'll find her," Morgan said.

"We better."

Traffic slowed as vehicles pulled into the Waste-to-Energy plant. Morgan sped up again after he passed the entrance.

"Is Agent Walker up there?"

"He was," Bynum said, "but he just left like a bat out of hell. Everyone's got somewhere more important to be than here."

"When you see him next, give him this name: Andrey Voronin."

"Who's that?"

"The lieutenant running The Hempstead."

Bynum asked, "Where'd you get this intel?"

"A source."

"Is it trustworthy?"

Morgan shrugged, even though Bynum couldn't see him. "I believe so. Anyway, the shooters don't work for him. They work for the Chicago boss. What's his name? Khrushchev or something."

"Hell if I remember. It's all alphabet soup, but I got it in my notebook. Hold on. Here it is. Viktor Kuznetsov. I think I'm pronouncing that right."

"Supposedly, Golubev and Semyonov are here to watch over The Hempstead for the big boss."

"God, these names are making my head hurt. Say the lieutenant's name again so I can write it down."

"Andrey Voronin," Morgan said. "Listen, I gotta jump off. I'm almost to the vet clinic."

"Remember," Bynum said. "Let radio know where you are."

They ended their call.

Morgan slowed when he approached a sign that read West Side Veterinary. He turned into the parking lot and saw a black Cadillac Escalade. It was the same type of vehicle reported leaving the shooting on Rosewood. He flipped a U-turn and left the parking lot.

Across the street was a gas station. Morgan found a spot which allowed him an unobstructed view of the vet clinic.

He called dispatch immediately as Bynum advised and informed them he had located the Rosewood shooters. Next, he called Nayla Senai.

"Where are you?" she asked.

"Watching the shooters. They're at a veterinarian."

"A discount doctor?"

He smiled. "That's my guess. One of them must have gotten hit. What are you doing?"

"The boys grabbed a couple runners. We're squeezing them now."

"Ask them about Andrey Voronin." Morgan said.

"Who's he?"

"The lieutenant running The Hempstead."

"You think he's responsible for the shooting?"

Morgan shook his head. "I think the order came from the big boss, but Voronin might be able to serve Chicago up on a platter for the FBI."

"All right," Senai said. "We'll ask. I'll call you back."

Morgan set down his phone and watched the vet clinic. He imagined himself a Great White shark lurking just offshore, waiting for a pair of swimmers to enter the water.

Chapter 43

Damien Truscott moved his car away from Vivian Basler's unit to the front of the apartment community. He backed into a parking stall and waited. Truscott lowered the volume on the police radio and called his wife.

When Tessa answered, she sounded upbeat. "What're you doing?"

"Waiting to meet with an FBI agent."

"FBI?"

Truscott bounced his fist off the bottom of the steering wheel. "I'll tell you about it later."

"Tell me about it now."

"It's a long story," Truscott said. "I probably shouldn't talk about it over the phone."

"Why are you calling then?"

"Because I might be late."

"I'm fine," she said.

"I know." He ran his palm around the steering wheel. "I'll be home as quick as I can."

Tess sighed. "Damien, we talked about this. It's okay. I'm okay."

Telling him things were okay wouldn't make it true. "I know," he said again.

"The doors are locked. I know where the gun is. Practice is almost over, so I'll pick up the boys in a bit."

Damien gripped the steering wheel and pulled himself upright in the seat. "Anyway."

Tessa chuckled, but it sounded forced. "Thank you for checking on me."

"Of course."

"I love you," she said. "More than anything in this world."

"I love you, too."

"Come home when you're done."

"Straight away," he said.

They ended the call, but he didn't put the phone down. Instead, Damien held onto it as if it allowed him to remain connected to Tessa.

His thoughts drifted as he watched cars enter and exit the apartment community. It was hard not to think about the day Tessa revealed the attack. She'd been running the trails near the Bowl and Pitcher, one of the many state parks she jogged.

A man had jumped out of the woods and overpowered her. He dragged her behind some trees and hit her. Tessa lost consciousness during the rape. When she returned home, she took a shower and washed her clothes—things she knew diminished the chances of recovering any evidence.

A man collecting trash walked by the front of Truscott's car. He bent, picked up a flattened pop can, and dropped it into the sack. The guy straightened and noticed the detective. He nodded once before continuing on his way. He scanned the area, found some more debris under a shrub, and headed toward it.

Truscott's thoughts returned to Tessa. When he returned home from work that night, she told him about the attack. She had to tell him about the rape because of the bruising around her eye. Truscott was furious. Tessa had destroyed critical evidence. He wanted her to go to the hospital for a forensic rape kit. She refused.

She had heard Truscott's doom and gloom stories about the prosecution of rape cases. Defense attorneys dragged the victims through the mud and put their lives under a microscope. This traumatized the victims a second time.

Truscott tried to convince his wife that the scenario she described wouldn't occur in her situation, but she refused to go to the hospital. He begged her to do the right thing because her attacker was still out there. Her assailant could attack someone else. Still, Tessa refused. It was already bad enough knowing Truscott would look at her differently. She didn't want their boys to do that, too.

So, they lied about what happened to her.

Keeping that secret ruined Truscott's time in the Special Victims Unit. He couldn't investigate sex crimes any longer. Every suspect took on the added weight of being his wife's potential attacker. His focus waned, and his attitude soured. Cases stacked up and his clearance rate fell. Before long, the administration suggested a change, and he didn't fight it. Besides, Truscott secretly hoped he would find his wife's attacker so he could kill the man. That result would ruin more lives than just his.

A black Jeep Wagoneer pulled into the community. It crept forward and nosed into the stall next to Truscott's car. Agent Walker sat behind the steering wheel. He spoke to someone via a hands-free kit. The other voice warbled through the walls of the vehicle.

When Walker ended the call, he faced Truscott, and the window descended. "Where's the girl?"

"She's in one of the apartments." Truscott waved over his shoulder. It was a stupid gesture. Walker could have surmised that by their meeting place.

The agent's face pinched. "Get her. I'll take her someplace safe."

"She's already safe."

"What kind of game are you playing, Detective?"

"No game," Truscott said. "She's a woman who's scared. I'm not putting her at any further risk."

"That's not your choice to make."

Truscott shrugged. "Right now, I think it is."

Walker's eyes narrowed. "You're interfering in an investigation."

"I'm keeping her alive."

"That's not how a judge would see it."

Truscott lowered his gaze. "Maybe not." He tapped the steering wheel. "But I'm willing to take that chance."

"Her boyfriend is dead," Walker said.

"She knows. I told her."

"Did he know her whereabouts somehow? Did they kill him to get the location of the safe house?"

Truscott looked away and quickly considered the ramifications of telling the truth. He wouldn't lie to the agent about this. "She called him."

Walker's eyes widened. "She what?"

"She used your agent's phone. He left it unsecured when he went to the bathroom."

"Jesus." Walker rubbed his face. "How'd she know where she was?"

"The grandmother of an old boyfriend lived two houses down."

The agent shook his head. "This town."

Walker's phone rang. A chirping sound came through the SUV's speakers. "It's your boss," he said before answering. "Chief Dillon," Walker said as he faced forward. "Please give me some good news."

The chief's voice boomed through the Jeep's sound system. "*Detective Morgan found the shooters. Our SWAT team is enroute.*"

"Outstanding," Walker said. "What's the location?"

"A veterinarian clinic on Geiger Boulevard." Dillon recited the address. *"We're marshaling in the parking lot of the Waste-to-Energy plant."*

"I'll head that way shortly," Walker said, "but don't wait for me."

"We won't."

Walker faced Truscott. "And chief."

"Yeah?"

"I'm with Detective Truscott. He's hiding our witness."

"Truscott? And the girl's safe?"

A woman in sweats and a flannel shirt pushed a stroller by Truscott's vehicle.

"That's what he says," Walker said.

"You haven't seen her?"

"He won't let me. He's keeping her secluded."

"The hell is wrong with you, Truscott? Let Walker see his witness."

The mother eyed the lawmen with curiosity as she pushed her baby away.

"Send some marshals," Truscott said. "They're trained for this. When there's enough protection, I'll tell Walker where she is."

"That's not your decision." Dillon's voice echoed out of the Jeep.

Truscott thought about not being able to help his wife. Right or wrong, he felt like he was helping Naomi Stapleton.

"She's safe, Chief. When the marshals are available, I'll turn her over."

Dillon sighed. It sounded funny coming through the speakers, like a football losing all its air. *"All right, Walker. You heard him. What do you want to do?"*

"I'll call the marshals and see if they've got anyone now," the FBI agent said, "but I hope you discipline your people for this type of behavior."

"*Trust me*," Dillon said. "*We will.*"

The driver's window rolled up, and the Jeep backed out.

Truscott had been unofficially dismissed.

Chapter 44

A kettle squealed in the kitchen and Vivian Basler stood from her position next to Naomi on the couch. "Last chance."

"I don't drink tea."

"That's no reason not to try it." The older woman walked into the kitchen and silenced the pot. "I'll make you a cup. If you don't like it, you don't need to drink it."

Naomi flopped back onto the couch and stared at the ceiling.

How'd she end up here? she wondered. How had her life taken such a hard turn that everything went so horribly wrong? It's not like she had a lucky touch or anything. Quite the opposite. Everything she touched turned to shit.

She tried college and quit halfway through the first semester. She told her friends and family it had been too boring, when it was actually too hard, too. All that studying and those tests. She couldn't smile and giggle her way through it like she had during high school.

Jobs had come and gone since then. She hated punching a clock, especially when the bosses were men who eyed her like a tiger watching its prey. Her mother said to ignore them and their ugly comments; it was the cost of being pretty. Naomi's mom had once been beautiful, but now looked haggard and unhappy. Naomi never wanted to end up that way.

She started to think about the men in her life, but Guille entered her thoughts. Naomi rolled her head on the back of the couch to watch Vivian in the kitchen. The tall, blond woman poured steaming water in two large mugs.

"When is Detective Truscott coming back?" Naomi asked. Her words caught in her throat.

Vivian glanced up and concerned filled her eyes. "I'm sure he'll be back soon."

Naomi stared at the ceiling again.

Try as she might, relationships entered her thoughts. Why did every guy treat her like trash? Something less than valuable? Even Guille did. A tear streamed down her cheek. Why was she okay with it?

Because everything she touched turned to shit, she reminded herself. She wasn't worth something or someone of value. A wave of emotion rolled through her body. Naomi shut her eyes and struggled to hold back an onslaught of tears.

"Here you go."

She opened her eyes to find Vivian holding a mug out. Naomi sat upright and accepted the cup with both hands. Warmth radiated through her palms.

"It's green tea," Vivian said. She settled onto the couch next to Naomi. "Good for calming your nerves."

Naomi nodded but didn't sip.

"Thinking about your boyfriend?" Vivian asked.

"And my life."

Vivian lifted her cup and sipped the tea. "What about it?"

The words flowed from Naomi then. All the thoughts she'd just been thinking spilled out of her like a tipped over milk jug. Some flowed effortlessly. Others gurgled out until Naomi rediscovered her rhythm.

Vivian remained mostly silent while Naomi spoke. When the topic of OnlyFans came up, Vivian nodded knowingly and said, "I understand better than you think."

By the time Naomi finished talking, the mug had grown cold in her hand. She finally sipped its contents. There wasn't much taste to it, but the liquid soothed her throat.

A lull dropped over the conversation and the soft jazz music filled its place.

Vivian dragged her finger around the lid of her cup, and her thoughts seemed elsewhere. Finally, she said, "Don't let anyone wag a finger at you."

Naomi cocked her head.

"I'm serious," Vivian said. "Nobody's opinion matters but yours. Do you understand?"

"I guess."

"Those friends who called you a whore. What do they do? Where do they work?"

"One works at a coffee stand. Another at a dentist's office. One used to be a boyfriend."

"A former boyfriend called you that?" Vivian rolled her eyes. "He's just mad he's not with you. Ignore him. Those other girls who called you a whore? They get paychecks. You're an entrepreneur, taking risks, putting yourself out there. Who's braver? Them or you?"

Naomi's brow furrowed.

Vivian set her mug on the coffee table. "At first, I didn't know why Jimmy suggested Truscott bring you here, but I know why now."

"Why's that?"

"Web cams," Vivian said. She gracefully leaned back on the couch and put her feet on the edge of the table. She stared up at the ceiling. "That's what we called them twenty years ago. We'd start a website, put a camera up in our bedrooms and charge guys a fee to visit."

Naomi's mouth opened, and she slowly glanced around the beautiful apartment. All this came from sex work? Her gaze returned to Vivian. "You're joking."

"I don't joke about it, because I'm not ashamed of it."

"How much did you make?"

"More than enough to invest."

"Do you still do it?"

She shook her head. "I aged out."

Naomi's face pinched. "You're beautiful. There are plenty of guys who dig MILFs. That means Mothers I'd Like to—"

Vivian raised her hand to interrupt. "I know what it means. I aged out because I found other ways to make money. I brought other girls in, set them up with their own apartments, their own cameras. It was good money while it lasted."

"What happened?"

"Bigger business. The girls no longer needed me when they could go directly to companies like the one you work with."

"Are you angry?"

Vivian shook her head. "Why would I be? I made money by myself. I made even more with those girls. All businesses have a cycle. Mine ran its course. I'm lucky I had a backup plan."

"Which was what?"

"Invest and save. That's why I stayed here. I liked my apartment, never got married, never lived above my means."

"But still."

"All that old content still gets seen now and then. I wasn't stupid; I saved it. I get residuals from sites."

Naomi blinked. Who was this woman?

"Don't let society put you in their box," Vivian said. "You're an entrepreneur. There's only one you and you only get one life. Don't live it for anyone else but you."

"Okay." She didn't feel confident when she spoke, so she said the word once more with emphasis. "Okay."

"If a guy can't love you for who you are, he doesn't deserve you. Never forget that."

Naomi tilted her head. "Are you with that Morgan guy?"

Vivian smiled. "No."

"Because he doesn't accept you?"

"He accepts me fully," Vivian said.

"Then why not?"

"Because he wants something else."

"What's that?" Naomi asked.

"The chase."

Naomi blinked a couple of times. "I don't understand."

"Not every guy wants to catch the rabbit."

"I'm still not getting it."

A knock came from the front door.

Vivian stood. "Someday you'll understand."

The older woman crossed the room and checked the peephole. She unlocked the door and stepped back. Detective Truscott entered.

"Everything okay?" he asked.

"Everything's fine," Vivian said as she closed the door.

Truscott entered the living room and looked at Naomi. "They've located the shooters."

"What's that mean?"

"Officers have locked down the scene, and SWAT is on the way. We're staying here until the US Marshals arrive."

"The marshals?" Naomi asked.

Truscott nodded. "They'll take you into protection. They know what they're doing."

"It'll be all right," Vivian said.

"Will I have to go into witness protection?" Naomi asked.

"I don't know." Truscott shrugged. "Maybe."

Naomi shifted her position on the couch. Witness protection meant moving somewhere new, getting a new name, maybe changing her hair color. She'd seen the shows and the movies. The news troubled her after the talk with Vivian.

"But what about my work?" Naomi asked. "Being an entrepreneur?"

Vivian sat next to her. "If a boulder in the middle of the road is blocking you from your destination, what do you do?"

Truscott eyed the women with curiosity.

Naomi shook her head. "What?"

"If a big rock—"

"I know what a boulder is." Naomi smirked. "I guess I'll go around."

Vivian shrugged. "There you go. Or you move the rock. But you won't turn back, right? Not if your destination is further down the road."

Naomi smiled. "Right."

Truscott's eyes bounced between the two women. "Clearly, I missed something."

Vivian nodded. "Yes, you did, Detective. Would you like some tea?"

Chapter 45

Morgan straightened in his seat.

A black Lexus sedan pulled off Geiger Boulevard headed toward the veterinarian's parking lot. Morgan jotted the license plate on his notepad. The clinic sat back from the arterial, and trees lined the two-lane road leading to it. However, Morgan had a perfect view from where he sat.

"Are you seeing this?" Morgan asked into his radio.

"We got it," Captain Gary Ackerman said.

Initially, the captain's involvement confused Morgan. Ackerman oversaw the Investigations Division. The patrol captain should have been on the phone if high-level brass was a necessity, especially since SWAT fell under patrol's purview.

Ackerman was Chief Dillon's right-hand man, his go-to in situations like this. Dillon was likely at the Waste-to-Energy plant, too, which meant Ackerman tagged along. Since a detective was sitting off the shooters, Dillon probably tasked Ackerman to be Morgan's go-between.

At least, that's how Morgan figured it. The two brassholes were probably sitting in the command van now—a dilapidated motor home they brought to active scenes like this. Some of the administration called it a war wagon, but a war wagon didn't have a coffee pot and snacks.

Where had Ackerman been earlier in the day? He missed the meeting with Agent Walker, yet he showed up now? Morgan didn't always understand how the administration worked, but this seemed odd to him. He let it slide, though. It was the least of his worries.

Morgan and Ackerman communicated via cell phone. Morgan had his on speaker, so he didn't need to hold it near his ear. Because of the sophisticated nature of the Russian crew, the brass stopped radio communications. Unfortunately, the BOLO for Andrey Voronin had already gone out over the air.

The SWAT team and members of the administration assembled at the Waste-to-Energy plant. Supposedly, a member of the SWAT team flew a drone above the vet clinic, an eye in the sky to keep watch over those comings and goings, but Morgan couldn't see the damn thing no matter how many times he looked for it.

The detective bent slightly to search the blue sky again. Morgan thought he saw something, then realized it was dirt on his window. He grunted.

"Did you get the plate?" Ackerman asked.

Morgan consulted his notepad before reciting it. The captain read it back for good measure.

"That's it," Morgan said.

Ackerman didn't say he was going to have an officer run it, but Morgan knew that would happen. Captains and lieutenants didn't dirty their hands with such trivial tasks.

The Lexus parked next to the Cadillac SUV and a white male got out. He wore a baseball hat and a hooded sweatshirt.

"What have you got?" Ackerman asked. His voice remained calm, as if he were watching a TV show after dinner. "We've got nothing."

"White male. Blue hoodie. Baseball hat." Morgan leaned forward, hoping the extra few inches might help his sight. "I can't make out any logos from this distance."

The driver paused before entering the vet clinic. He looked toward Geiger Boulevard, then he tilted his head back as if searching the sky.

"We got him now," the captain said. "Clear as day."

"Can he see you?"

"Not unless he's Superman. We're way up there."

The driver lowered his gaze, checked his watch, and entered the building.

Ackerman said, "The car is registered to Riverside One, LLC."

"That's the company who owns The Hempstead."

The captain leaned away from the phone. "Call Crime Analysis and have them look into Riverside One, LLC." Some indistinct chatter came from someone else. Probably an officer kissing ass and telling the captain they were "on it!"

"Call Senai," Morgan said. "She was already working it."

"Copy," Ackerman said. He said something away from the phone again. "Looks like we've got facial recognition. It's Andrey Voronin."

"How'd you get that?" Morgan asked.

"We texted a picture to Agent Walker. He's on his way now."

Morgan frowned. He would have thought the FBI man would have already been there. Showed where the FBI's priorities lay.

Ackerman said, "So we've positively connected The Hempstead to the murder of an FBI agent."

"I thought that was already done. With the building on fire and its residents in the wind, I think Chicago is trying to cauterize this wound."

The door to the vet clinic opened.

"We've got movement," Morgan said.

"We see it." Ackerman turned from the phone. "Load up!"

Morgan started his car.

Andrey Voronin stepped out, and he held the door open. A man in a red tracksuit followed him. Sergei Golubev's left arm was in a sling. He shuffled toward the passenger door of the SUV.

A man wearing a green tracksuit stepped out and pushed the door closed. Mikhail Semyonov yelled at Voronin and pointed repeatedly at him.

"They're leaving," Morgan said.

Ackerman directed his voice away from the phone again. "Hurry up! Let's go!"

The Waste-to-Energy plant was only a couple of minutes from the veterinary clinic, but if the shooters got out to the arterial, it would likely turn into a pursuit. More lives could be endangered.

Andrey Voronin flicked his hand and turned toward his car. Mikhail Semyonov stopped yelling and moved toward the driver's door of the SUV.

The Lexus backed out of its parking stall. A moment later, the SUV reversed as well.

"Is SWAT enroute?" Morgan asked.

"They're leaving now," Ackerman said.

They'll never make it.

"I'm engaging," Morgan said.

He tossed his phone into the driver's seat, but he could still hear Ackerman hollering, "Stand down! Stand down!"

The Charger's engine whined as it shot across Geiger Boulevard. Morgan missed colliding with a semi hauling a double load of fuel. The Charger entered the two-lane roadway toward the vet clinic.

Morgan activated the emergency lights in the car's grill and the siren under the hood. The Russians knew the cops were coming now.

The Lexus leaped forward, and the two cars suddenly closed the distance between each other. Morgan had only a second to make a choice. He could stay in his lane, which would allow Andrey Voronin to pass him by and make it to Geiger Boulevard. He'd then be forced to make the same decision with the SUV. Or he could try to clog the roadway.

Morgan jerked the steering wheel, and the Charger swung wildly into the Lexus.

The world exploded as the two cars collided. A cacophony of screeches and crunches filled Morgan's ears as the airbag deployed. He didn't have time to register the sensation of landing in the hard bag because the SUV crashed into the side of his car.

Morgan slammed about the car's interior like a rag doll shook by an angry child.

When the Charger stopped sliding, Morgan slumped against his seatbelt. His head hung and blood ran from his nose. A smile played across his lips. He wasn't dead.

Move.

He blinked.

It wasn't his voice. It was one from his past—a drill instructor.

Move, maggot!

He lifted his eyes and looked ahead. There was nothing there but trees. He looked to his right, out the passenger window. The SUV was there, its nose crinkled. The driver's door popped open. A millisecond later, the passenger door swung open.

Now, maggot!

Morgan scrambled to get his seatbelt off. His thumb pressed the button several times until he yanked the belt out of its latch. He opened his door, rolled out, and saw his dilemma.

He was stuck between the Lexus and the Cadillac. Morgan drew his Glock as gunshots rang out. Staying in the middle of a crossfire was a nonstarter. He needed to find cover fast. He squatted and ran toward the Lexus, keeping his gun up and ready as he moved.

Andrey Voronin lay on the steering wheel of the Lexus, a deflated airbag underneath him. Either the man was dead or unconscious, but Morgan didn't care. Voronin was out of the fight.

More shots rang out.

Morgan moved to the trunk of the Lexus. He didn't pop his head up because he thought that might give Golubev or Semyonov a target. Instead, he leaned out from behind the trunk and stared at the man in the green tracksuit as he came around the rear end of the Charger.

"*Vot!*"

Morgan rolled away as bullets slammed into the sedan's trunk. He rose to a knee, prepared for the man to pursue him.

A roar came up the roadway off Geiger Boulevard, but Morgan didn't look back. He knew it was the cavalry. SWAT was on the way.

The Russians shouted at each other now. Morgan flopped to his belly and looked underneath the Lexus. The two Russians had taken up positions behind the sedan.

Additional shots rang out. They were firing at the arriving SWAT BearCat now.

Morgan aimed at Semyonov's feet. He knew whose shoes they were because of the green tracksuit. Morgan took a breath, aimed, and squeezed. A bullet ripped through the tennis shoe's fabric. The Russian gunman fell to the ground. When Semyonov landed, he didn't scream. Instead, he rolled toward the direction the shot came from. Morgan shot him twice in the chest.

Golubev must have watched his friend fall because he moved behind a tire. That didn't help him much, because in a moment his body collapsed in a burst of gunfire from the SWAT team. Morgan rolled away from the car and stood.

Behind him, a SWAT officer stood upright through the BearCat hatch and hunkered behind its hatch. Several other officers gathered behind the steel-plated driver and passenger doors. All had their weapons pointed in his direction. A team of SWAT officers ran toward Morgan's position.

He moved toward the front of the Lexus. Andrey Voronin stared straight ahead. His hands were on the steering wheel and his face was ashen white.

The driver's door squealed when Morgan pulled it open.

"Andrey Voronin," he said. "Please step out of the vehicle."

Chapter 46

Damien Truscott sat quietly in a chair and watched the two women on the couch. While he was outside, a dynamic had shifted. Vivian Basler had assumed a mentor role, and Naomi Stapleton seemed to relish the advice.

For the past twenty minutes, their conversation bounced across several subjects. Nurturing investments, developing an abundance mindset, and surrounding oneself with people seeking success.

Truscott wanted to ask what Vivian did for a career, how she could afford to be home in the middle of the day, but he remained quiet. Naomi needed the confidence boost Vivian gave her.

His cell phone rang, and the two women stopped talking.

"Excuse me," Truscott said.

He pulled the phone from his pocket and checked the screen's display—Captain Ackerman. Truscott had spoken to the man before; that's how he had his number in his phone. Usually communication went through the chain of command. Getting a call from the head of the Investigations Division was irregular.

Truscott stood as he answered the phone. "Truscott," he said.

"Ackerman. The chief told me you have the girl?"

"That's correct." Truscott moved away as Vivian and Naomi restarted their conversation.

"What the hell were you thinking?" Ackerman's tone had a sharp edge to it.

"We got her to safety."

Naomi glanced in his direction. Concern filled her face. Vivian continued to talk.

"We?" Ackerman asked. "Who's we?"

"Me."

"Someone else helped you," Ackerman said.

Ackerman turned away from Naomi. "A neighbor woman."

"You involved a citizen?"

Truscott wasn't going to mention Morgan. He had no affinity toward the man, but aligning himself with Morgan seemed worse than admitting he involved a citizen. Truscott remained silent.

"We're going to review this," Ackerman said. "You know that."

"I'd suspect nothing less."

"Watch the tone, Detective."

Truscott put his hand on the doorknob. If the reaming continued, he'd step outside. Even though Vivian and Naomi couldn't hear the captain, Truscott didn't want to feel humiliated.

Once again, Truscott remained silent.

"We've located the shooters and they've been—" Ackerman paused. "They're dead."

"Both of them?"

"That's correct."

Truscott straightened. He looked at Naomi. She and Vivian stared back at him.

"Was anyone on our side hurt?"

"They fired at officers, but they hit no one. Thankfully. We've got the scene locked down. County detectives are on the way out."

The Spokane Police Department and the Spokane County Sheriff's Office had an interagency agreement on officer-involved shootings. Protocol dictated the outside agency investigate the shooting to keep a level of impartiality. Justice and the citizenry demanded it.

"That's good news," Truscott said.

"Have the marshals arrived?"

"Not yet."

"When they do, report to the scene of the shooting. Chief Dillon and I are in the command van. We'd like a debrief on the day's events."

"Yes, sir."

Ackerman ended the call. Truscott stared at his phone for a moment.

"Everything okay?" Naomi asked.

"Yeah." He slid his phone into his pocket and returned to his chair. "They found the shooters."

Naomi's face whitened, and her lower lip trembled. "Okay."

"Sounds like they died in a shootout."

Naomi hugged herself as if she'd suddenly gotten cold. Vivian moved closer to Naomi and put an arm around her shoulders.

"Was anyone else hurt?" Naomi asked.

Truscott shook his head. "Just them."

"What's going to happen now?

"Our officers have locked down the scene," Truscott said. "Now, we've got to investigate the shooting."

"With me," Naomi said. She glanced at Vivian. "What's going to happen to me?"

Truscott shifted uncomfortably in his seat. "The marshals are still going to take you somewhere safe."

"What about here?" She glanced at Vivian. "Can I stay here?"

Vivian opened her mouth to speak, but Truscott interrupted her.

"That wouldn't be smart for either of you. The person who started all this, the guy who killed Nick—"

"Nick," Naomi nodded.

"He's still in Chicago. You're a witness to a murder he ordered."

She lowered her gaze. "The golden witness," she muttered.

Truscott cocked his head. "What's that?"

"That's what Agent Smith said I was." Shame passed over Naomi's face. "The golden witness."

Truscott grunted. He'd never heard the term before. Maybe it was an FBI thing.

"I wish I never saw it happen." Naomi closed her eyes.

Vivian pulled her in tighter. "But you did."

"So many people are dead now." Tears welled in Naomi's eyes as Vivian stroked her hair.

"They knew the risks," Truscott said. "The shooters who worked for the Novy Brat Nation. They knew what they were involved in. Agent Smith, too."

Naomi sniffled. "Not Guille."

"No," Truscott said. "Not Guille."

Guille hadn't wanted Naomi to call the police. He wanted her to bury her head in the sand. Had she done that, the shooters would have arrived at her house and killed both Naomi and Guille. Truscott knew Naomi didn't need to hear any of that now, though. She was struggling with her grief and needed to work through it.

A knock at the door caused Truscott to look away. "I'll get it."

Vivian nodded and continued to stroke Naomi's hair.

He crossed the room to look through the front door's peephole. On the other side stood three people—two white men and a Hispanic woman. All three held up wallets containing circular badges.

Truscott opened the door.

The tall man in front wore a blue windbreaker over a light blue button-up shirt. The windbreaker bunched behind the gun on the man's hip. He appeared to be in his early fifties with short, salt and pepper hair worn in a businessman's cut.

"Marshal Criddle," the man said.

Truscott leaned in to check out Criddle's wallet. The small badge and ID card clearly identified him as a United States Marshal.

Criddle jerked his head toward the side. "Marshals Hayward and Martinez." Both marshals wore the same style of windbreaker as Criddle.

Truscott introduced himself, and the two men shook hands.

"We're here for Naomi Stapleton," Criddle said. "May we come in?"

Truscott stepped back and allowed the three agents to enter.

Criddle moved out of the way and allowed Marshal Martinez to enter the apartment first. Hayward followed close behind. Criddle remained at the door and scanned the complex.

Truscott looked beyond the agent and saw a tan SUV idling in the parking lot. The driver's door was opened, and a man wearing a US Marshal windbreaker stood just behind it.

"Hi, Naomi," Marshal Martinez said, "I'm Elise. We're here to get you someplace safe."

Naomi slid off the couch and stood. She glanced about, clearly unsure of what was about to happen.

Vivian stood next to her.

"Do you have everything?" Martinez asked.

"I don't have anything."

Martinez stepped back and motioned for the front door. "We'll brief you on the way."

"Where am I going?"

"For your safety, it's best if we don't share with the others." Martinez's smile was practiced. "I hope you understand."

"It's okay," Vivian said. "Here." She pulled Naomi into a hug. "It's been wonderful to meet you."

Naomi clung tight to Vivian. "Can I come see you sometime?"

"When they say it's okay, of course you can."

They broke their embrace.

Martinez stepped toward the door and paused. "After you."

Naomi nodded and led the way. She stopped near Truscott and hugged him. "Thank you."

"You're welcome."

"I hope you don't get in trouble."

She let go and glanced around a final time. Then Naomi Stapleton stepped outside. Marshal Criddle led the way to the tan SUV. Martinez and Hayward followed Naomi. When they were in the SUV, it sped away.

"And just like that," Vivian said, "she vanishes from our lives."

Truscott extended his hand. "Thank you for your help."

"It was nice to meet a friend of Jimmy's." Vivian held his hand with both of hers. "I do hope everything works out. For all of you."

Chapter 47

James Morgan sat on a curb with his elbows on his knees. He was benched, a spectator to the activity flowing about him.

Two officers hurriedly hung yellow CAUTION—POLICE—DO NOT CROSS tape around the vehicles. The tape fluttered in a light breeze as the officers tied it to the trees on the opposite sides of the roadway. They strung four straight lines of tape—two on each side of the cluster of vehicles—to create an inner and outer perimeter. However, all the straight lines did was add to the confusion. A sergeant stood nearby with the officers and discussed how to better identify the perimeters.

Fifty feet away, Agent Walker interviewed Andrey Voronin. Chief Dillon and Captain Ackerman stood quietly behind the two men. Several other FBI agents had arrived to monitor the investigation.

The decision to sideline Morgan was for no other reason than policy, and Morgan hated it. As soon as Morgan shot one of the Russian thugs, his day was done. He was automatically placed on a seventy-two-hour administrative leave. Killing the man didn't add any additional time.

A single SWAT member sat on the curb opposite Morgan. He was the man responsible for killing the second shooter. Like Morgan, he was waiting for further instructions.

It wasn't Morgan's first Officer Involved Shooting. He knew what would happen next.

No one could interview him for the next three days. That cooling-off time was union negotiated and supposed to allow him to recover after a critical incident, so he could get his thoughts in order. Morgan thought it bullshit. His thoughts were fine, and he'd prefer to be interviewed now, while his memory was fresh, but this rule needed to be maintained.

Morgan understood the importance of the policy. Some other officers might not have held themselves together after a scenario like this. Those officers might spout off and say something stupid to an investigator. The union was wise to get them seventy-two hours to go home and calm down.

When the crime scene techs arrived, they would collect Morgan's gun. They might also confiscate his clothing. It happened at his last shooting.

The techs impounded his Dodge Charger following his previous incident because several bullets had hit its side. Morgan almost got himself in trouble then because there were drugs in the trunk—his street currency. Luckily, he had managed to get into the trunk before a tow truck arrived.

Morgan had no worries about a similar situation playing out now since he'd given Laszlo Nagy his narcotics back a couple of hours ago. Sometimes, he thought, it was better to be lucky than good.

Unfortunately, he'd never get to use the Charger again.

His gaze shifted to the veterinary clinic. Officers stood outside the building and interviewed one white male and two white females. A doctor and two assistants, perhaps? Was it sexist to assume the doctor was the male? The wounded shooter had gotten help at the clinic, and Morgan guessed the doctor was male. Maybe it was biased to assume a criminal doctor was male, but Morgan didn't care. He wanted the women to be innocent in the whole affair.

He dropped his head. "Shit," he muttered. He was getting too old to be in the department. Maybe even the world.

Morgan pulled his phone from his pocket. He'd missed several calls from Nayla Senai. He dialed her number. When they connected, he asked, "How's it going?"

"Better than you, it sounds. You okay?"

"Never better," he lied.

"Uh-huh," she said. "You going to be there a while?"

Morgan's attention shifted to two unmarked Chevy Impalas entering the roadway off Geiger Boulevard. They couldn't make it very far because of the congestion of police vehicles gathered before the crime scene. No one was getting out of there for some time.

"I'm not going anywhere," Morgan said. "How are things there?"

"Fire is still working on it. They're going to be here for a while. They don't need our help."

"I missed some calls from you," Morgan said.

"The boys squeezed those runners. Thought you might want to know what we learned about Andrey Voronin."

The driver's door opened on the first Chevy Impala and Major Crimes Detective Shane McAfee stepped out. Detective Tim Chambers exited the second. Morgan knew both detectives from the Spokane County Sheriff's Office. He wasn't fond of either, but that wasn't surprising. He didn't like any investigators from Major Crimes, regardless of the agency. All were stuck-up pricks, unless they were women. Then they were stuck-up bitches.

The Officer Involved Shooting protocol dictated an outside agency investigate the incident. The Spokane Police Department got to have their own investigator involved, but only as a shadow—someone to ensure the case was handled with care. Detective Dallas Nash shadowed Morgan's previous shooting, which created some unexpected problems. Morgan hoped Nash wasn't next up on the rotation.

A third unmarked Chevy Impala entered the roadway. It stopped behind the two county cars.

"You still there?" Senai asked.

"What's that?" Morgan leaned to get a better look at the latest arrival.

"Andrey Voronin. A couple of the runners talked. They said he was one of the original coders in Viktor Kuznetsov's first— What are we calling these operations?"

"Digital sweatshops," Morgan said. He didn't see any reason to glorify it.

"Yeah, so when Viktor Kuznetsov wanted to decentralize his operation, he sent Voronin out west."

"Why'd he pick Spokane?"

"Kuznetsov had connections or something. Not sure if it was family."

Morgan nodded. Spokane had a large Eastern European population. The demographic exploded in the region after the collapse of the USSR in the early nineties.

Whoever was in the third Chevy Impala hadn't gotten out of the car yet.

Detectives McAfee and Chambers talked with Captain Ackerman now. Chief Dillon still lingered around Agent Walker as he interviewed Andrey Voronin.

"Why'd they burn the building?" Morgan asked.

"They knew we were watching it."

"What?"

Senai laughed. "Voronin was already shutting down operations when the OnlyFans girl shooting happened.

They were scrubbing their systems while we watched from the across the street."

"You're kidding me," Morgan said.

"If those bozos hadn't shot that FBI agent, Voronin would have quietly opened the doors, and everyone would have walked away without us knowing anything. How about that?"

"Voronin ordered the building burned because he figured we'd charge in after the shootout?"

"That's what the runners are saying. It was always their contingency plan."

The door to the third Impala opened and Detective Marci Burkett climbed out.

"Christ," Morgan muttered.

"What?"

"My day just got worse. Listen, I gotta go."

Morgan ended the call as a short, dark-haired woman approached the county detectives. Burkett wore a black pantsuit with a red shirt. Her eyes scanned the scene. When her gaze hit Morgan, she paused only briefly and then continued as if his situation didn't matter.

The stuck-up bitch, he thought.

All the petty fights they'd had over the years were about to haunt Morgan. She was one half of the Glory Hounds, the Major Crimes team the administration fawned over. Morgan hated Burkett and her partner the most. She smiled as she shook hands with McAfee and Chambers.

Agent Walker called over an officer who led Andrey Voronin away to a patrol car. Walker said something to Chief Dillon, then headed toward Morgan.

Morgan stood.

"I gotta hand it to you," Walker said with a quick scan of the crime scene. "You made a helluva mess."

"I had help."

The FBI man motioned over his shoulder. "We hit the jackpot with Voronin. He's gonna give up Kuznetsov. The Chicago office has been trying to take him down for years and we're gonna get him in days."

Right now, Morgan needed an ally, and Walker seemed like he wanted to be friends. Morgan nodded politely.

"How are you?" the agent asked. "You okay? No ill-effects from the shooting?"

"Just the political ones."

Walker frowned.

"Not my first shooting." Morgan glanced at Chief Dillon, who now spoke with the three Major Crimes detectives.

"You did it by the book?" Walker asked.

"I think so, yeah."

"Would a commendation help?"

"It wouldn't hurt."

Walker stuck his hand out, and Morgan shook it.

"If you can add the rest of my team to that commendation," Morgan said, "I'd appreciate it. They're out at The Hempstead with a couple of Voronin's grunts. They're talking up a storm, too. I think you'll like what they're saying."

The agent pumped Morgan's hand twice more. "No honor among thieves, huh?"

"Has there ever been?"

Walker pulled out his business card. "Would you call someone from your team? Ask them to contact me. I'd like to have those men brought downtown to our office for interviews."

"Will do," Morgan said.

The agent patted his shoulder. "Everything will work out fine, Detective. You did good work."

Walker spun and headed toward his car.

The Major Crimes detectives approached the crime scene then. McAfee and Chambers looked at Morgan, but neither approached. They knew the no-contact rule. The interviews would occur later.

Besides, Ackerman had already done a tactical debrief when he first arrived on the scene. The captain asked basic safety questions about outstanding shooters, Morgan's direction of fire, and how many rounds did the detective send down range? Once Ackerman got that information, he ceased the interview.

Burkett, however, looked straight ahead, ignoring Morgan.

She's loving this, Morgan thought.

Captain Ackerman approached again. "Forensics is on the way. Won't be much longer."

Morgan nodded.

Ackerman studied him. "The chief thinks you made the right choice, by the way. Stopping them before they could get onto the arterial, I mean. Who knows what might have happened out there?"

Morgan's gaze followed the three investigators. "I hope they'll remember that during their investigation."

The captain frowned. "Listen to what I said." He turned and walked off.

Morgan replayed his words and finally settled on what was important.

The chief thinks you made the right choice.

Morgan relaxed then. He knew how the investigation would go now. He lowered himself to sit on the curb once more and waited for the crime scene technicians to arrive.

Chapter 48

Damien Truscott entered his house and quietly closed the door. He missed the days when the boys ran to greet him with smiles and hugs. Jace and Cole hadn't met him at the door in years, not to mention anything about a hug and a smile.

The television was on in the living room. He headed toward the sound. It was the news. On the screen was footage from the arrest at the veterinary clinic. The video showed detectives working behind yellow caution tape. The news crews had arrived too late to capture any of the action.

Tessa lay asleep on the couch. She wore blue jeans and a pink T-shirt. Her feet were bare, and they crossed each other. She breathed deeply, on the edge of a light snore.

Truscott cocked his head, listening for the boys, but he didn't hear them. He turned his attention back to the television.

The newscaster chattered on about the cooperation between various agencies that resulted in the apprehension of a dangerous Russian mobster.

Mobster, Truscott thought. He hadn't thought of the Novy Brat Nation as a mob, but the definition could fit. Truscott had thought of them as a gang or a crew. A bunch of digital thieves collaborating under the leadership of one man. Mob worked just as well as any other term, and the FBI would likely slap that title on Viktor Kuznetsov so they could charge him with racketeering. That's usually how they brought down criminal organizations.

Truscott had stopped by the vet clinic crime scene after the marshals collected Naomi Stapleton, but there wasn't anything for him to do there. The county detectives didn't need his input. They weren't investigating Alexei Nikolaev's murder—Truscott had started that, and Chicago PD finished it—well, the FBI had. Agent Smith's murder was being investigated by someone in SPD. The county detectives were solely focused on Morgan's shooting.

Detective Marci Burkett had barely acknowledged him. He didn't take offense to it, though. They weren't friends. Never had been. Her job was to shadow the county detectives. It wasn't to make nice with Truscott. Besides, she was usually intense and didn't acknowledge him at the station. Why would it be any different at a crime scene?

Captain Ackerman pulled Truscott aside and told him to get some rest. "Be in early tomorrow," he said. "We need a debriefing."

Truscott read between the lines. The administration would make two determinations during that conversation—if he violated policy, and what the department's exposure was if he did. Officers had violated written policy before while protecting a citizen. If no one outside the department knew about it, the administration swept it under the rug with a letter of documented counseling.

Letters were strongly worded scoldings and were tantamount to saying, "Don't do it again." They meant little until it came time for the department to cover its ass. If an officer got into larger trouble, the administration could point to the officer's file and say, "Look how responsible we are. We acted by writing those letters."

Chief Dillon appeared on the television. "We're proud of our—"

"What time is it?" Tessa asked. She shifted on the couch and reached for him.

"A little after seven."

She groaned. "You're kidding." Tessa sat upright and rubbed her eyes. "I fell asleep."

Truscott smiled. "I see that. Long day?"

"Every day is long when you're scraping teeth. Have you eaten?"

"No, but I'll fix something. You rest." He kissed the top of her head.

"Your plate is made. I just need to heat it. You rest. You had a longer day."

She stood and grabbed his hand. They walked together into the kitchen.

"Where are the boys?" Truscott asked.

"They took off a while ago for the basketball court."

A lone plate remained on the kitchen counter. Tessa removed the aluminum foil cover to reveal a piece of chicken, some cubed potatoes, and green beans. "It'll only take a minute or so to reheat."

Tessa grabbed a paper napkin, set it over the meal, and stuck it in the microwave. Soon, the machine whirred to life. She watched the tray spin inside.

"Want to go for a walk after?" Truscott asked.

"That'd be nice."

Tessa quit running outside after the attack. She hadn't stopped going places, but she only went where there were other people—work, the grocery store, the mall. She joined a gym so she could jog on a treadmill, something she previously hated.

Truscott settled onto a barstool and watched his wife.

"I saw there was a shooting on Geiger Boulevard," Tessa said. "The news has shown it several times."

"If it bleeds, it leads. Isn't that what they say?"

She shrugged a single shoulder. "You weren't anywhere near that, were you?"

Truscott shook his head. "Opposite side of town."

"That's good. I don't want to worry about you getting into things like that anymore. That's why I like you being a detective."

He smiled. "I know."

The microwave dinged, and she opened the door. "If it's not warm enough, I'll put it back in."

"It'll be fine." It could have been cold, and Truscott would have eaten it.

Tessa put the plate on the counter before him, then she pulled a fork and knife from the drawer.

"Want me to sit with you," she asked, "or can I get changed for our walk?"

He waved her on. "It'll take me a minute to finish this, and I'll be right behind you."

Tessa lightly touched his shoulder, then hurried away.

Truscott cut a piece of chicken and shoved it into his mouth. While he ate, his thoughts drifted to Naomi Stapleton. He wondered where the marshals might have taken her and what her life might be like now.

Vivian Basler had said, "And just like that, she vanishes from our lives."

Would Naomi still end up in witness protection if Viktor Kuznetsov was in custody? If she did, Truscott realized he would never know what happened to her.

He ate another piece of chicken.

Naomi was no longer his concern. He'd done his job and kept her safe.

Unfortunately, he couldn't say the same for the love of his life. The thoughts of Tessa's attacker bothered him again. He continued to chew, but the food had lost its taste.

Truscott eventually pushed away the plate and set down his knife and fork. About two-thirds of his meal remained. He would finish it after the walk, after the thoughts of his wife's attacker faded.

He slipped off his stool and headed toward the bedroom to put on his walking shoes.

Chapter 49

"Where do we go from here?" Officer Hoffman asked.

Morgan lifted his head from the passenger door window. He hadn't fallen asleep, but he had closed his eyes as his thoughts overwhelmed him. "Here's fine. I'll walk the rest of the way."

Hoffman had just pulled his patrol car off Magnesium Road and into Morgan's apartment community.

"You sure?" the officer asked.

Morgan shifted upright in his seat. "Yeah. This is good." He waved at the little office building guarding the front entrance. The walk would do Morgan good since it would allow him to clear his head.

Hoffman pulled the car parallel to the office and stopped. "Have a good night, Detective."

Morgan grunted. He opened the door and poured himself out. His muscles ached and his bones felt weary, an aftereffect of the collision and the adrenaline dump he experienced during the firefight. Morgan had felt this before. It would go away after a good night's sleep.

He closed the door, then tapped on the window as a friendly gesture. Morgan had barely said a dozen words to the officer on the ride home. He would call the officer later to say a proper thanks.

Morgan stepped back and watched the patrol car speed out of the neighborhood. He looked into the night sky. The moon was out, at least part of it. Some of the stars were visible, but not many. The lights from the city destroyed the opportunity to see more.

He dropped his gaze and began the long shuffle toward his apartment. Morgan snickered to himself. "Getting old."

He could pick up the pace if needed, but there was no one to chase.

Morgan knew he was slacking. He should have lifted his head high, pulled his shoulders back, and thrust his chest out. Act like a man with a purpose, he thought, and move smartly. But Morgan did none of those. He simply put one foot in front of the other and let his early thoughts return.

On the drive home, he'd replayed the events of the past few days—mostly he thought about those incidents where he'd crossed the line. He could justify those decisions to himself, but could he do the same to another investigator?

Internal affairs often sniffed around him, looking for reasons to jerk his chain. This might give them another excuse to come calling. Yet Morgan believed he could defend his actions at the veterinary clinic. If Chief Dillon was on his side, the investigation probably tilted in Morgan's favor.

However, a detective with an ax to grind was a wild card. He wished someone other than Marci Burkett had been called to shadow the shooting investigation. He knew the adage about catching more flies with honey than vinegar. Unfortunately, he'd hurled vinegar at the woman for years.

Morgan passed Building D and looked up at the third floor. A light remained on in Vivian Basler's apartment. It wasn't that late. Maybe a little after ten. Why wouldn't she still be up?

He proceeded toward her apartment. As Morgan walked, he lifted his head higher and his shoulders pulled back. His chest puffed out.

Morgan was once again a man on a mission.

He ran his fingers through his hair. Perhaps he should run home and grab a shower. Get a different set of clothes. Right now, he wore an old blue T-shirt, faded jeans a little tight around the waist, and dirty running shoes. They were the emergency clothes he kept in his locker. Morgan dismissed the shower and nicer clothes.

Fortune favored the bold, he thought.

His pace quickened, and he bounded up the steps, two at a time, to her apartment. When he made it to the third floor, he was out of breath. He grimaced—more in shame than in discomfort.

Morgan inhaled deeply several times, then he knocked lightly.

Several moments passed. So many Morgan thought about knocking a second time.

The door opened. Vivian Basler stood in the doorway. She wore a long sweater and white shorts. Her tanned feet were bare. She looked like the classy models in the *Playboy* magazines he coveted as a boy—if the women had been in their early forties.

"Jimmy?" she cooed. "What are you up to?"

Morgan thumbed over his shoulder like an idiot. "I just got home and saw your light on."

Vivian took him in then. Her gaze traveled his length, pausing for an extra moment on his ratty running shoes. She chuckled. "Did you have a date tonight?"

A wave of embarrassment flashed over him. Perhaps he should have gone home and changed. He felt like a teenager talking with his high school crush. "I was working."

"I know. I'm teasing." She smiled, and her eyes sparkled. At least, that's how Morgan would describe it if anyone asked. "So, why are you dressed that way?"

"They took my clothes."

"Who took your clothes?" Vivian's smile faded and eyebrows pinched together.

Morgan dumbly thumbed over his shoulder again. "The crime lab."

"Why would they do that?"

"Standard procedure. They do that after a shooting." Morgan pulled his shoulders further back. "Not sure if you saw the news." He was about to tell her about the firefight at the veterinary clinic, but Vivian interrupted.

"I did," she said.

"Oh."

Morgan waited for Vivian to ask if he was okay or to inquire about what happened. Any other woman in his life would have asked that, he was sure of it. They would have invited him into their apartments by now, too.

But Vivian watched him, waiting. The sparkle in her eyes returned. Morgan knew what was occurring because she was playing his favorite game—the push and pull. He knew how to play it, too.

He shrugged. "Well, I just wanted to stop by. You know, to see how it went with Naomi."

"It went fine." Vivian crossed her arms underneath her breasts. "She's a nice girl."

Morgan looked down at Vivian's feet. He had to stop staring at her eyes, and he was afraid he might glance at her breasts. But damn if Vivian's feet weren't sexy, too. "The marshals got her okay?"

"They did."

There was a pause, but Morgan didn't look up. He searched for something to say next, but Vivian beat him to it.

"Detective Truscott was nice."

Morgan's head snapped up. "Truscott?"

"Mm-hmm." Vivian smiled. The way she moaned her answer made Morgan jealous.

"He's all right, I guess." Morgan shrugged.

"Quite handsome, too."

"What?" Morgan nearly choked on the word.

"Both Naomi and I thought so."

Morgan's face warmed. He was afraid to say anything for fear of blurting out something stupid.

"Too bad he's married."

A throbbing began at Morgan's temple.

Vivian's mouth parted slightly like a hungry panther sizing up her prey right before the attack. Morgan wanted to be the aggressor in this relationship, but perhaps it needed to be the other way around. Maybe Vivian needed to take him down. If that were the case, he'd act like a wounded gazelle.

"What are you going to do now?" Vivian asked, interrupting his thoughts.

"Huh?"

She stared at him. The sparkle in Vivian's eyes had vanished and her lips were tightly closed.

Morgan glanced over Vivian's shoulder into the apartment. Why hadn't she invited him inside yet? She usually would. Was there a man in there? A woman? Vivian had occasional lovers, Morgan was sure of it. She usually kept it quiet. She knew about Morgan's women because he usually met them in the apartment community. It was an improper balance that drove Morgan crazy. He wanted to know what went on in her love life.

"Jimmy?"

He refocused on her.

"What are you going to do now?"

Morgan thumbed over his shoulder a third time. "Go home. Maybe make something for dinner. You know." He winced at how stupid it sounded.

She nodded. "Sounds like you got your night all planned out."

"Not really." Morgan waited for her to offer something better. When she didn't, he asked, "And you?"

"I'm going to shower," Vivian said. "Then climb into bed."

Morgan had fantasized about her doing that many times before. Those images popped immediately into his mind.

Vivian stepped out of the apartment. When she moved toward him, he closed his eyes and smelled her perfume. She kissed him on the cheek.

"I'm glad you're safe," she said.

He opened his eyes.

"Sleep well," Vivian said and stepped back into the apartment. She closed the door.

Morgan reached out but stopped short of touching the door. Was she waiting on the other side of the door? Did she want him to knock again? Doing so would seem desperate. But was that what she wanted?

Had she invited him inside, Morgan would have accepted gladly. Vivian was incredible, and Morgan might never find another woman like her in the entire world. Had she suggested they be together, it would have ruined everything.

They already had the perfect relationship, and Morgan was sure he loved her for it.

Nobody played the push and pull like her.

After a moment, Morgan dropped his hand. His shoulders slumped, and he shuffled home.

Did You Enjoy the Book?

Thank you for reading *The Golden Witness* and visiting the 509! I hope you enjoyed meeting some of the recurring characters. This is a continuing series with other characters occasionally stepping into the lead role. There are two parallel series to the 509 Crime Stories—the Flip-Flop Detective and the John Cutler mysteries. I hope you'll check them out.

I'm always grateful when a reader takes time out of their day to comment on one of my novels. If you do write a review, please email me, and let me know.

I'd love to say thanks!

About the Author

Colin Conway is the creator of the 509 Crime Stories, a series of novels set in Eastern Washington with revolving lead characters. They are standalone tales and can be read in any order.

He also created the Cozy Up series which pushes the envelope of the cozy genre. Libby Klein, author of the Poppy McAllister series, says Cozy Up to Death is "Not your grandma's cozy."

Colin co-authored the Charlie-316 series. The first novel in the series, Charlie-316, is a political/crime thriller that has been described as "riveting and compulsively readable," "the real deal," and "the ultimate ride-along."

He served in the U.S. Army and later was an officer of the Spokane Police Department. He has owned a laundromat, invested in a bar, and run a karate school. Besides writing crime fiction, he is a commercial real estate broker.

Colin lives with his beautiful girlfriend, three wonderful children, and a codependent Vizsla that rules their world.

Find out more at colinconway.com.